Bittersweet

BITTERSWEET REVENGE.

The second book in the "Bittersweet events" series.

Bittersweet Revenge.

Welcome to my second novel, Bittersweet Revenge.

After writing Bittersweet Summer and it's success I decided I quite liked being an author, and that my first novel definitely needed a sequel!

So here it is. The follow up.
The next chapter in the Bittersweet story!

Dedicated to a brave lady Rosy Wildsmith, who battled hard but ultimately lost her fight.

You will always be my "Madame" and it was a privilege to know you!

I hope you get the chance to read it "up there!"

Bittersweet Revenge

CONTENTS

4) Marco.

16) Barry's Confession.

27) Ronnie Kray.

34) The truth Michelle.

41) The Villa.

45) Just checking dear boy.

51) It wasn't an accident.

55) Rosy.

62) High Class Hookers.

73) Colonel Mustard.

78) Lazlo Kiss – No that is his name!

86) The signalman.

92) Marco comes to the U.K.

99) The 4th of July.

109) Detective Sergeant Nicholson.

126) Nikki turns killer.

137) Ruth.

149) Nikki is dead.

157) Ken.

162) I fucking own you.

181) What went wrong?

191) Your worst nightmare.

204) I want to make you a deal.

215) Broken Ribs.

223) The rendezvous.

237) Dead!

256) The investigation begins.

267) The Warren.

275) Crossbow Charlie.

283) Annie.

288) Giles liked young girls.

292) Charlie Summers death.

307) The Chief Super.

317) Take me to bed detective.

333) Ken calls in some help.

342) I know who he is.

348) Wind it down.

Marco.

As the plane touched down and the two friends smiled at each other, their husbands back in England were doing just the same.

"A toast, dear boy," boomed Giles and raised his glass, "To power, knowledge, and the ability to deal with problems!"

Tommy smirked. He had dealt with that prick Charlie Summer alright. However, Charlie had a son, who Tommy had already run into once, and who he was fairly sure wouldn't be as easy to get rid of as his father had been. Still, for now, he would drink the toast just as Giles had said, and let his mind worry about other events when Michelle returned. As the evening wore on, Tommy was bored. He wanted sex. And Nikki was at the club. He told Giles he was leaving, and made his way to his nightclub.

Giles had no intention of going there. Nasty place, but the new girl behind the bar at the golf club, Gigi, looked like she would do just fine for his relief this evening. He bid Tommy farewell and went back to the bar. "Gigi darling," he smiled, a lecherous grin, "pour me another would you, and why don't you have a little cheeky one yourself, just for me?"

Gigi blushed as he winked at her. She didn't much like Giles, but she also knew he had a lot of contacts, and the job here was nothing more for her than a stepping

stone... She fluttered her eyelashes and murmured, "Thank you Mr Williams."
"Call me Giles my dear," he said loudly, "Are you here till late?"
Gigi smiled, "I'm here till closing."
"Good, good," Giles grinned. "See you later on," and he marched off to his office. As he looked back he beckoned Gigi. She pretended to look shocked, but she knew exactly what the dirty old man had in mind. And if a blow job here and there got her what she wanted, so be it.

Michelle and Valerie arrived at one of Anesh's villas (he had several!)

Anesh was there to greet them. He had such a warm smile, and as he hugged Michelle she felt overcome with sadness and he held her just a little tighter until the moment had passed. "Welcome ladies!" he beamed. "There

is Champagne in the fridge, and the meal tonight is on me, I will collect you both around 8." He kissed both girls and toddled off.

Valerie looked at Anesh as he left. "He is such a sweetheart," she sighed. "Such a pity he is gay!" And she giggled like a schoolgirl.
Michelle laughed, "Gay or not," she said, "he isn't the most handsome fellow!"
Valerie shot her a look, "I agree," she replied, "but he has a handsome heart."

Michelle stopped laughing. "Yes," she replied thoughtfully, "and that counts for so much actually." And she went back to Charlie and his sense of fun and enjoyment for life. "Time for a glass of that bubbly I think!" she exclaimed, as she closed the door. As the two women sat in the sun on the terrace and enjoyed the bubbly, they both knew that the peace would be shattered at some point. The recent events involving Charlie especially, had driven Michelle to vow that she would avenge his death, and that no matter how powerful her husband thought he was, if he truly was behind it, he would be made to pay for what had happened to the man she had fallen in love with.

Valerie could sense the edge to Michelle's mind. "Just relax for now. Enjoy this place, let your hair down, and let's do things the right way," she spoke calmly, with steely determination. "We both know who was responsible for the crash, but we can't just go in all gun's blazing. It has to be structured, and done so that when the retribution happens, it's both swift and final." She touched Michelle's hand.

Michelle looked back at her friend.

"You are right, of course," she replied. And raised her glass, "To Charlie and Jamie!" she shouted.

Valerie smiled. "To Charlie and Jamie," she said softly. The sun was still warm as they dressed for dinner.

Anesh had style, and the two women were pretty sure the restaurant he was taking them to wouldn't exactly be down market, so they dressed accordingly. Liberal outfits containing Yves Saint Laurent, Chanel, and matching accessories. Just as they finished making themselves look perfect, the Bentley arrived. A beautiful sweeping two door, four seat convertible in the deepest metallic blue with white leather inside, and the top down. And Anesh resplendent in white trousers and a fuchsia coloured shirt. Valerie waved from the window, and the ladies almost ran down the stairs to meet him. He stepped out of the car to allow access to the back seats, and held out his hand to assist the women getting in. He squealed with delight as he closed the door. "Hello ladies," he beamed, "I have booked a table at Marco's!" And he clapped his hands together. "It's my treat after all you two have been through."

Valerie smiled. "You are an angel!" She exclaimed. "It's just a pity you are gay, you would make a wonderful husband," and she laughed heartily.

Anesh smiled in the rear-view mirror, "Dahhhling," he paused for effect. "I make a wonderful husband anyway!" and he joined in the laughter.

Michelle smiled. Her mind still wandered back to Charlie. It had been almost six months since the crash, and though she and Tommy were now leading almost separate lives, and had never spoken about the accident, she knew inside that she needed to take revenge. And when she did, it would be sweet, if she could ever find a way to make sure it was complete. She shook her head, and laughed, joining the conversation late, she said, "I think you are just perfect as my gay husband!"

Anesh looked at the sadness behind her eyes. "Not with this shirt on dahhhling!" "It would clash with those eyes!" They arrived at the restaurant. A small, yet totally immaculate and perfectly presented establishment, with a celebrity following and a waiting list measured in months. But not for Anesh.

As he stepped from the car, Marco shouted, "Anesh my brother!" And embraced him tightly. "And who are these beautiful ladies?"

Anesh beamed broadly…"These are two of my dearest friends, this is Valerie, and this is Michelle." And he swept his hand majestically as he bowed like an actor taking applause. The two women looked at each other and smiled.

"Very pleased to meet you ladies," Marco boomed, and his belly laugh made Valerie shudder slightly as she thought of how similar it sounded to Giles. The two women curtsied and smiled again.

"Come in, come in," Marco gushed, and he clapped his hands, "CHAMPAGNE!" He exclaimed.

A small girl dressed in all black said quietly, "Yes Marco," and scuttled off. Marco showed the party to a small discreet table in a secluded booth. He winked even more theatrically, and whispered, "A little privacy for you," as he looked at Valerie and discreetly studied her up and down. Marco was a larger-than-life character. Happy, always smiling, and a little larger in build than perhaps he should be, but it fitted his persona perfectly.

Valerie studied him up and down too, and smiled as her eyes reached his fitted trousers.

Marco winked, and left them shouting, "Cristina, whatever Anesh and his lovely guests want!"

Valerie smiled. She looked at Michelle and mouthed, "His cock is huge!" And laughed out loud. Michelle went red, she had no idea why, and replied, louder, "You are so naughty!" And grinned.

Anesh caught the words and joined in, "She can be dahhling!"

Cristina returned with menus and refilled their glasses with Champagne. As the three friends chatted about life, reminisced about the past, it was clear that no one wanted to talk about the events of the last six months.

Anesh began in the end, "So, Michelle dahhhling," he said theatrically, "what will you do with the villa?"

Michelle turned sharply to him. She wanted to be angry at him, but she knew deep down she had to make a decision sometime, and much as she wanted to put off even thinking about it, she was grateful to Anesh for kicking her into thought.

"I want to keep it," she answered. "After all, it's paid for, and Callum is covering the expenses, so right now, I want to leave things just as they are." She felt a sense of relief come over her. She had not actually set foot in the villa since Charlie had bought it. She had chosen to stay in a couple of Anesh's properties on the occasions she had come over since the crash. She suddenly blurted out,

"I want to see the villa." And again, the wave of relief swept over her.
"You do?" Valerie asked.
"I do," Michelle returned.
"Good," Valerie said firmly. "It's about time girl." Valerie knew only too well how grief can overcome a person, and she had let Michelle take all the time she needed. But Valerie needed Michelle back to full strength. Because if the future was going to go the way she planned, she would need her friend firing on all cylinders to help her.
Anesh beamed. "Im sooooo happy dahhling," he chirped. "Let's go tomorrow!" And he raised his glass. "To us," he said loudly.
"To us!" The girls shouted in unison. The evening slipped by in a slow drunken haze of friendship, laughter, and a little remorse and sadness.
Michelle left the conversation at times, letting her mind go back to Charlie. Her eyes filled with tears, as she said to herself, "He would have loved this."
Anesh looked at her. "It's OK," he said softly.
And Michelle was back. She knew that she had to fix things. For Charlie. For her. And because it was time for Tommy to understand the woman he had now made. At around 2am, and with legs that most certainly were a little more wobbly than when she had entered the restaurant, Michelle asked, "How are we getting back?" Valerie was deep in conversation with Marco, and laughter filled the booth and Valerie's hand wandered along Marco's trousers as his enormous cock stiffened at her touch.

"Stay!" He bellowed. And looked directly at Valerie.
"OK," she whispered. And they both gently helped Michelle to the stairs.
Anesh looked at his oldest friend, and said firmly, "Look after them Marco, I will be back in the morning." He embraced the man he had grown up around fondly.
"I will dahhhling!" Marco laughed as he tried to imitate his friend. "They will be safe here." And he crossed his hand across his heart.
Anesh rose from his seat. "I know my friend," and he left. As he did so, the young man at the bar followed, and Marco couldn't help but smile. Anesh was a good friend. Despite him being gay!

He went back upstairs, and opened the door to the guest room where Michelle was already sleeping soundly. Valerie was still awake. "Would you prefer to share my bed?" Marco asked softly.

"Only if you introduce me to that monster," she smiled. A naughty, horny grin appeared on her face. Marco unzipped his trousers. Released his cock, and Valerie reached out. It took both her hands to cover his length.
"Come and say hello," he whispered. And quickly turned and left.
Valerie slipped from the bed. Ensuring Michelle was covered, she followed Marco to his room. As they went inside, Marco turned the key in the lock, and dropped his trousers to the floor.

Valerie knelt, unsure how much of this massive shaft she could get in her mouth. But she wanted it. She looked up at Marco. "Be gentle," she said.
"To start," he returned, and she took him into her mouth.

    Valerie woke up with Marco laying close. She smiled. And thought back to how big he had felt inside her. She had longed to just fuck. After her experience with that god awful sex site, she knew now that if she needed sex, she would find it for herself. And without the help of the internet. She remembered screaming as Marco had fucked her hard. It felt good. And was just what she had wanted. She felt awakened again. And though she didn't much care for Marco as a relationship, what he had hanging between his legs more than made up for any shortcomings elsewhere. She went to the bathroom as she needed to pee. When she came back she kissed him softly on the forehead. Gathered her clothes, and went back to the guest room.

    Michelle was still sleeping, but as Valerie shut the door she woke. Rubbing her eyes, she asked, "Where the hell have you been?!" And laughed like a schoolgirl.

    "He is enormous!" Valerie gasped. "I have never seen anything like it, or felt it come to that," she laughed. "And I feel fucked!"

    As they both gathered themselves, Valerie's phone lit up. Anesh. "Shit!" she exclaimed. "He will be here in twenty minutes!" She rushed off towards the bathroom.

Michelle swallowed hard. The villa. Charlie. The dreams they had wanted to fulfil. She wanted to cry. But something was stopping her. She didn't know what, but she knew Charlie would want her to go back to the villa and sort out this mess. And she was bloody determined to make sure she did.

The sun was already warm as the two girls left Marco's and climbed back into the Bentley. As the car left, Marco looked out of the window. He smiled as Valerie looked up and waved. She felt warm inside, and held Michelle's hand.
    Anesh exclaimed, "I'm so excited DAHHHLING!" He squeaked, "The Villa is beautiful," and he swished his hands in dramatic style. It took around 30 minutes to get there.
    Michelle gripped Valerie's hand tighter as they approached. And she could feel the fear and sadness. She had to do this. As they swept into the driveway she was greeted by a typically Spanish villa. Terracotta coloured, and with orange and lemon trees lining the drive. She gasped. "It's beautiful," she whispered.
    "It's yours, dahhhling."
Michelle felt the tear softly roll down her cheek. "He would have loved this," she said softly.
 "Let's go inside," Anesh beamed. And he turned the lock, and swiftly unset the alarm. A beautiful entrance hall, white and immaculate, greeted them, with heavy oak doors leading off it and a central staircase. Valerie took Michelle's arm and they began to explore.

Anesh went to the kitchen and poured the Champagne he had left there the night before. He made his way outside and sat on the terrace. There was a huge plush sofa next to the pool. And loungers dotted around. He had made sure the place was perfect. He liked Michelle and had liked Charlie too, despite only knowing him for a short time. He let the girls explore and took out his phone. "My brother," he whispered. "Do you still have your old contacts?"

The voice boomed with laughter. "Of course I do my brother, I choose not to use them, but they are still there."

Anesh smiled. "Keep them close," I may need them." As he put the phone down, the ladies appeared. "A toast dahhhling, bless this beautiful house."

The two girls took a glass each and smiled.

"Bless this house," Anesh laughed. "Bless the Jaguar in the garage too!"

"What?! Michelle looked puzzled.

"Charlie took care of everything for you, dahhhling," he said. There is a BMW Z4 in there, and a Jaguar. My friend got them for me. All in your name. All paid for, all taken care of."

Michelle smiled. She felt a new strength inside her. "Time for me to take care of things too."

And the three of them laughed. But Valerie could see the steel in Michelle's eyes. She knew this woman was hurting, and needed to make sure she did it the right way, but also knew Michelle was ready.

"I have to run girls," Anesh said as he drained his glass. "Enjoy your house Michelle." And he kissed both women on both cheeks before skipping outside back to the car. Valerie looked at Michelle. "It's your turn."

Barry's confession.

For the first couple of weeks after the funeral Michelle had slept badly. Her mind still couldn't cope with the sounds she had heard as the conversation with Charlie had been so cruelly ended. She had spoken to the police three times. Each time she told the same story. Each time she cried. He was such a fool to leave it so late. Why did he take that bloody car? Why did he have to speed so much? Her mind was nothing more than a whirling tumbling confused state. She had needed Valerie more than ever. Valerie had been her rock. The woman at her side.
And Callum, Charlie's son, had been amazing. Initially he had shown anger towards Michelle. He blamed her for his father wanting to leave. And ultimately that had caused his death. But she knew, and he knew that wasn't the case. He had seen his father happier than he could imagine and knew this lady had been the reason. So once Michelle had calmed, and Callum had made sure of all his father's arrangements, they went out for a drink. They needed to talk about it. And to both let their emotions out. They had both loved this man so deeply. And found strength in the solace they could offer each other. Slowly, they had formed the bond that would have grown naturally if Michelle had become Charlie's life partner. She had felt that from early on. This man was put on earth for her to be with. And there were no words that

could describe how deeply saddened she felt that he had been taken from her.

Callum was still angry. He was seeking revenge, for he didn't for one moment believe the police report that the cause of the accident had been excessive speed. He knew only too well his father's capabilities behind the wheel, and, despite his dad becoming a little older and slower, he still had it. There was no way Charlie just crashed and died. He had a bloody good idea who had been responsible too. It wasn't a coincidence that Harvey's son had left the garage almost as quickly as he had wanted to join. Callum wanted answers. He had told all his fears and thoughts to Michelle.

She initially had not believed any of it. Kept saying, "The police found nothing." And that was true. It had been a small country lane, there were no skid marks; no CCTV to view, and no witnesses. The car had ended up upside down, in a field just after a tight bend, which the police concluded Charlie simply had been going too fast to make the turn, had lost control and crashed. The nature of the field meant the car had rolled over, and somehow caught fire. Callum had gone back there several times. He just couldn't believe it. He had even bought an old Saab just like his father's and had driven it along there. Faster, and faster. Eventually he fell off the road at around 60 miles per hour. The car went through the gate and ended up in the field. But there was no big roll over. No fire. No matter how fast he had gone, all the way to over 70 mph, it was the same result. By now three months had passed since the crash. He couldn't let it go. But had to concede, without any proof, and with the reputation Tommy had, unless he was certain, he would have to take his time and find another way.

Valerie and Michelle had spent more and more time together. It was becoming clear that their husbands were perilously close to being out of control. The Amsterdam deal had gone to plan. The nightclub was ticking along more than nicely. And both men were almost arrogant in their attitudes at being invincible. The only saving grace was, they were so busy preening themselves and displaying their prowess like a peacock in full 'show off' mode, they had been far too busy to pay any attention to how much time the two ladies had been spending together.

The two ladies had planned another spa day. They were enjoying each other's company more and more, and what had started as an accidental meeting of minds in the ladies loo, had become a true and deep and close friendship. One that now was beginning to explore just how far their husbands might be prepared to go to keep their empire juggernaut rolling.

As Valerie and Michelle entered the steam room at the spa, and hung their robes, Valerie had said simply, "How are you?"

Michelle had looked at her. "How do you think I am?" She answered, almost sarcastically.

"Well, you best snap out of your pity!" Valerie snapped back.

"I'm sorry," Michelle returned. "I didn't mean to sound so sarcastic, but my head doesn't want to think about it."
"I know, and you can take all the time you need, but you are going to have to think about you now, and about Callum, and where your life goes."
Michelle sighed. She knew perfectly well that her friend made total sense. She just didn't know how to get her mind to focus.
Valerie raised her hands to both of Michelle's shoulders. "Come on woman," she said. "I'm here to help, and you need to get your shit together for your own sake, now come on!" And she gently shook Michelle. Secretly, Valerie wasn't quite sure she should have pushed so hard, but if it made Michelle at least snap back into the present, it was worth the risk.
"I will," Michelle whispered softly. "I'm going to need your help, but I will."
"Good," Valerie beamed.
"Can I tell you what Callum thinks? Michelle said softly.
"You can tell me anything Michelle, you know that."
"He doesn't think it was an accident," she blurted out a little too angrily.
Valerie pretended to look shocked. "He doesn't?" Valerie wanted to know exactly what Callum thought.
"No," Michelle continued, "He thinks someone caused that crash, he just doesn't believe his dad would have lost control like that. Valerie didn't either, but there was no way she would let on yet. Michelle carried on with the story of how Callum had even gone and bought a similar

car and tried to replicate what had happened to his father but to no avail.
Valerie listened intently. "And what do you think?"
Michelle's eyes grew wet. "I am not sure anymore, I just have this feeling that it was more than an accident," she hung her head. "Don't ask me why, I have no proof at all. But something tells me it was. And she sighed. A deep resigned sigh.
Valerie took stock. She had no real experience of Charlie's driving, other than when he had taken her out in Jamie's Maserati. But she knew even then that this man knew his way around a car. "Well," she said slowly, "if there is anything sinister going on, we are going to need as much proof as we can find. Because there is no way the police will want to know unless we do."
Michelle snapped her head around. "If this is anything to do with Tommy, or Giles," she snarled, "the police will be the last people I involve, now let's go and have a drink." And she grabbed her robe.
Valerie smiled, she liked the fact her friend was becoming angry, it suited her, she grabbed her robe and followed suit.
As they made their way to the green room, a voice behind them said "Miss Valerie." Valerie stopped. "Barry!" She exclaimed, surprised to see her slightly ageing driver there.
"Can I have a word in private?" He shuffled uncomfortably.
"Of course," Valerie replied, a note of concern in her voice. And she led him to a small office off the main

corridor. "You carry on Michelle," she waved her friend on. "I will catch you up, you know where you are going," and she smiled.
Michelle looked puzzled, but did as Valerie had asked. She slipped into the private room, and found the gin. As the ice "chinked" into the glass, and she sank into one of the huge and comfortable armchairs, she reflected on the last few months. Tommy; the drugs and the deals. Charlie. Spain. Valerie. Giles. The circle was toxic, and she needed to get out. Spain was still very real. But also, Tommy needed dealing with. Since the crash he had become unbearable. Hit her on numerous occasions, she knew he knew, but wouldn't give him the satisfaction of showing him she was hurting over Charlie. He was still having sex with that cheap slut at the club, and she and Tommy now slept in separate beds, which suited her just fine. He had told her to get out more than once. But she had been strong enough to face up to him. And her name was on the house. When they had first met, she had made sure she would have some rights. And being on the mortgage hadn't been a big deal. So, Tommy had gladly agreed. As the relationship had taken its much darker turns, until ultimately, she had been ready to leave, he had begun to regret both what Michelle knew, and also what and how she could make things very difficult for him. And only when Charlie had died, did he suddenly see the error of his ways. He should have let her bloody go with him. One way or another, he needed to deal with Michelle. But for now, things were fine the way they were. He had control of her, her money, and though she

was spending far too much time with that bitch Valerie, he could say nothing. Giles adored his wife (at least he pretended to). Tommy had already been put in his place once before. He needed to tread carefully if he was to deal with Michelle. And right now, he had bigger things to worry about.

"What is it, Barry?" Valerie asked, concerned. Barry was getting on towards 70, but she couldn't do without him. He was her confidant, and she considered him a friend. "Are you OK?"

Barry looked at her, a pained expression on his face. "I'm not sure Miss Valerie," he said softly, "but I don't think Mr Charlie's car crash was an accident." He bowed his head, almost as if paying his respects.

"What makes you think that Barry?" Valerie immediately paid attention.

Barry always played his cards close to his chest. But Valerie could see sadness in his eyes. "I had to take the Mercedes for some repairs," he said slowly. "I went to a place I had been using for years. When I arrived, I saw a black Mercedes van having some work done. The door and wing were off, they were badly damaged. And I overheard voices saying, 'Tommy wants this back perfect.' I saw the damaged panels. They were covered in silver paint."

Valerie went cold. She too had had her suspicions, but there was just no evidence. "Thank you, Barry," she said gently. She leant gently against the wall, she needed just a little support.

"I'm sorry Miss Valerie," he smiled at her. "You know I don't like bringing bad news." Barry wandered off with his head bowed.

Valerie was in a state of shock. She knew there could have been a chance it wasn't an accident, but in her mind, this pretty much proved it. Valerie composed herself. The one thing she needed to do was find the right time to tell Michelle. She made her way to the green room. Michelle smiled as the 'secret' door slid open. She loved the secrecy. And loved even more that Giles had funded it all. Valerie took a deep breath. Now was most certainly not the time. One thing was certain, Tommy and Giles were dangerous. And if they would go that far, whatever the two women might decide to do, it would need to be permanent, or she may live (or perhaps not live), to regret doing anything at all. So, for now, she would keep it to herself. Gather her thoughts, (and information), and make a plan. She wasn't the only one sick of Giles and Tommy and their behaviour. And much as she loved the life, and the lifestyle, after what Michelle had gone through, and with Jamie's death too, it had made her re-evaluate what was important in life. Her love for Jamie had confirmed she could love someone. One day Valerie hoped she too could love again.

She opened the door. "*Gin darling?*" she said rather too loudly as she beamed at Michelle. Almost *too* theatrically. But Michelle didn't seem to notice.

"Was Barry alright?" Michelle enquired.

"Oh yes," Valerie replied. "The silly old sausage has doubts about his age every now and again and tells me he wants to retire and move to the coast. I just have to pat him on the shoulder and tell him he can't leave me, who would look after me?"

Michelle smiled. She could see Barry saying just that, and then feeling all warm inside at feeling wanted by Valerie. In truth, Barry had no one. His wife had died a few years before he got the job with Giles. When he first took the job, it was just as Giles had begun his real rise to power, so Barry had been so grateful just to have a reason to live again. His wife had been his world. They had never had kids, and as she had become ill, he had quit work and cared for her till she died. His heart had been broken, but not his spirit, and he wanted to make the most of the time he now had ahead of him. He had very quickly bonded with Valerie, and she had complete trust in him. So much so that, after a couple of years, Giles had wanted someone younger and more dynamic, but Valerie genuinely didn't want to lose him, so she persuaded Giles to keep him on as her personal driver and to potter about the place doing a bit of weeding and the small, odd jobs that came up. It had worked well for almost 10 years, and the truth was Barry had come to her and said he was too old. But Valerie considered him a friend and had indeed persuaded him to stay. And the information she had just received made her doubly sure it had been the right thing to do. She took a large swig of Gin. "Goodness!" Michelle exclaimed, "Thirsty?" She asked laughing.

"Oh gosh yes! The thought of Barry leaving terrified me!" Then she burst into laughter, hoping against hope Michelle couldn't hear how forced it was.

"I'm sure you can persuade him, he is lovely, and I would miss him too!" She knew only too well how good Barry was at seeing 'nothing' and imagined he was very well rewarded for his silence if nothing else.
Valerie filled her glass again. She needed the gin more than Michelle could imagine. As she took another big swig, she asked, "So, what is the plan now?"
Michelle came crashing back to reality. She felt herself well up slightly. "I... I do, doon, I don't know." She stuttered.
"Oh for Christ's sake!" Valerie snapped. "Pull yourself together woman."
Michelle was genuinely shocked. "Well thanks for the fucking sympathy!" She snapped back.
"You have had enough sympathy!" Valerie barked. "Now get your bloody head together and decide what you are going to do with that animal you are still married to, and where the rest of your life is going to end up. I told you I will be here to help, but you have to help yourself, and if you want the truth, you need to sort your head out."
Now Michelle burst into tears. Not tears of sadness, but tears of anger. She knew Valerie was right. And suddenly felt a weight lifted from her shoulders. And an anger and resentment towards herself. She thought to herself, "Charlie wouldn't want this." "OK!" she shouted. "What the fuck do you want me to say?"
Valerie looked at her. A hard, meaningful stare. "I want you to stop wallowing in pity, snap out of your sadness, and realise you have, no, WE have, a chance to make a

difference. We have both seen what love can do, and, despite the fact we have both lost the men we love, we haven't lost each other. I'm bloody sure I'm not going to go back to 'yes dear' when I know there can be happiness to be found, whether that's with someone else or alone." And she drew a massive breath and slumped into the chair draining her glass. "I can't keep living in misery and self-pity. If you are with me, then it's time," she said angrily.

Michelle finished her gin. Poured the next one straight and downed it. "OK!" She blurted. "It's our turn, but, against those two, what the hell chance do we stand?" Valerie smiled. It was a menacing, devious smile. "We have each other, and a friendship," she replied. "And that's something Tommy and Giles will never have."

Ronnie Kray?

It was true. Despite the two men having the drug business, and even playing golf together, there was no love lost between them. Tommy wasn't the brains, and, certainly at the beginning, he didn't have the money to back up the undoubted talent he had for dealing with trouble, and also with providing the perfect outlet for the cocaine.

Giles on the other hand was the squeaky-clean businessman; a pillar of the community. He had rebuilt the school nursery using his construction company. Was the chairman of the golf club and gave thousands to charity. Yet inside he had always wanted to be Ronnie Kray. A desire to control; to rule with fear, it excited him. Made him aroused. Sadly, he had neither the physique nor the mental capacity to actually harm anyone. But when Tommy had opened that club, he had begun to frequent it whilst it was still (as he called it) an 'establishment'.

And he had found in Tommy the perfect ally. A hard, dangerous individual, not afraid of risk, and even more so if it came with a big reward. The drugs had begun in a small way in the club. Giles had still been a member and enjoyed supplying his high-class friends with a small amount of cocaine to see them through the night. However, he quickly accepted that whilst he hated the idea of a night club, he would never be able to shift enough coke to make him a serious player unless he found better outlets.

Tommy had suggested over a round of golf that he change the place into a nightclub. Younger clientele, teens needing a high. It didn't have to stop at coke. Pills. E's. Whatever they needed. He had contacts that could set them up with decent gear. And, providing Giles could control what the law knew or needed to know, Tommy could provide the transport and the muscle to ensure that their precious cargo would always get to its destination.

Giles had initially not been interested. It was too close. Too dangerous. And could be traced back to them. But Tommy had insisted he could make it work, and over time Giles had listened to his business plan and come on board. Giles was both powerful and influential. And despite living in a small village, the surrounding towns and city owed much to him in terms of construction, as well as the seedier side of life. Drugs and occasional girls had been distributed for his very powerful friends. It had rendered him almost untouchable, or so he thought. Tommy had been the icing on the cake for Giles.

He had always made sure Tommy would be first in line should anything go wrong, and Tommy had always believed it was just because he did such a good job. His ego was stroked by an overweight and ultimately weak individual who lived out his 'Ronnie Kray' but kept his distance just in case. But both men would admit, neither of them was a 'friend'. It had developed into a mutually satisfactory business arrangement. But it was no more than that. Giles liked Tommy grudgingly, and respected his contacts, if not always his methods of dealing with things.

Tommy was less complimentary in his mind about Giles. He hated the fact Giles was the 'money', and particularly at the beginning he had wanted too much too quickly. And Giles had told him in no uncertain terms, if he couldn't piss with the big boys, keep his cock away until he could. Tommy had felt the anger well up inside him even then, but he also knew Giles was right. He needed time to get his empire together. And Giles was just the man to make it happen. Not to mention his 'friendship' meant that doors opened where once they had been closed. Whether that was simply a nice restaurant and the best table, or a box at the racing, Giles had an influence that cast far and wide. And Tommy had used it. As much as he possibly could. But especially because (much as he hated it) it gave him an air of respectability by being associated with Giles. People genuinely liked the fat bastard, and thought he was almost Jesus Christ with the amazing gifts and charity work he did. If only they knew the truth. But people liked Giles the man too. Even if he was a bit overbearing and had a weird liking for very young girls. Tommy knew that, as the business had progressed, Giles had nurtured their relationship, and Tommy had grown stronger and stronger. Yet he hardly needed reminding of the beating he had been given not so long ago, and which Giles had ordered. 'Just to keep him in line'. It had actually surprised him at the time. He never really thought the old man had it in him. But it had made him even more determined to make sure that the Amsterdam deal had happened. He now wanted more. Wanted to take over. For Giles to step aside and let him show him how it should be done.

Giles knew this of course, and was having none of it. No matter how much Tommy thought he could run the business, the truth was Nikki had told Giles how nervous he had been in Amsterdam. Giles couldn't trust Tommy. He was a loose cannon. But also, a useful one. It would only be a matter of time before Tommy went too far. And Giles had always been quite sure to keep a distance. If ever there was anything discovered, he had made sure Tommy would always fall first. And with any luck, Giles would walk away squeaky clean. So far, other than the taxman sniffing around sometimes, he had kept everything above board. Golf with the Chief Constable always helped, as did a bottle of the finest single malt for him at Christmas. Not that it was a bribe of course, just two old friends celebrating the season of goodwill. At least if anything came out, he could deny all knowledge. And of course, the Chief would have to. Another perfect arrangement. Giles needed Tommy for sure. But Tommy needed Giles more.

In truth, they were both in it up to their necks. And the drug business was threatening to get out of hand. More and more dealers and pushers were needed. And with that came more and more risks.

Giles didn't like it. He wanted to scale things back a little. But then he wasn't snorting some of the profits.

Since Tommy had become more and more dependent on cocaine in particular, his mood swings had gotten even worse. And when he had tried the new 'LSD' drug, spice, he had briefly felt totally out of control. Thankfully, the spice trial had ended as quickly as it had begun. Neither Tommy nor his clients particularly cared for the 'Zombie' drug as it had become known. And Tommy certainly would not be using it again. Despite its highly addictive nature, he was more than happy with his coke hit whenever he needed it. Giles had been happy about that. At least he could control Tommy on the coke. The spice had been too dangerous. Too unpredictable. But Giles was concerned about how much Tommy was using now. And the cheap little tart he called his 'General Manager' at the club, couldn't manage to tie her shoelaces without instruction. But she did make Giles's cock hard and sucked it well. So he had to forgive her for some things. He loved his wife. But sexually she did nothing for him. The only way he could get hard was young flesh. Preferably 20s but he had forgiven Nikki, as being early 30s she was still young enough to get him hard. And despite the fact he couldn't think of her as anything more than a cheap slut, she served a purpose now and again. She had also given him the idea to take the business into something far safer, certainly in terms of if he did get caught. Pornography was the lifeblood of the world, with more internet searches for porn than almost anything else in the world.

    However, he had to be careful. It was an industry he knew nothing about. But he knew people who did. And they would be his guide. Keep him away from all that child stuff. It disgusted him. Despite the fact, at over 60, he preferred a 19 or 20 year old to fuck him. He wasn't a hypocrite. They were legal after all.

He had said that to Tommy. At 15 years Giles junior, Tommy had called him a paedophile. Giles had been angry at that. He had never overstepped the age limit, but he could have. He told himself he never would. Another of his 'perfect' arrangements. And now that little minx at the club, what was her name again? Ginnie? Something like that. She wanted in on the porn scene too. He was beginning to find the right sort of girls. And, with just a little coaxing, they would do as they were told. And if they had a coke addiction... it just made them easier to control. Yes, right now, the business was ticking along very nicely, Tommy was a loose cannon who could go off at any time, but

Giles had his measure, and as long as that little tart Nikki kept delivering the goods, and his porn business could begin to grow, he would do very nicely indeed.

Tommy couldn't see things the same. The cocaine addiction had become absolute now. And he couldn't survive a day without it. Once he was high, he felt immortal. Even if there had been too many occasions when his cock wouldn't work because of the drugs, and he had to resort to using a wine bottle to make Nikki satisfied. She didn't care. She just was now fulfilling all her fantasies. And that idiot Charlie had been responsible for it all! She was now exactly where she wanted to be. Not a care in the world. All the cocaine she could take. A decent fuck, when he could actually get it up. And the prospect of unlimited cock and pussy if Giles ever got his arse into gear with the porn business. She was a very happy girl. So it seemed that, six months on from Charlie's crash, the three people who were (at least indirectly) responsible for the accident were completely free, and beyond suspicion. They felt safe in their little bubble. They had totally taken their eyes off the two people who they should have been keeping the closest eye on.

The truth Michelle.

After probably the 6th gin, both women were inebriated. They began to be a little freer with each other. Despite their differences, they had become firm and loyal friends; had a relationship based on honesty and trust that their husbands could only dream of. There was no bullshit. Valerie in particular didn't hold back. But that had only made Michelle see how meek and mild she had become, that Valerie had given her the drive to change and become her own woman again. Back to that fiery teenager. But this time with a little more control. Michelle was enjoying finding herself again.

"Anooother oone?" Valerie slurred slightly.

"Why not?"

"*Good!*" Coz I have something to say." Valerie's face fell. Michelle looked troubled as she poured the drinks.

"What's wrong?"

"Sit down Michelle."

Michelle brought the two tumblers over to the sofa. She sat down softly. Looked deep into Valerie's eyes. "*What?*" she said abruptly.

Valerie sat up straight. Suddenly very sober despite the gin, and said calmly, "The accident." She paused. Michelle was about to say something, when Valerie put her finger to her lips. "Let me finish," she said. "The accident. It wasn't one."

Michelle didn't know what to do or say. For the last few months, she had been desperately trying to believe that it had just been Charlie driving too fast. She had even convinced Callum of the same. She exploded into tears.

Angry, resentful tears. Her fists clenched. "*WHAT THE FUCK DO YOU MEAN?!*' she screamed in her friend's face.
Valerie slapped her. Michelle reeled.
"Calm down," Valerie spoke softly. "I do *not* want anyone knowing anything until I am one hundred percent sure I can prove it."
The slap wasn't hard. But it was enough to shock Michelle.
"*You hit me*!" she snapped.
"You needed it." "Now, do you want to know all I know, or are you going to be hysterical again?"
Michelle let out a deep breath. "I don't know how you do it?" she said to her friend. "How can you deal with it so calmly?"
"It's simple," Valerie replied, in a very matter of fact tone, "I take in all the information. Process it. *Then* go hysterical if it needs it. You should try it, it will save you a fortune in mascara," she laughed.
Michelle couldn't help but smile. "*Bitch*," she laughed. "OK. I'm calm. Tell me."
Valerie relayed the story Barry had told her. Michelle sat dumbfounded. As the story unfolded, she could feel the anger rising again. This time she absorbed what Valerie had said. But stayed calm. Even if the fire of anger in her belly was making her blood boil.
When Valerie had finished. Michelle said simply. "So what now?"

Valerie smiled. "I'm impressed," she noted, "a much better response. Now you understand, I hope. Listen. Absorb. Process. Then react."
Michelle smiled back. "Yes, I get it, I'm sorry, I just got so angry. I knew he couldn't have just crashed."
"I knew it too. From the day he took me out in Jamie's Maserati I knew he could handle a car."
"I know," Michelle nodded in agreement. "Callum couldn't believe it either. And now I know he was right." A tear left her eye. But this time there was no big commotion. She just let it flow, and steeled herself for what was to come.

"You *cannot* tell Callum yet," Valerie said firmly. "Not until we are 100% sure. He is a little hot-headed and we need to make sure this is done properly and finally."
Michelle nodded again. Processing what Valerie was saying, understanding it, and ultimately, in total agreement. "So, what do we do next?"
Valerie laughed. "We have *more* gin!"
Michelle smiled. She already knew that meant, enough chat now. Let's just have a good time.
As Michelle poured the next, Valerie said, "We will do this properly, it's our turn," and that almost evil smile returned. "I have had enough, and I am pretty certain you have too!"
Michelle nodded. Swigged her gin and tried to replicate the same evil smile.
Valerie picked up the phone, clearly, she had changed her mind about letting things go. "Rita," she paused, looking at Michelle.

Michelle blushed remembering her first encounter with Rita.
Valerie knew it too. "Would you be a love and find Barry for me? Thanks." She replaced the receiver. "I will get Barry to tell all. You can hear it for yourself."
The door opened. "Hello Miss Michelle," Barry said brightly. "How nice to see you." Michelle smiled. He was such a sweet man.
"You too Barry, it's lovely to see you." Michelle straightened a little. "I understand you might have something to tell me about Charlie's accident?"
Barry looked crestfallen. He stared at the floor. "Yes, Miss Michelle," he said humbly. He shuffled his feet.
"Take your time Barry," Michelle comforted him. "It's OK, I need to hear what you know."
Barry looked at Valerie.
"Go ahead Barry," she encouraged. "And if you remember anything else, make sure you tell us everything."
"I will," he said shakily. "If you are sure."
Valerie nodded.
"You know me," he continued. "I don't like to upset anybody."
"BARRY!" Valerie snapped. "Tell the bloody story!" Barry sat up straight.
"Yes Miss Valerie," he said. "Well, it all started for me the day of the funeral," he turned to Michelle.
"It's OK, Barry," she said softly. "Please carry on, I need to know."

Barry sighed. "Well," he began again. "I had taken you to the funeral, and I was going to have my little snooze," he blushed.

"It's OK, Barry," Valerie smiled. "I don't mind your little snooze!" His face lit up. "Anyway," he carried on, "I settled the seat down. And just as I was about to pull my cap down, out of the corner of my eye, I saw a Black Mercedes Van. I noticed it because it was parked but with the sliding side door open." He paused, Michelle wasn't sure whether it was for breath or effect, before continuing. "So I pretended to pull my hat down. As I watched, I saw that black fella with the bad arm lean out of the open door. He had his phone out. And was taking photos. I made sure I wrote down the registration number of the van." He reached into his pocket and pulled out a piece of crumpled paper. "You see," he said, holding it aloft.

ASP 15E was written on the paper. "Except," Barry went on, "it was spaced out like this." He turned the paper over, A SPI5E.

Michelle knew it belonged to Tommy. It was used for the dancers at the club. He wanted the "SPICE" type number plate, but this had been the best he could find. "Anyway. As the service ended, and you all came out of the church I saw the door close and the van leave. As it drove past, I made sure they hadn't noticed I had been watching them, but at the time I found it odd. I only saw one side of the van and didn't notice anything unusual about it at the time. A few weeks later, I went to take the Mercedes in to have a little repair done," he stopped and hung his head again. "I might have had a little bump in it," he said.

Valerie smiled. "Barry dear, you do so much for me, one little bump is nothing," and she winked at Michelle. Mouthing, "It's not the first!" Michelle smiled.
Barry continued. "Anyway, I saw this black Mercedes van in the same place. It had no number plates on it. And a big dent along one side with silver paint all over it. It looked like a nasty bang," he nodded to himself.
Michelle nodded too. She was trying to be patient, but Barry could drag a story out.
"I asked when mine would be ready, and the bloke said about a week. As he did so I heard a voice from the other side of the black van say, 'Tommy needs this perfect, no trace of damage'. And he walked around to where I was. He immediately went quiet and went back inside. It was only as I was leaving that I saw the number plates inside the office. A SPISE or whatever it is. I didn't really even click then. But then I cast my mind back a couple of weeks. I was out walking, and I saw this silver Saab going mad past me, near where the crash had happened. As he got to the corner, he was going way too fast, and ended up skidding off and into the field where Charlie's car had been found. I stopped to watch, and a young man got out. Checked all the car over and drove it back out again."
Michelle asked, "Who was it Barry?"
Barry looked her in the eyes this time. "It was Mr Callum," he said slowly. "I didn't quite understand at the time, but, as I kept thinking about it, I worked out he must have been trying to understand how his dad had crashed so badly. So then I thought about the van, and

the silver paint." He hung his head again. "So I can't prove anything Miss Michelle. But I don't think the crash was an accident." He bowed his head.
Michelle put her hand on his shoulder.
"It's OK, Barry," she said softly. "I had always had a suspicion but couldn't prove anything."
Barry stuttered. "No, no, no, no," he said. "I can't prove it," he shook his head.
Michelle comforted him. "I know you can't Barry, but you have just made my mind up, I need to find out. So please, don't be too hard on yourself, I'm very grateful." She stopped. "Barry?" She asked. "What happened when you went back to collect the car?" Barry looked up. "The van wasn't there, Miss Michelle," he said. "But the damaged panels were laying in the yard, I saw them as I drove out. I stopped at the gate, and as it lifted up, a voice shouted, 'I'm going to deliver the Merc.' "My ears pricked up. So, I pulled out, and watched this fellow walk to the yard next door. He got into a black Mercedes van. And as he left, I saw the number plate. And I knew where it was going." Michelle grinned. An evil grin. "Thank you, Barry," she said kindly. You have done the right thing letting me know.
Barry shuffled his feet. "Go get a nap," Valerie smiled. Barry left the room.
Michelle felt the anger rise again. "So, what do we do now?"
Valerie returned her evil grin. "Now my dear Michelle, we take our time, and make sure it's our turn."

The Villa.

Michelle woke up with a start. The Spanish sun was already warm, and she could hear Valerie downstairs. The Villa was truly beautiful. And she felt a tinge of sadness, but also a joy that Charlie had done all this for them. She slipped out of bed, and as she put on the thin robe, she could smell coffee. She shouted down "Yes please!" And smiled to herself.
"Come on!" Came the reply.
And she grinned more broadly. Despite all that had happened. Her friend never failed to make her smile. She walked into the immaculate kitchen.
"Hello sleepyhead," Valerie laughed.
"I think it's the first time in six months I have slept all night," Michelle replied. "And it felt good."
Valerie nodded. "I hear you. When I lost Jamie, I think it was about the same time frame for me. But you need it. Without it, you become lazy, slow, and lose your lust for life!" And she threw her head back with laughter.
Michelle smiled and stepped into the magnificent garden. The loungers were slightly off white. Perhaps not the most practical, but certainly in keeping with the amazing building and gardens. She took a huge deep breath. It was a good feeling. Valerie joined her by the pool. They sat in silence and just smiled.

As Valerie sipped her coffee Michelle spoke softly. "I want to make Tommy pay." Valerie wasn't quite ready for the conversation, and almost choked on the hot liquid in her mouth.
Michelle continued, "I need to prove beyond all doubt it was him, and when I do, I want him gone permanently." There was a steely determination in her voice.
Valerie smiled. "It's about bloody time! So how do you intend to do this?"
Michelle looked at her friend. "Right now, I don't have that answer." Valerie smiled again. "But I intend to find it."
"Well!" Valerie spoke in a determined voice. "If you are sure, then perhaps we need to have a chat with Anesh and Marco." Michelle looked puzzled. "Marco doesn't just have a huge cock," she laughed as the words came out of her mouth and she thought about how big he had felt. "He is also very well connected to just the sort of people that Tommy would love to get to know, she paused, "he has been a very bad boy in the past."
Michelle put her hands on her hips. "And just how do you know all this?" She questioned. "I told you before dahhhling," Valerie smiled. "I make sure I get everyone I get close to checked out." And an almost evil smile came across her face. "He may have the restaurant and be the golden boy, but he has a very dark past that I hope we can use to get what we want," she paused. "And it also means I get to have that beast of a penis again!" She laughed as she stood up, dropped her robe and slipped

quietly into the pool. As she did so she gasped, the water was a little colder than she was expecting!

Michelle smiled and dropped her robe to join Valerie. Naked swimming in her own pool, in her own villa. She felt the grief pass over her, and wished again Charlie was here. But she at least now knew she had the strength to fight back.

The two women swam for maybe twenty minutes before Valerie's mobile began to ring. As she stepped out of the pool, Michelle looked at her and realised how far they had come as friends. She felt a warmth inside, which became the fire of anger as she let her mind go deeper. Valerie put the phone down with "Excellent, see you then," and turned to Michelle. "Let's see just how good your BMW is shall we?"

Michelle looked puzzled.

"We have a date with a huge penis and your gay husband!" And she strutted toward the house.

As she did so, a young woman appeared. "Who are you?" Michelle snapped, taken by surprise at the stranger.

"My name is Ruth, I am your maid, and I come to the house every Tuesday and Friday." The accent was undeniably Spanish, but the wording was perfect English.

"Oh!" Michelle answered a little abruptly, not wishing to appear foolish. "Of course, I had forgotten what day it was, nice to meet you Ruth," Michelle smiled. Ruth returned a sheepish smile. "Carry on," Michelle said, before realising she was naked. She thought for a moment that she should feel embarrassed, but decided it was too late for that! Ruth smiled again and went over to the pool and began clearing the few leaves that had fallen into it.

Michelle smiled. Charlie had thought of everything. Valerie watched from the upstairs bedroom window. She could see the confidence. She whispered to herself, "At last."

45

Just checking dear boy.

Back in the UK, Tommy and Giles were planning the next shipment. The Amsterdam contact, Lars, had been impressed with how the deal had gone, but this had seemingly only massaged Tommy's ego even further.

Giles had secretly been impressed, but he wasn't about to tell the jumped-up thug that. "Well done dear boy," had been all that Tommy had received as congratulations. Giles had known very little about the death of Charlie Summer. He always made sure there was a distance between himself and any, as he called it, 'nasty business'. He had told Tommy, "You do what you think you need to do, but I assure you it will be something you will regret."

"Yeah, yeah," had been the response. What the hell did that doddering old fool know? He had never done any work, let alone dirty work.

Harvey had earned well out of using his son to find out all of Charlie's travel details, and he had told Tommy that he wanted to quit now he had enough money to get out. Tommy had told him in no uncertain terms the only way he was getting out was dead. "Take some time off," Tommy said, "but I suggest you and your kid come back." Harvey wasn't especially scared of Tommy, but since his wife died, his only son Aaron was all he had. And Harvey had already got him involved in Tommy's affairs. "I will be back Tommy," he had told him grudgingly.

"Know your fucking place," Tommy had replied.
Harvey could feel the anger. He had served in Afghanistan, and a jumped-up little prick like Tommy was nothing. However, since the bullet had taken most of the use of his right arm, and Tommy had been the only one to give him a job, Harvey had always been in his debt. Big mistake. Harvey left the room seething. Tommy knew it, but he couldn't care less. He was in total control. Giles needed to be careful. Tommy was almost ready to take over.

"Peggy darling, be a love and find Eugene and Geoff would you? Get them to come to my office."
Giles was in a bad mood. Valerie was distant, and despite the business booming, he felt flat. He was the lord of all he surveyed, yet he was far from happy. Tommy was at the root of all his unhappiness, he knew that. The mess of Charlie Summer could affect the whole enterprise. He had arranged a round of golf with the chief superintendent just as a precaution. As his mind went deeper, the two men arrived. Giles smiled. "Boys," he said slowly, "we have to be very careful of Tommy, I feel he might want more than just a share of the business." Neither Eugene nor Geoff were entirely sure what Giles meant. Giles opened the safe. He took out two envelopes. "You work for me, and only me," he said quietly. "Call this a productivity bonus, but make sure Tommy's club gets a visit, and make sure all of our merchandise and its outlets are secure."
He waved them away.

The two men picked up the envelopes and left. Inside there was a note. "Don't bother to count it, there is ten grand. Just make sure you let Tommy know who is boss. I don't care what you do, or how you do it, but do NOT kill him. Right now, we still need him."

They had both given Tommy a small taste of what they were capable of some time ago, but always relished a chance to put him back in his place when, or if, Giles said so. Neither of them wanted to get too involved with Tommy's right hand man Harvey. Hard bastard. No matter. A smile crept over their lips. "No problem," they said as one. They walked out together. Geoff had always thought of himself as the 'boss', in

their working relationship, but the truth was that, despite Eugene's much thinner and wiry build, he actually liked doing the dirty work. Geoff did it for money. Eugene did it for pleasure. He touched the pistol tucked in its holster under his very expensive tailor-made suit. Geoff laughed, "You are one sick fucker you know!" he bellowed. "You like it don't you?"

Eugene's face twisted into a grin. "I love it," he said quietly.

Geoff shrugged his shoulders. "Come on, let's go see what that prick Tommy is up to." Eugene didn't need telling twice. He strode towards the Mercedes parked close by. Geoff always drove, but Eugene didn't care a damn about that, he wasn't lazy, but would use all his energies for the right thing. Let Geoff drive if he thought it made him a bigger man.

Eugene had seen action in Afghanistan too, not with Harvey's regiment, but he was nonetheless not fazed by death, or anything associated with it.

Geoff's background was much simpler. A child of a failed society. Kicked out of school at an early age, he started boxing. It became his outlet for his anger. Bare knuckle fighting meant big money too. But it also meant pain. A lot of pain! Then, one night in Tommy's club, Geoff had bought his cocaine in the club, and was just cleaning up his nose, as Tommy walked into the toilets. As Geoff left, his small comment, "Well that was shit," made Tommy turn in anger.

Just as he was about to say something, Giles walked in. He saw the anger in Tommy's face, "Calm down," he had spoken quietly, but forcefully. Giles didn't have many 'tough' qualities, but when he spoke people listened. Even Tommy. Geoff left the room, Giles followed, and asked him what he had said.

"The coke he serves up is shit."

Giles smiled. "I'm sure," he said. Giles went back into the toilets and saw Tommy seething. "Got some balls that lad!" Giles smirked.

"Shut it Giles," Tommy snapped.

"Who is he?" Giles continued.

"Some boxer, bare knuckle mostly. He fucking says anything about my merchandise again, and he will be boxing me."

Giles laughed. "It's not yours dear boy," he uttered the words slowly, and deliberately. "At best, it's ours, and you best learn that fact bloody quickly. And he walked out. Going to the bar, he bellowed, "Large G&T!" And drank it down fast. He left the club and made sure he found out more about the young boxer. He would be perfect for his protection. Giles had already employed Eugene, after meeting him in a doorway. As Giles went to kick him out of the way, this thin empty looking man grabbed his ankle and pulled him down to the floor.

Giles had never been so embarrassed, as the man he now knew as Eugene, had simply said to him, "Have some fucking respect."

Giles stood up, and said to Eugene, "Do you want a job?" And that was how it all started. From having nothing after coming home from the army, Eugene had now become a very valued member of Giles growing empire. Between Eugene and Geoff they both protected and controlled all of the unpleasant business affairs that Giles didn't wish to. It had become a good relationship between the two men. Neither one really liked the other, but they both knew their job, and did it well.

As they arrived at Tommy's nightclub that evening, both men checked their guns. Whilst Tommy had Harvey to handle all his unpleasantness, and Harvey had employed one or two other men in order to keep everything in check, both Eugene and Geoff did not underestimate their counterpart. Harvey was a decorated war hero, and he took no prisoners.

Eugene especially knew what Harvey had been through. So as Geoff parked the Mercedes, Eugene simply said, "Be professional."

Geoff laughed. "Whatever." And he stepped out of the car.

Eugene said in a low tone, "You may think you are some big shot, but trust me, Harvey may only have one arm that works, but he would kill you in a heartbeat and not think twice about it." And without looking back he strode towards the club.

Geoff looked slightly disappointed. For although he too was a hard bastard, he had never encountered war and all the sadness and anger it could bring. He knew deep down Eugene was right, but typically he laughed it off.

"Whatever," he said again under his breath. And followed Eugene to the back entrance to the club.

It wasn't an accident.

The Spanish air was still warm despite it being late in the evening. However, the temperature in the bedroom above Marco's restaurant was red hot. Valerie moaned loudly. "*Give me that massive cock of yours harder!*" She screamed as Marco fucked her from behind. No matter the pain she just wanted to embrace it. And the deeper Marco went, and the more it hurt, the more she lost herself in the amazing sex. She was determined not to fall in love, but the sex right now with this man's massive appendage more than made up for it! She smiled to herself, and as she did, the orgasm hit her. Unexpectedly, and overwhelmingly, she gasped, Marco forced his cock as deep as it would go, and her pussy exploded. She screamed again and squirted all over him. He grabbed her arse, and she felt him come inside her. His body shaking and quivering as he did so. He withdrew and lay beside her as she collapsed into his arms. He kissed her forehead, smiled, and whispered, "You are quite some woman"

Valerie grinned. "You are a whole lot of man!" She laughed like a schoolgirl.

He bellowed a deep guttural laugh.

As he did so, Michelle was downstairs in the restaurant with Anesh. "My Daaahhhhhling Michelle," he paused theatrically, "how are you now?"

Michelle couldn't help but love this man, she barely knew him, but she found such comfort in his total love for life, people, and especially how he had taken

Charlie into his friendship, and all that brought with it. "I am good Anesh. *Much* better than I have been. But," it was her turn to pause, though less for theatre and more for clarity of thought.

"But?" he asked curiously.
"But I am disturbed," she replied. Before Anesh could ask anymore, she put her finger to her lips. "Let me finish," she said abruptly.
Anesh crossed his hands into his lap. "Of course."
Michelle took a deep swig of her gin. "I don't think Charlie's death was an accident," she blurted out.
Anesh sat, unmoved. Michelle looked puzzled. He smiled. "Neither do I," he said softly. Michelle looked shocked. As shocked as anyone could be. Anesh smiled a much broader grin. "The question is"... he paused again for more theatre. As he did so, he took a sip of his brandy. "What do you want to do about it?"
Michelle took another deep swing. Drained her glass and stared.
"How the hell do you not think it was an accident?" Anesh whispered.
Calm down Michelle, she thought to herself. She instantly thought of the speech Valerie had given her. "Absorb. Process. Evaluate. Then go ape shit if necessary."
"Sorry Anesh, I guess it still hurts and makes me angry." Anesh smiled. He had a broad and rather ungainly smile, but it was always warm. "It's OK, Michelle. Just use that anger in the right way."

Michelle said, "Get me another gin would you please?"

Anesh needed to do nothing more but smile at Cristina. The petite attractive waitress arrived instantly, "Dos Grande por favor," he smiled, and pointed to the two glasses on the table.

"Gracias," came the demur reply.

"So, are you angry enough to want to do something about it?"

Michelle shot him a vicious look. "Oh yes!" she spat. "I am definitely ready to do something about it."

The waitress returned.

"Gracias," Michelle smiled.

"Then perhaps once Marco and Valerie are available…" he paused and laughed deeply. "We should all talk about the best way to do just that."

Michelle grinned. "You are a beautiful person Anesh."

Anesh looked back and could see the sadness still in her eyes.

"So are you lovely lady, and if I wasn't gay, I would look for a woman with all the beauty and determination you possess. "However, I am gay, and muscles and big cock are more my thing!" He laughed so loudly, half the bar turned to see who it was. Anesh waved at them all and laughed again.

Michelle exploded in fits of laughter, and as she did so, Valerie and Marco appeared.

The broad grin from Marco was for Anesh, the grin from Valerie was for the memory of what she had experienced a short time ago with Marco.

"MY BROTHER!" Marco bellowed. And they sat at the table.

Michelle blushed a little as Valerie whispered, "Gosh I'm fucked!" She smiled at her friend, and thought of just how much the tables had turned in the last few months. She felt an enormous happiness for Valerie, yet this also enveloped her in her own sadness.

Marco boomed "UNA BOTELLA DE MEJOR TINTO!" He sat, then shouted "NO!, DOS!" And laughed again. The four friends talked and laughed late into the evening, not talking about anything in depth, and just enjoying the company, but all the time in the back of their minds, all four of them knowing there was far more to talk about than how amazing Marco was in bed, or how Anesh looked so good in his outrageous shirts.

As the bar thinned out, Marco beckoned them all to the back. "I think it is time for some privacy my brother," he said in a low menacing voice.

Anesh suddenly changed from the laughing and jovial character, and displayed a side Valerie had only ever seen once. Anesh returned, "It's time." It was equally as low in tone, and as he leant forward, the outline of the small Beretta 9mm could be seen beneath his shirt.

Michelle smiled. Looked at Valerie. "He is a dark horse," she smiled at Valerie.
"Marco is hung like one," she returned, and laughed again as they slipped into the back office, taking with them another bottle of red, and as they made themselves comfortable, Marco locked the door.

Rosy.

Geoff entered Tommy's club first. Harvey immediately got onto his radio, discreetly whispering into the microphone, "Giles obviously wants to look around."
A grin appeared on Geoff's face. "He doesn't miss a fucking trick the old bastard," under his breath as he strode forward. Geoff was right. Harvey knew full well that Geoff being in the building meant only one thing, Giles was having issues with Tommy. The only thing puzzling Harvey was where on *earth* was his sidekick Eugene? The answer was simple. Eugene was already halfway to Tommy's office. His mind was far sharper when it came to cunning and deceit, a trait of his time in the forces.
Eugene knocked.
And a voice said, "Wait."
Eugene did nothing of the sort. He opened the door and let it crash against the filing cabinet behind.
Tommy looked up startled, as the white powder was still both on the table and all over his nose. "WHAT THE FUCK DO YOU WANT?!" he bellowed.
Eugene calmly took out the pistol and screwed on the silencer. "Giles sent me," he said in a completely monotone voice.
"NO FUCKING SHIT SHERLOCK!" Tommy almost screamed.
Eugene smiled again. Raised the pistol. Tommy gulped.
"Giles says you are getting out of hand." He spoke again in a dull soft voice. "Says you might be more trouble than you are worth."

As he finished the sentence he heard "Daddy can I have some please?" A bright almost childlike female's voice. Nikki turned and saw the office door open. She ran the few steps and entered the room.
Eugene calmly pointed the pistol at her. "Perhaps you are the problem?" He said. There was still no change in his voice.
Meanwhile Tommy was seething with rage. He was desperately trying to open the drawer of his desk.
"Leave the fucking gun alone!" Eugene snapped, angrier now. "I was sent here to try to make you see, it's time to get back in line Tommy." He paused, smiled, then spoke again. "Dear boy," and a smirk flashed across his face more briefly this time. "I could beat the shit out of you," he was back to monotone.
Tommy began to speak, "You couldn't fucki…"
Eugene pressed his finger to his lip. "Be quiet," he said. "But what's the point of that, when all I needed to do was waltz in here unannounced and I could have taken you or the coke without anyone being any the wiser?"
Nikki whimpered. Eugene spun around. "What's the matter, you little slut?" He whispered. "Daddy not such a big man now?" And again, he smiled. Nikki froze. "I will leave you two cunts in peace." And he stowed the pistol.
"Why don't you fuck off you prick," Tommy said with no conviction at all.
Suddenly there was a loud thud, and Harvey appeared. "Where the fuck have you been?" Tommy barked.
"He was keeping my colleague under surveillance like the good boy he is," laughed Eugene.

Harvey said nothing. It had all been over in less than 5 minutes. Geoff had simply stood at the bar smiling. Eugene spoke again.
"The old man wanted us to remind you who is boss again, however, I think we have seen all we
need to see. I will go back to Giles and report your security shortcomings," he looked at Harvey and smirked. "And perhaps he will need to see you again." He looked around the room. "I would suggest you have a rethink of your business plans, because..." And he paused again enjoying the brief feeling of power. "Dear boy, you definitely have neither the brains, nor it would seem the brawn to carry off what my boss thinks you are intending. So, be a good boy, clean your act up, and let's say, golf at mid-day tomorrow? We have been here once too often Tommy. Either you sort yourself out..." He stopped mid-sentence.
"Or what?" Tommy snapped.
"Or Giles will." And he swept out of the room.
Tommy stood up from the desk. As he did so he caught a glimpse of himself in the mirror. An overweight, slightly red-faced man with cocaine smeared across his face and a wasted expression.
He turned to Harvey. "I suggest you get the boys together," he whispered.
Nikki looked at him. The show of aggression from Eugene, dark, brooding and menacing, had terrified her far more than anything Tommy had ever done to her. She spoke gently. "Tommy, I think I might need to leave the club."
Harvey smiled. He knew the next line.

"What did you just say?" He adjusted himself and wiped his nose. He knew now just how ridiculous he looked. Nikki said again slowly, "I think I might need to look for a new job."
Tommy calmly walked towards her. As he got to within a couple of inches of her face, she could see the last remnants of the cocaine on his face. She couldn't help herself, and almost instinctively licked the white powder from his skin. He laughed, grabbed her hair, twisted her neck until she began to feel just a little faint. "Just remember bitch," he snarled, "I fucking own you." He let her go and she fell to the floor. "HARVEY!" Tommy shouted. "Get the boys together, I am not taking this shit from the fat arrogant old bastard anymore."

Geoff and Eugene got back into the Mercedes. Eugene was shaking ever so slightly.
"What's up with you?" Geoff asked.
"I can't stand that prick," his colleague replied. "I wanted to shoot him then and there." Geoff for once didn't laugh. "The old man told us to let him know who is boss, not to kill him."

"I *know!*" Eugene raised his voice, unusually, "but I would have done it for nothing." Geoff started the car. He said nothing more, but watched his counterpart fidget and constantly touch the holster he kept the pistol in. Like a firework about to go off, Eugene couldn't stop himself. He didn't much care for the drugs, or the women, or anything really. But after the day in the doorway, he had always had respect for Giles. Even if he didn't really like the arrogant fat bastard either.

They arrived back at the golf club late. There were not many staff on now, and even fewer customers.

As they stepped into the bar, a new face appeared.

Older, more tanned than anyone in England had a right to be, and with a beaming smile and ruby red lips, and bright red hair. She smiled. "Good evening gentlemen."

"Who are you?" Eugene demanded.

"I'm Rosy, Rosy with a Y not an IE, so just make sure you remember me." She laughed loudly, "I'm the new bar manager."

Eugene and Geoff looked puzzled.

"Is Giles in his office?"

"He is my love, but I think he may need a few minutes, he asked Gigi to take some notes for him."

The two men looked even more confused. "Notes?" They said as one.

Rosy looked at them with a smile. "Well at least I think that's it," and she winked provocatively. "He told me Gigi was taking something down for him," and as she did so she dropped two tumblers of scotch on the bar.

Both men grinned. A cheesy, Christ! I didn't see that coming type of grin.

"Welcome to the club Rosy," said Geoff as he raised a glass.

Eugene and he chinked glasses and downed the warm liquor. As they replaced them on the bar, Giles' office door opened. A petite young woman came out as they looked down the corridor. She wiped her mouth and made for the staff changing areas.

Rosy grinned. "I will just make sure Giles is er… ready for you boys," and she teetered off in bright red heels.

The two colleagues looked at each other, smiled, and Geoff reached behind the bar, grabbed the scotch bottle, and poured two more.

"I have no idea what's happening," he turned to his colleague. "But I have a feeling it's going to be a hell of a ride."

Giles' shirt wasn't quite tucked in as the two men entered the room. They both grinned like naughty schoolboys, as Giles coughed and said simply, "Well?"

"You certainly look well," they said almost as one and smirked.

"Oh for Christ's sake!" Giles bellowed, "What did you discover?" And he slammed his fist on the desk. Both men stood to attention.

"He couldn't lace your shoes, boss," Geoff muttered.

Eugene laughed.

"What he means Giles, is that Tommy might want to take control, but, unless he sorts his act out, he couldn't take out the rubbish."

Giles smiled. "And the merchandise?"

Geoff chimed in, "He is in control for the most part. The distribution and storage is more than OK. He just uses too much and loses his focus."

Eugene answered back. "Tommy needs to lay off the gear and get his head back in the game Giles, but he is still dangerous. However, I am pretty confident he will snap out of it," and smiled an evil grin.

"Good work boys," Giles finished.

"I have told Tommy golf tomorrow at 12 o'clock."

Giles grinned. How many more times was he going to have this conversation with the brawn in their relationship?

The two men left the room and Giles followed.

As they left the club together, Rosy smiled and turned off the lights. "Gigi!" She shouted, "come on let's go."

Gigi appeared. "God I hate Giles," she blurted.

Rosy smiled. "Fat man, small cock?" She laughed.

Gigi smiled. "Yes," she snapped, "and it's bloody awful!"

The two women set the alarm and left the club.

High Class Hookers.

Tommy swept into the golf club. Angry. The Aston Martin engine note matched his demeanour. He didn't bother to put the roof up or even lock it. He stormed into the bar. Rosy was there to greet him. He looked at her with disdain. "Rum," he said arrogantly.
"Rum, what?" Rosy replied sternly.
"Rum and be quick about it!" Tommy's mood darkened.
"And who the fuck are you to talk to me like that?"
Rosy smiled. "I'm the woman with the rum you so clearly want," she said softly. "So have some fucking manners." She bent her head low to meet Tommy's gaze. Tommy stood up. His fist clenched, just as Giles walked around the corner.
"Tommy dear boy He boomed. Giles looked at Tommy, "isn't she marvellous?" He grinned and looked back at Rosy. "You are not having any trouble with Tommy are you my dear?"
Rosy stopped. Turned softly. "Oh! Nothing I can't handle," she smiled and glared at Tommy.
"Good, good!" Giles bellowed. Tommy looked in disbelief.
"I say old boy," Giles chuckled. "Why don't we have a round and a chat."
Tommy replied softly "Why don't we," and left the bar. Giles winked at Rosy. "Good girl," he whispered. And he shuffled off to follow Tommy.

As the two men began their round of golf, Tommy blurted out "Who the fuck do you think you are?"
"You know very well who I am dear boy," Giles spoke softly yet sarcastically, "I'm the brains." Tommy's fists clenched again. Giles continued. "So, let's not get into this situation again shall we? I have had a chat with the chief super, and as far as the police are concerned, the accident to the Summer fellow was just that, so, it would seem that you did a good job. However, once again dear boy, you have let standards slip, and I will not tolerate it again. So, let's clear the air, and move forward, shall we?" He swung the driver and connected perfectly with the ball. As he did so, he shouted "Fore!" Then he turned to Tommy. "Rather good that, what?" And he belly laughed.
Tommy was beside himself with rage. He briefly thought of using the club in his hand to beat Giles to death with, such was the force within him. However, he restrained his inner animal. Giles was right in some respects, he had let things slip a little. The prick Harvey was his head of security, but he now doubted the man who had worked for him from the beginning. "You are right Giles," he said, the words almost making him feel sick as he said them.
"I knew you would see it my way dear boy," Giles smirked as Tommy hit his ball just as cleanly.
That lightened his mood. He looked at Giles. "Game on old man," he grinned, "shall we say £100 just for fun?" And he held out his hand.
Giles shook it warmly. "Why not dear boy," and he gripped Tommy's hand and shook it vigorously. The rest of the

day would pass without incident. Neither man paid any attention to the small figure that had actually been doing nothing. Just wandering about with a small dog that was occasionally annoying the golfers, yet this small figure was observing, studying, and planning.

Rosy was still behind the bar when the two men swept in. Tommy, much brighter now, having beaten Giles and claimed his winnings, he approached the bar a little more politely. "Rum for me please Rosy, and a Scotch for the old man."

Rosy smiled. "Just on the rocks gents?"

"Please." Tommy returned, "And have one for yourself."

Rosy smiled again. "Take a seat gentlemen, I will bring them over."

Giles was already sitting at the far end of the long room. His table. Tommy smiled. Every now and again he marvelled at how this overweight, arrogant, self-important man had almost everything. One day he vowed. And strolled down the long room to join him.

"So, what's with Rosy?" Tommy questioned.

"She will control my new business venture," Giles said with a little too much pride. "She is my manager, with a hint of Madame!" And laughed loudly.

Tommy looked puzzled. "A what?" he questioned.

"Dear boy," Giles said patronisingly, "Porn. High class hookers. It's a market I have always wanted to get into and it's VERY lucrative." He sat back in his leather high backed chair. Looking like an overweight golfing catalogue model, and smiled.

Tommy looked even more puzzled. "But we already do very well out of our merchandise."

"We do, dear boy, but at a rather large risk, and besides," he paused and grinned, "Gigi is definitely going to be a star." And as he winked a lecherous smile crossed his face. "So, are you in dear boy?"

Tommy needed a little time to process.

As Rosy arrived with the drinks, Giles pinched her arse, "Just been telling Tommy here about my new plans," Giles laughed.

"Oh Giles, you are naughty," Rosy laughed.

She looked at Tommy. "Well," she said, after my experiences in both France and Spain, "I just suggested to Giles that perhaps his more exclusive clients here might need a little more relaxation than the wonderful spa Giles currently has, can offer." And she playfully patted Giles' knee. "And of course," she continued, "they might also need something to relax them." She turned on her heel and walked back to the bar.

Tommy began to get the picture. He looked at Giles as he took a sip of the smooth dark rum.

"So, how does this all work old man?" He questioned.

"Simple, really dear boy," Giles looked particularly pleased with himself. "You build another Spa, but it's almost hidden. In fact," and he laughed heartily, "it is hidden, it's underground."

Tommy almost spat the drink out. "You have already built it?"

"Nearly finished dear boy," Giles replied. "It's about 20 miles from here. I have had the land for years, never quite knew what to do with it. Met Rosy on my cruise, got chatting at the bar, she told me all about 'celebrity whorehouses', so to speak. And it went from there.

The moment I got back, I got on to David at the planning office. A couple of lobster and Veuve Clicquot lunches later, and amazingly planning was granted." He laughed again.
Tommy was simply beside himself. How on *earth* did Giles manage to do this.
Giles continued. "I had already had my man Karl drawing up designs for something underground there as I knew anything on the surface would ruffle too many feathers. And my construction company had been discreetly just doing a little excavating here and there." He wheezed. "Amazing what money lets you get away with isn't it dear boy."
"Isn't it just." Tommy scowled. "So, how far into this are you?"
"Oh, it should be completed in the next three months or so with any luck!" And Giles chortled almost to himself.
"And just how do you propose to keep it discreet if it's had to go through planning?" Tommy posed.
"Dear boy," Giles sat back once again. "David, the chief super and I go back a long way. Nothing is too much trouble for my good friends, and they tend to reciprocate." Tommy was dumbfounded. Giles carried on. "It's perfect you see. Everyone gets what they want. Lots of people in the public eye need something private. I can offer that, at a price of course, and they can be confident of complete discretion." He sat back, sipped his scotch, and looked far too pleased with himself.
Tommy was almost speechless. He drank in the information. Drained his glass. And said, "So where the hell do I fit into these plans?"

Giles looked at Tommy. "Protection dear boy," he said simply.
"Protection?"
"Yes, dear boy!" Giles boomed. "You may not be the brightest star in the sky, but you definitely know how to look after people," and he laughed, "just ask that Summer fellow," as he did so, he raised his hand and waved. Tommy looked over, Rosy (with a Y not an IE) *God!* It was so corny, smiled and waved in return.
"Plus," Giles continued, "you will have to find the right merchandise for my clients."
Tommy smiled. This he could do. He had met Lars in Amsterdam, who had introduced him to a Spanish guy. Tommy would never forget his name. Lazlo. Lazlo Kiss. I mean really? *Lazlo Kiss for fuck's sake.* However, Tommy had spoken to him at length about having something other than the cocaine and cannabis to make money with. His experience with the SPICE had left him disillusioned, and he had gone back to what he knew. Now, his mind went straight back to Lazlo, and he smiled to himself. As the drinks arrived, he grinned at Giles, "I know just who to talk to," he said.
"Good, good," Giles muttered. "So you see dear boy, once my luxury underground Palace is open, I will most definitely need your help. However, I do think you need to have words with Harvey, he seems to be a bit slow these days."
"It's in hand," Tommy snapped. "There is nothing wrong with Harvey, and we both know what a hard bastard he is. You simply caught him by surprise, and, if it hadn't been

anything but your two goons then he would have been able to handle it."
Giles waved him away patronisingly. "Just sort it, dear boy," he said dismissively.
Tommy nodded. He finished his drink.
"Another?" Giles enquired.
"I have some calls to make," Tommy stood up. "Leave the merchandise and the er... protection, with me."
Giles smiled. "Of course, dear boy," he said. And raised his hand and waved.
Tommy smiled. "How the *fuck* do you manage to get everyone liking you?" He said aghast.
"Charm dear boy." Giles bellowed with laughter.
Tommy turned on his heel and marched out of the club.
Rosy delivered Giles his drink. "All is in place my dear," Giles said softly.
Rosy bent down. Her short black skirt rode up enough to expose her hold ups. Giles didn't much care for older women, and Rosy was now in her late sixties, but he couldn't resist running his hand up her thigh. Rosy bent lower. "Not here Giles," she mouthed gently, and stood up as she placed the glass. "Would you like it in your office?" She winked as her heels made their way back to the bar.
Giles smiled. Life was definitely good.
Tommy started the Aston. His phone linked to the car. And he shouted "Lars!" As the number dialled, Tommy puzzled to himself. He hadn't had a fix of anything for a couple of days, and he couldn't work out if he felt better or worse. He stopped before the exit of the club. Opened the glove box; took out the small packet, and prepared a couple of lines. He snorted hard. As the drug

hit him, he felt the power course through him. The phone connected.

"Tommy!" Came the voice of Lars, "What a pleasure, what can I do for you, my friend?"

Tommy smiled. "I need to get in contact with Lazlo, I have a different kind of merchandise I will be needing in a few months' time."

Lars laughed. "You are branching out?"

Tommy smiled. "You could say that."

"I will send it over to you," and he ended the call.

Tommy accelerated hard. He drove fast to his nightclub. He needed to speak to Harvey. He swung in behind the club, and marched through the back door. Harvey had been with him a long time. He knew all about Harvey's past. But couldn't overlook the fact he was getting older. Whilst he had nothing but admiration and respect for him. He needed Harvey to find at least one other who both he and Tommy could trust. Harvey's kid was no use. He was OK with getting the information Tommy needed about that prick Summer, but he was too thin, too weedy, and at times too bloody needy since his mother had died.

Tommy shouted "HARVEY!" and stormed to his office. Harvey could hear Tommy's voice from a mile away. There was no mistaking he was definitely in the shit. Grudgingly he shuffled towards Tommy's office, he really wasn't in the mood for this conversation especially when he would have to tell Tommy that the guy he had been interviewing had a surname of Mustard!

As he reached Tommy's office, he swallowed hard, then knocked on the door and heard the growl from the other side "Get the fuck in here now."

Harvey opened the door. "You wanted to see me?"
"Fucking right I wanted to see you!" Tommy bellowed. "What the fuck is going on with this place?"
Harvey was kind of ready for the fight. "Well maybe if you spend less time snorting the fucking stuff and more time looking after it, I wouldn't have to nursemaid you every five minutes."
"Who the fuck do you think you're talking to?" Tommy raged.
Harvey smiled. And in a tough yet soft tone he replied. "We have known each other a long time, you gave me a job when no one else would, and I have served you faithfully for many years. But what I see right now is the man I once admired and didn't mind doing his dirty work trying to be Mr Big Shot yet letting everything slip through his hands. Because it's fine distributing it, but you can't take it as much as you do and expect to keep your eye on the ball. That's what I see…"
Tommy turned his head to one side, went to the cabinet, took out the rum, and as he turned back said to Harvey. "Sit down." Tommy poured two large glasses and handed one to Harvey. "So what the hell do we do now?" Tommy asked.
"I have a new guy," Harvey replied. "My son has known him for a couple of years."
"I'm listening," replied Tommy.
"His name is Alan Mustard." Harvey grimaced as he said the words.
"Are you taking the piss?" Tommy laughed.

Harvey smiled. "No Tommy, I'm not taking the piss and that's not his real name, but it's the one he chooses to use just so nobody ever will know exactly who he is." Tommy grinned again and took a deep swig from the glass.

"Okay, give me the story," he said as he leant back in his chair.

Harvey began. "My son met him in a bar. He was standing on the door, thin and wiry, and didn't look much. Anyway, two guys decided to kick off. This thin door man wasn't the quickest, he has a damaged leg, but he reaches the first guy, hits him just once and puts him out cold. The other guy decides to run, and it's pretty obvious that thin doorman is never going to be Linford Christie, but he calmly opens his jacket takes out some fucking Chinese weapon thing and throws it as hard as hell. It hits the runner on the back of the head and wraps around his neck, and he collapses on the floor. The doorman walks over and drags him out of the club leaving him on the kerb. He then does the same to the other fellow. Aaron couldn't believe what he had seen. Once everything had calmed down Aaron went up to talk to him and asked if he could buy him a drink at the end of the night. The guy was ready to hit him, thought Aaron was gay and coming onto him. Aaron told him who I work for, and the guy began to listen. He told Aaron "The club closes at two, buy me a drink then." Turns out he's an ex motorbike racer who had a bad accident, kind of a Barry Sheene job. His leg was badly damaged and so was his mind. So much so that he never raced again. The team dropped him, he ended up with nothing and fell onto hard times.

Eventually ended up in a bedsit and doing odd jobs for money. One of the guys he did some work for was a martial arts trainer, and this guy Allan asked him to teach him. That was about ten years ago. Once he had mastered all he thought he needed, he began working on the door anywhere he could. Got a reputation as a horrible bastard with a heart."

Tommy laughed out loud. "No one who works for me has a heart."

Harvey smiled. "The only person who doesn't have a heart is that crazy bastard Eugene who works for Giles. He has never had anyone to have a heart for, except the army, and they threw that back in his face."

Tommy almost choked on his rum. He knew only too well what Eugene was capable of. Come to think of it, he was thin and looked nothing too. "I want to meet Colonel Mustard," he joked.

"Good," Harvey said, "coz he is here."

Tommy looked surprised.

"I knew this was coming," Harvey returned. "I still don't see why you and Giles have to have this fucking power struggle, and it will only end in tears, but, I will go get him." And he stood up and left.

Colonel Mustard!

Allan entered the office. Tommy smirked a little at the young man. "So you think you are Mustard do you?" he laughed.
The reply was short and swift. "No" he said softly, "I know I am!"
Tommy smiled again. "A cocky bastard too eh?" He questioned as he approached. "Well, let's see how fucking cocky you are now." He swung his fist. As he did so the young man swerved the punch, crouched down, kicked Tommy hard in the gut, making him bend double, and as he did so, a swift chop to the back of his head had him falling to the floor.
Harvey laughed. Tommy didn't. And Allan stood motionless. Tommy got to his feet. "Want a drink?" He asked.
Allan shook his head.
"Well Colonel Mustard, it's all well and good you doing that, but have you ever had to handle a gun?" Tommy moved surprisingly quickly, and opened the drawer at the side of the desk.
As he reached down, Allan jumped over the desk using one hand for leverage. He swung his legs high and across it, missing Tommy's face by millimetres. In fact, he got so close, Tommy felt the tiny rush of wind as the shoes went past his nose.

Allan landed back neatly on the other side of the desk. "I could have broken your nose, or cheek, or whatever the fuck I wanted," he said, but I figured that might not be the best job interview."
Harvey laughed again.
"Shut it Harvey!" Tommy bellowed. "Now you explain to the Coleman here how we do things, and that, IF he wants to join my payroll, he understands the rules."
Harvey looked decidedly puzzled. "Coleman?" he questioned.
"Well I ain't gonna keep calling him fucking mustard!" Tommy snapped. "Now fuck off."
Harvey laughed again, putting his good arm around Allan's shoulder. "I think he likes you," he wheezed, "come on son, let's go have a chat." And both he and Allan left the room with a smile on their face.
Tommy wasn't smiling. Despite actually being impressed with the 'Coleman's' abilities, any new face in his organisation made him nervous. He needed a drink.
As he walked to the bar, Nikki came out of her office. "Where have you been?" She asked almost sarcastically, but with a wink and a smile on her face.
Tommy looked at her with disdain. "What the fuck is it to you where I have been?" He answered dismissively.
"I was only playing Tommy," she answered meekly.
Despite loving the drugs and the lifestyle she had been allowed to create, there was no doubt in Nikki's mind that her days were numbered with the way Tommy was treating her.

Tommy looked at her with a mixture of pity and lust. He opened his fly, and said harshly, "Play with this," as he took out his cock.

Nikki looked up and smiled. She turned back to her office door, and turned the key in the lock. She walked inside, and, as she did so, raised her skirt, put her fingers in the waistband of her thong, and bent over slowly slipping her knickers off as she did so. "Yes Daddy," she said.

Tommy followed, his semi erect penis still poking out of his zip. As Nikki removed her knickers completely, Tommy grabbed her hair and pulled it hard. Nikki whimpered, inside she loved the pain, but she was never certain how Tommy would be.

His cock grew harder. And he pushed her to the floor. He grabbed two large handfuls of her hair, and looked down and simply said. "Suck it till I cum."

Nikki said nothing, but took his erect shaft into her mouth. Tommy held her head and pushed his cock as far as it would go. Nikki gagged hard. This only made Tommy fuck her mouth harder. Nikki was gagging more than ever now as Tommy pushed his cock deeper. She had her hands on his arse as his cock hit her throat, making her lose her breath and her head go light. She was close to passing out now, as he pounded her mouth but she was scared how much she liked it. Her head was spinning like she was in some sort of trance as she felt Tommy's rock hard shaft begin to twitch. She felt a little angry, but was powerless to stop him now. His cock exploded into her mouth as he pushed it deep once too often, and suddenly everything went black. She slumped to the floor, her mouth and blouse covered in both her saliva and Tommy's semen.

Tommy stood up. Just briefly he worried that there may have been something more sinister than her just passing out, but he looked at her chest, saw the rise and fall and realised she wasn't dead. He calmly put his cock away and left the room. Nikki was still a crumpled mess on the floor as the door closed, and Tommy strode back to his office. He now needed his cocaine and a rum more than ever.

As he opened his door, Nikki began to stir. Her head drowsy from the lack of oxygen. She scanned the room, looked down at her cum soaked blouse, looked around the room and muttered, "You bastard," as she came to.

Tommy opened the cupboard, poured a large glass of rum, and took out his mobile. He began to message Giles. "When is opening night?"

Giles was at home. Normally he would have been at the golf club, but he too had been making progress, and his love of pornography and especially young girls (he would only admit to lusting after girls 18 years old plus of course, but Tommy had his suspicions). Instead tonight, with his wife out and the house being empty, he had been doing what he claimed was 'research.' With porn on the computer in his office, situated behind his study in the vast house he and Valerie occupied, and also on the TV in his study, Giles was clearly taking his research VERY seriously indeed. With his cock in his hand, and naked young women displaying all he loved, he wanked himself slowly to orgasm, and fell asleep. Having made doubly sure the study door was locked, 'just in case,' after all, he couldn't risk his wife coming home and finding him! When he woke, it was gone 2am. Giles looked around, quickly switched off the TV, did the same to the computer, having first deleted his history, and slowly crept up the stairs to bed. Valerie's bedroom door was shut, and he sighed with relief. Closing the door to his own magnificent bedroom, he lay down, and fell asleep almost immediately. He didn't see Tommy's message.

Lazlo Kiss... no, that is his name!

Lazlo Kiss. You couldn't make it up. But he had used his name and his charm; never mind his dark good looks, for many years to both excite and manipulate women, and, at 42, he felt in the prime of his life. He had never intended to be a drug dealer, but life had just turned out that way. He had an empire dealing in very niche drugs, but that he supplied in enormous quantities to the porn industry. With orgasm enhancing poppers, and as much crystal meth as he could handle, he had initially only really dealt into the gay scene. But as he got deeper, despite, or perhaps because he was straight, he looked for ways to allow his merchandise to please women too. He now even had a factory making Amyl nitrite and business was booming. He puzzled over the loud Englishman Tommy, and what on earth he was up to. Drugs into England were always hard work. He didn't care much for it. But a sale was a sale.

    Anesh took out his pink mobile. He didn't care who knew he was gay. And despite his slight build, and his almost typically camp demeanour, he and Marco had grown up in the poorest of areas, and had nothing, so had learned to fight for all they had. Friends for over 35 years now, and almost never having had a crossed word, they had seen and felt all of the anger and anguish that young children can, and it had made them bitter and tough men. Mentally for Anesh, and physically for Marco.

The blend of brains and brawn a perfect match for anyone who dared cross their path. As they grew up together, so their friendship became an almost brotherhood. This allowed them to become, for a time, very powerful and controlling. Overseeing a small yet efficient organisation of drug dealers, pimps, and brothels which had made them huge amounts of money in a very short space of time. As their business grew, they carefully extracted the money, putting it into legitimate business, or giving to charity. Anesh went his own way; with property, cars, and enjoying all the wealth he had created.

Marco took a different path; opened his restaurant, and spent a huge amount of money making it totally exclusive. The two men had little to do with the dark past that had allowed them to have almost anything they wanted, but they were still in contact, still respected, and most of all, still feared. As Anesh's fingers flicked over the keys, his blue mobile lit up. "My brother, I think you should come over for a chat."

Anesh smiled, it almost infuriated him at times how Marco could almost read his mind. He put down the pink phone, he only used that now for his most important calls and messages, and replied, "We do my brother. Let's make it 10pm tonight shall we? Your place?"
Marco replied, "See you then."

Valerie woke around 8am. Refreshed, she had gone to bed early when Giles had gone to the study. She was not interested in what or who he was doing. Her mind was still full of Jamie, Charlie, Michelle, and of course that

massive Spanish penis of a man Marco! Oh how her desire for fun and laughter had been awakened by him, never mind her body. His cock really was enormous, and she very much wanted it again. She looked around the bedroom, and sighed. Her life had always been this way. She had met Giles at a dinner party organised by her mother. It had been dreadfully dreary, but Giles stood out. He was a little brash, a little flash, and had a glint in his eye. In fact, she thought he was a bit like Tommy was now. Though clearly with more upbringing. She smiled to herself, and thought, "God! You are a snob Valerie," and allowed herself a little chuckle. Her mind wandered to Jamie. And she felt sad. A wave of emotions hit her and she almost instantly went from a smile to sobbing deeply. The events of the last year swept over her. She cried, hard. As she did so, she could feel the anger building. Valerie had always been strong. Despite her privileged upbringing, she was no prude, or indeed blind to the world. Her mother had left when she was around 15. She had been having an affair with her father's best friend for years. When daddy found out, their marriage became what she now saw she was living in. A complete sham. But a very wealthy one. The tears stopped as quickly as they had come. She reached for her mobile, opened WhatsApp. Sent, "Girl we need a drink," and made her way to the en-suite. Her phone lit up before she got to the door.
"We do," came the reply.
Valerie smiled. Today would be a good day.

Tommy was in less of a good mood. His head couldn't get around the fact that Giles had once again gone behind his back. He thought they were partners, though he also, after the two visits he had been paid by Giles, grudgingly understood that Giles was still in control. The drug business was good, the club was good, he had all he wanted, yet he was angry. Almost constantly. He had fought hard to be where he was. Yet he still wasn't in total control. And the more he thought about it, the more he hated it. His mind began to race. How could he get rid of Giles? He shook his head. He couldn't of course. Not yet. Let the old bastard have his den of iniquity if that's what he wanted, Tommy could supply all the booze and drugs Giles needed. Tommy's time would come. He smiled, an evil smile, and thought back to Charlie Summer. Tommy's mind turned to Michelle. She was becoming a problem. He had no idea yet how he would deal with her. But he knew he must. With a million thoughts of anger, almost rage, his fists clenched and as he did so his mobile rang. Tommy looked down and smiled. He grabbed the phone. "LAZLO!" He bellowed.

Giles swung the driver and shouted, "Fore!" As the head of the club connected with the ball. "I say old boy," he said to himself, "rather good that." And bent to pick up his tee.

The Chief Superintendent smiled. "You get too much time to practice Giles," he commented as he put his ball down.

"Well one has to relax, old chap," Giles laughed. "I mean, all work and no play and all that".

The policeman swung the club and connected perfectly, sending the ball soaring into the clear sky, and he turned to Giles. "Indeed," he said. "And goodness knows we could all do with a little play," he laughed. "Especially that new girl behind the bar you old devil," and he winked theatrically.

Giles smiled to himself. The timing couldn't be any better. "Well Oscar," he began. "I have a new venture, which you just might think is right up your alley." And he put an arm around the Chief and in his booming voice said, "Let's go find our balls old man," and he waddled off laughing.

Neither one saw the blonde haired, rough skinned, heavily tattooed man deep in the undergrowth. The small dog he had with him was a perfect cover for anything anyway. But he walked slowly through the trees. Intently watching both Giles and Oscar as they marched to retrieve their golf balls. Taking in as much information as he could. The man turned as the two players resumed their battle. He looked down at the dog, made a small hand signal, and went back to the road. The battered Land Rover was never locked. He didn't care. No one would steal it. The dog jumped up onto the passenger seat, and as Brian put the key into the ignition, he looked at his four-legged friend and smiled. He started the engine. A loud, rough, uneven sound. Brian didn't care. He had been deaf since birth. Living in a world of silence that had made him calm over the years. He had been bullied at school. And made sure he fought his battles as hard as he could. As he grew older, he learnt that fighting could earn him real money. He began to use his fists to fund his life. Now, at almost 70, he considered himself retired. He had known Marco for years. Brian lived by himself save for his dog, on a narrowboat just outside of town. But 20 years ago, he had lived the high life in Spain, with a big yacht and an apartment on the harbour. He had met Marco when a deal had turned sour. The boat delivering the goods had been followed. Marco was caught in the crossfire and Brian had pulled him clear of the gun battle. The police eventually made two arrests, and the boat's precious drugs cargo was seized. But Marco was never found by the police. Brian removed the bullet from Marco's shoulder and let him stay on his boat for a couple of days. They had been friends ever since.

Marco knew better than to call on Brian since he had retired, and Marco himself kept out of the gangs and deals now. But when he met Valerie, and as much as he tried, he couldn't help himself liking her. And the fact his brother Anesh hated Valerie's husband made it all the easier to help her. Valerie had been insistent, she needed help to put right Charlie's death. And Marco could help. Marco smiled. He thought of fucking her again. The smile turned to a grin. Perhaps a trip to England was on the cards. He took out his mobile. There was little point in dialling the number, so he sent a WhatsApp message. "Do you have room on that boat for one more?" Marco smiled. He could feel the blood pumping through his veins, and he looked out of the restaurant window. The sun a brilliant yellow in the clear blue Spanish sky. His phone lit up. A simple message.

"Anytime."

Marco replied. "See you Friday."
"I will get some wine," came the message back.
Marco smiled again. His fingers whizzed across the screen. "I am going to England."
Anesh replied almost before the words had landed on the screen. "Be careful my brother, Giles may be a fat arrogant man, but he isn't stupid."
"I will be just fine my brother." Marco replied. And he opened a bottle of expensive red, poured the glass, and drank it slowly. Savouring the feeling of power returning to him. Much as he loved his restaurant, and all of the background stuff, secretly Marco had missed his dark past. Anesh loved the theatre and the drama, all of the planning and setting up of deals, and making it happen. Marco loved the violence. The physical act of making someone suffer to extract what you wanted. He even loved the killing. He took another swig of wine. As he did so, Christina arrived. She blushed a little at Marco. He smiled and poured a second glass. "Come sit," he smiled. Christina did as Marco asked. She took a sip of the wine. Marco looked at her. And she could see him getting hard. She had been fucking him for a while now. And despite the fact she thought she should be used to the size of him, his enormous cock always made her gasp. As Marco undid his zip, she took a bigger swing of wine, lowered her head, and put his cock in her mouth.
Marco allowed his head to fall back. He gently touched her hair. "Suck me," he commanded.
Chrsitina did as she was told. The head of his cock in her throat. She gagged. He loved that. He pushed a little

deeper. She could never get it all in her mouth. Faster she worked her magic. Her tongue flicking over the head. Her hand wanking him when she lost her breath. He knew it wouldn't take long to come. He had been thinking about Valerie all morning. His mind wanting her. His cock needed release. As Christina looked up, Marco smiled. And exploded into her mouth. She choked. The hot sticky semen hitting her throat. Her eyes a little wet from taking him so deep. She gasped, as she swallowed the last.

Marco took his cock out of her mouth. Kissed her softly. Poured a little more wine and said, "We must get ready for our day!" A deep bellow that almost made Christina jump. She felt dissatisfied. She had wanted Marco to fuck her. He stood up. Saw her expression. As he mouthed, "Later," another waitress knocked at the door. Marco smiled. "You see?" He laughed.

Christina shook her head. Her mind understood. Her pussy was still hungry. And she was angry. She stormed out and went to the kitchen.

The other waitress looked a little puzzled as Marco smiled. "Come Stephanie, let's get ready for opening!" Stephanie smiled. And looked down. His cock still semi hard, she grinned.

Marco smiled back, touched himself, and then said, "Let's start with the booths at the back." He winked provocatively. Stephanie blushed. And followed him to the back of the restaurant.

The Signalman.

The plane landed at midday. As Marco stepped off, the rather warm day surprised him. Certainly, for the time of year he had not expected it to be so mild. As he made his way through the airport, and to the exit, it didn't take him long to see the white-blonde hair of the man he called 'The Signalman'.

A short wave, and Marco and The Signalman walked in silence to the battered Land Rover. They got in and drove in silence to a secluded spot on the canal. There, moored as it had been for years, was 'Silent Revenge'. A seventy feet long Narrow boat. The Signalman had lived on it for a long time. He opened the boat, and Marco followed him inside. Only now did the old friends begin to talk, as Brian poured the deep rich Cabernet Sauvignon. As the evening wore on, the conversation turned to darker subjects.

Marco explained how he was friends with Valerie, and all about the accident with Charlie.

As he listened, Brian grinned. He downed the glass. And said simply, "I'm retired." Marco's face fell.

Just as he was about to remonstrate, Brian smiled. "But, my brother, his hands explained. "For you, and a big pay cheque!" And he laughed at his own joke. "I will make an exception." He reached for another bottle. Sat back down. His dog joined them both. And slowly, they began to put the world to rights.

Marco had learned to use sign language after Brian had shown him kindness and he felt it the least he could do

was to be able to communicate properly with him. Marco smiled. "Good!" he signed.
"So what do you want me to do?"
"I need you to find a way to eliminate Giles and Tommy," Marco scowled. "They are getting out of hand, and Lars is concerned that their lack of care could put operations in danger."
Brian smiled. He had always enjoyed retribution. It made him feel whatever happened had some justification. He nodded. "I have been watching the fat man," and he used his hands to simulate an enormous stomach. He laughed as he did so, then suddenly became serious. "He plays golf with a policeman."
Marco smiled. "How else would he get away with all he does?"
A wry smile appeared on Brian's face. "How much?" He said simply.
"Name your price."
"This is serious," Brian signed.
"This is serious my brother," Marco returned.
"250," came the reply.
Marco pondered for a moment. "Let me speak with Anesh," and he took out his phone. Sent the simple message "250."
The reply was instant. "125 for each. If he doesn't complete both, he only gets what he has finished."
Marco smiled, and turned the phone to Brian.
Brian looked at Marco. "Tell him he is a wanker, but he has a deal!" And he laughed loudly.
Marco sent the reply, "The deal is done," and drained his glass and yawned. "I need sleep my friend."

Brian pointed down the boat. Held up two fingers and poured more wine.
Marco took his bag, and made for the direction Brian had indicated. "Good night my friend," he signalled.
Brian smiled. Patted the seat, and as the dog jumped back on, he waved at Marco.

Giles leaned back in his chair.
Rosy smiled. And knelt. As she unzipped his fly, she looked up at him.
"Now my dear, let's just check your credentials, shall we?!"
Rosy took out Giles cock. And slowly went down on him. Thank God she had made him shower!
Gigi stood at the door. No matter how many times she had done it, she loved to learn and watching Rosy suck Giles expertly was just the education she needed.
Giles' hands rested on Rosy's head. He pushed her down. She resisted. He pushed harder.
And Rosy stood up. "Either you let me do it my way," she paused, "or you can suck your own cock."
"I'm sorry my dear, Giles said sheepishly, "got carried away."
"You will be," she replied. "in a bloody bag" And softly knelt once more. Gigi laughed. And Giles turned to the door.
"WHAT ARE YOU DOING?!" he bellowed.
Rosy stood again. "She is learning how to please your customers," she sighed sarcastically. "Now will you shut up and let me finish you off?"
Gigi laughed again.

"Come in my dear," Giles beckoned.
Rosy smiled. "Yes, that's a good idea," she said with a grin.
Gigi closed the door… Turned the key, and walked slowly over to Giles desk.
Rosy instructed her to kneel down and Gigi obliged. Giles looked slightly disappointed. Rosy put her finger to her lips. Giles stayed silent. His cock now softer since the interruption. Gigi took it in her hand. And began to slowly lick it.
Rosy smiled. "Good girl," she said, and she too knelt in front of Giles.
He smiled. The blood coursing harder through his veins now. His cock began to stiffen and first Rosy then Gigi licked along its length. Rosy took it in her mouth. And with just a few deep throat gulps she made Giles orgasm in her mouth. She stood up, went over to the sink, and spat the semen out. Giles was speechless.
Rosy smiled. "Come on Gigi, let's close up."
Gigi smiled. "Yes, let's," and she followed Rosy.
As they got to the door, Rosy smiled sweetly and said, "I'm sure your customers will pay very well for that." And she swept out of the room taking Gigi with her.

Tommy shut the door. He hadn't spent much time at home lately. He was either at the club, or too busy trying to get hold of Lazlo to organise the first shipment. His mood was almost constantly dark.
Michelle kept out of his way, which was ironically easy now. He slept in the master bedroom. She used the guest room. It was nothing more than a shell of a marriage. And

Tommy had plans to get rid of his wife, in much the same way as he had got rid of her lover. After all, she had no one now. He smiled. And perhaps the Coleman would be just the man to do it. Tommy still hadn't forgotten how he was embarrassed by him not so long ago. The more he played the thoughts out in his mind, the more they appealed. He poured a large rum, and went into the den. As he flicked the TV on, the local news announced a new police officer for the county. Who promised to stamp out the growing threat of drugs spreading 'like a cancer' across the area. Tommy laughed. Said to himself, "Giles you fat cunt, you have work to do." As he flicked the TV further and the music channels appeared. "Valerie" appeared. Amy Winehouse. Tommy froze. He had no idea why. But that name suddenly made him realise, Michelle did have someone. A very dangerous ally. Valerie fucking Williams. He swigged the rum hard. Perhaps getting rid of Michelle wouldn't be quite as easy as he had hoped. He smiled. Said to himself, "I always like a challenge," and as he put the glass down, he slowly closed his eyes. It had been a long day. Tommy fell asleep at 3.12am.
At 3.12 am The Signalman opened a shallow cubby hole in the bottom of the boat. It was dark, and a little dusty. But he smiled as he shone the torch. The glint of cold steel brought him more joy than it should have. The machete and numerous knives had been thrown in without care. But he looked at them like they were old friends. He reached in and moved the knives. And there, wrapped in a hessian sack, was his crossbow. Brian didn't believe in using guns. In fact, he used nothing that made a noise.

Having been deaf since birth had taught him that you could achieve much with silence. Stealth. Cunning. If he was to carry out Marco's wishes, it would be in silence. He lifted out the weapon and grabbed the bag of bolts. It was time to get prepared. He went to bed with the weapon. The dog climbed on to the end of the bed and curled up at his feet. Brian closed his eyes and smiled. £250,000 would be just fine.

Marco comes to the UK.

Valerie kissed Giles lightly on the cheek. His snores were almost deafening. For God's sake! Why had she not run away with Jamie? She felt her emotions overcome her. And closed the bedroom door.
Michelle's mobile went off. "Fancy a coffee?" She smiled. Hell yes, of course she did! "See you in an hour!" She sent back.
"Perfect," came the reply.
Valerie smiled. As she did so, her mobile lit up. "Coffee?" She dropped the phone. Said to herself, "Fuck!" Then grabbed the phone again. She sent the reply. "It's a long bloody way to go for a coffee!"
Marco's face lit up.
"Not if I am in England!" And he bellowed out loud. Brian and the dog continued to snore.
Valerie blushed. Her mind couldn't help but think of Marco's massive cock. Her head span. Shit. Michelle. Marco. Shit!!
Marco stepped off the boat and sat in the camping chair. He smiled and looked at the bright sky. He sent back.
"It's short notice I know."
Valerie returned. "Just give me a couple of hours, would you?"
"Of course," he replied. "I am staying with an old friend on his boat. Let me know when you are around," and he sipped his black coffee. Life felt good for Marco.

Just as he closed his eyes and allowed himself to relax. He felt, and heard, the bolt rush past his ear. His head whipped around to find Brian smiling, and Toffee the dog almost laughing at him. He turned back to see the bolt embedded in the small spindly tree just to the left of where he was sitting. "You bastard!" He signed.

Brian laughed. He pointed to his ears. And mimicked, "Keep these open," as he closed the window and made his way to Marco.

Marco stood up. Made a fist and pretended to be ready to hit his friend.

Brian shook his hand and went to the tree to retrieve the bolt. He smiled as he returned. Held up two fingers. "125k each," he laughed. "I only need two." Toffee looked up at him. He gestured to the dog and went back inside.

Marco smiled. He knew he had the right man for the job.
Valerie's head was spinning. What on earth was Marco doing here? She didn't care, she needed to see him. As Michelle pulled into the car park, Valerie could no longer contain her excitement. She almost ran to the car.
"Marco is in the UK!" She squealed with delight.
Michelle laughed.
"What are you talking about?" She replied.
"I have no idea right now!" Valerie laughed. "But he is in the UK and wants to meet up!" She felt like a schoolgirl whose favourite crush had just asked her out.
"OK, OK, calm down," Michelle smiled. She could see the excitement in Valerie's eyes. "Why is he here?"

"Anesh is angry. After we told him the whole Charlie story, he spoke to Marco. Marco has never quite left his past. And Anesh had always wanted to get revenge on Giles for the way he had treated him."
Michelle's surprised look said it all.
"So he is here to get even with Giles?"
"I hope he is here to fuck me too!" Valerie laughed again. "But yes, he has come over to speak to an associate of his, and decide the best way to avenge both Charlie's death, and also allow Anesh to finally put paid to the past."
Michelle sat silent for a moment. "Avenge Charlie's death. You mean kill Tommy?" She said softly.
"Yes," Valerie replied sharply.
"*Merde,*" Michelle breathed the word. The sudden realisation that the possibility of retribution for Charlie's death was upon her, filled her with joy. But also, she suddenly understood that this man was either here to kill her husband, or find someone to do it.
"So, I am going to meet him in an hour or so. And hopefully we might have some more answers!"
The truth was Valerie hadn't given either Giles or Tommy a second thought. Frankly, she didn't care. She wanted to feel Marco. Have him naked next to her, and to feel alive.
Valerie smiled. She flashed her fingers across her phone. Hotel booked. Out of town. Just for a few hours. Perfect to have Marco. And let him have her. Her smile told Michelle all she needed to know.
"I best let you get on," she smiled. "I can see you have things to do. Let's catch up after you have seen him."

Valerie looked at her friend. "Thank you," she mouthed softly. And she made her way back to the Mercedes, where Barry was waiting.
Michelle sat, slightly empty. Yet understanding why Valerie wanted to leave. She had been there many times. Her mind drifted back to Charlie. The wonderful times they had spent together. How deeply she had fallen for him, and how quickly. She missed him. And as she allowed her mind to remember, the anger built. Tommy. The car crash. Charlie's screams as the flames took hold. Then the silence. Her fists clenched. Suddenly Marco being here was just fine. She wanted to know details. But she needed vengeance. She smiled to herself as she made her way back to her car. One way or another, it was most definitely going to be her turn. As she pulled out of the car park, she turned the music up loud. And drove fast. "It's my fucking turn!" She shouted to no one in particular.

    Valerie closed the hotel door. Marco smiled. Slowly he undressed her. Her body fizzed at his touch. He lay her on the bed and began to explore her body with his hands and mouth. She closed her eyes and let him take her. Her mind lost. Nothing but pleasure for the next few hours. Marco took full advantage. He liked this woman. And liked even more what she did for him.
    Brian was quietly preparing the weapons. He loved the precision. The peace. Taking out the knives, one by one, he poured a little oil onto the sharpening stone, and worked the knife gently across. Back and forth. Slowly. With care. He saw the steel go dull in colour. And ran his

finger across the blade. Rough to the touch, he turned and threw the knife expertly. It embedded itself in the tree. The smile on his face said it all. He would make sure he got his pay day. He looked down at Toffee. Patted his friend on the head. And went back to the knives. He chuckled to himself. This was too easy.

Geoff and Eugene were in the car. They had followed Giles at his request.

Today was the day he got rid of the Bentley. He wanted a Range Rover. At £300,000 it wasn't exactly cheap. But Giles was tired of feeling left behind by Tommy with his Aston Martin. He knew he couldn't fit in the Aston. But a Range Rover SV would do very nicely indeed. Giles swept into Lookers and parked slap bang in the middle of the forecourt. As fast as he could make his exit from the Bentley, the salesman, Jordan, came rushing out. As he was about to open his mouth, Giles smiled, "My dear boy!" He bellowed in his inimitable style. Sticking out his right hand he shook Jordan's vigorously.

Jordan looked slightly bewildered but smiled politely.

"Here to pick up a Range Rover!" Giles barked.

Jordan looked even more puzzled.

Just as he was about to open his mouth, a small, dapper man with a handlebar moustache and trousers too short for his legs appeared and held out his hand.

"Giles!" He exclaimed.

Jordan was bemused. The General Manager coming out?

"Hello dear boy!" Giles beamed, "Is she ready?"

The small man scuttled off, muttering, "Oh yes, she is ready!" And he disappeared round the corner of the building.

Jordan smiled awkwardly and went back inside, leaving Giles alone.

Just as he was beginning to feel himself get flustered at almost being ignored, the menacing, black car appeared. Giles' face broke into a grin. "Oh yes," he muttered softly. "Oh yes!" He boomed a second time.

The car drew alongside him. The darkened window lowered. And the small man with the moustache grinned. "Here she is Giles," he beamed.

"Here she is indeed," Giles exclaimed, and he slowly walked around the car.
When he got back to the driver's side, Frankie Winter, General Manager, was waiting.
"Shall we do the nasty business of paperwork?" He laughed.

"Why not dear boy!" Giles laughed. And followed Frankie inside. As he did so he waved at the Mercedes. And Geoff left the car park muttering, "He has too much fucking money," and roared out onto the road.
Eugene grinned. He didn't care about money. But Geoff was right, Giles had way too much of it.

Marco came inside Valerie hard. Her head bent down, buried in the pillow as his enormous cock fucked her hard from behind. She would never get used to this monster cock. But she loved the pleasure and pain he gave her! As his cock finally stopped ejaculating, he took it out and lay on the bed next to Valerie. Spent. Thrilled. Drained.

Valerie smiled. Between her thighs was swollen, a little sore, and completely fucked! She looked at Marco. "I will never stop enjoying feeling you," she grinned.

"Be careful," Marco said in a deep sombre tone, "I can't have you falling for me!" He laughed.

"Don't flatter yourself," Valerie smiled. "I just want your cock!" And she joined the laughter.

"That's just fine," Marco replied, "you can most certainly have my cock!" And he put his arms around Valerie, kissed her forehead, and gently touched her hair.

"Don't fuck it up Marco," Valerie said softly. "I need to know that whatever you are planning, it will be final."

Marcos' expression changed. "The man I have spoken to is the best." He said softly. "He has been a friend and associate for many, many, years, and I trust him with my life." He paused, "So I won't fuck it up," the words came a little more harshly.

"That's all I can ask for," Valerie smiled. "Now. Get dressed and I'm throwing you out," she laughed. "Giles may not give a shit, but he still calls the shots." Her voice tailed off.

"For now," Marco grinned.

The 4th of July.

Callum woke up with a start. Sam was softly sleeping beside him. He was sweating. And his mind couldn't stop playing over and over his father's death. He knew he had to remain calm. But his nature made that almost impossible. And, ever since Tommy and that bloody car, he was beginning to lose patience. He felt the anger building.

As he did so, Sam opened her eyes. She saw the sweat on his brow, his fists clenched. She smiled at him, and her hand touched his thigh. She proceeded to make her fingers stand upright. And began to walk them upwards. Smiling widely, she mouthed, "Good morning," and her hand reached Callum's cock.
Callum looked down. "Good morning, you." He grinned.
Sam slowly wrapped her fingers around him. "Do you need help calming down?" And her tongue slowly licked his inner thigh.
 He smiled again. "Oh, I think I could use a little help." Sam licked higher as her hand felt Callum's cock begin to stiffen. She wanked him slowly and raised herself to kiss him. "Let it go for now," she spoke gently, knowing the pain he still felt. Her mouth rested on his, and her tongue found his. As they kissed, Callum's cock became fully erect, and Sam rubbed it harder. Callum closed his eyes. Sam's breasts pressed against his chest. Her stiff nipples running across his skin. She opened her legs and softly lowered herself onto him. "I love you Callum

Summer," she said, as his cock slid inside. Her head threw back. And she began to ride him.
Callum put his hands on her arse. Slowly pushing in time with her rhythm. "I love you too Samantha." He whispered softly. "Fuck me Sam."
Sam did as she was told. Riding him with a rhythm she knew he liked. Watching his face enjoy her. Something she hadn't seen much of since Callum's father had died. She rode him harder now. Her own orgasm building. Callum lost in the sex for once. His mind focussed on nothing but the woman pleasing him. Harder she fucked him. Wanting her own orgasm. She had missed Callum and the sex. The passion. The love. Her breath became shorter. She held the bed frame. "FUCK!" She screamed loudly, "I'm going to come!"
"Fuck me Sam!" Callum's own orgasm close. He hadn't felt sexually aroused like this in a long time. He wanted to come. Hard.
Sam squealed. As his cock released inside her.
She screamed. "Oh fuck!"
Callum's head went light. Slightly dizzy. His cock exploded. He briefly lost control of his mind. And then the tears came. He held Sam tighter than he ever had. And cried. Hard. Hurting tears. The sex tipped him over the emotional edge. And the release, both sexually and now mentally, suddenly gave him a lightness. He softly kissed Sam. "I needed that!" He exclaimed.
"So did I!" She replied. They lay down.
"I have to go to work," Callum said. "I'm going to shower," and he got out of bed.

Sam watched him. She really did love him. But couldn't help but worry. She couldn't change the past. And was powerless to help with the emotions in his mind. But she could make sure his future had a better path. And she would make bloody sure it was.
"See you later!" Callum shouted as he left.
"You will," Sam replied.
Callum got into the yellow BMW M3. It was old, but his favourite. He left, as usual, with the car sliding sideways and angry.
"Take it easy," she laughed.
Callum arrived at the workshop within twenty minutes. Parked the car. And decided he would just go check on the barn. He walked slowly down the lane. Smiling to himself. What a way to start the day!

As he opened the door, the small dog running around in the next field made him smile again. The little dog was going crazy and having a great time. Callum turned off the alarms and stepped inside. Just as he did, the dog grabbed the round object and took it back to his master. The weathered skinned, blonde-haired man smiled. Signed "Thank you," to his pet and raised the crossbow again. As he pulled the trigger on the specially made weapon, the bolt leapt from it, and sped across the ground. It hit the round, cloth covered ball and embedded itself deep into it. It wasn't a ball, for The Signalman,
it represented a human head. He had several of them. And always practised. Toffee loved the game. If the head fell off its perch, so much the better, he didn't have to jump. But this time, the hit had been so clean,

the bolt simply thundered into the head and stayed there. Toffee leapt. And expertly grabbed the bundle. Trotting back to his master, he dropped it at Brian's feet. They had been here for an hour now. Brian patted his four-legged friend. Signed, "Let's go," and made his way back to the Land Rover.

As Callum locked the barn, he saw the puff of black smoke across the open field. Heard the engine start, and grinned to himself. "Bloody farmers," he said to himself. "You are supposed to look after them!" And he went back to the workshop.

Brian pulled back out onto the main road. Now all he needed was Marco to tell him when. He would decide where. He smiled and patted Toffee.

Marco got out of bed, made himself a coffee, took out his mobile. Dialled Anesh.

A strange voice answered. "Elo?"

"I need to speak to Anesh," Marco said, slightly puzzled.

"He has his hands full!" Came the reply, along with laughter.

"His mouth too I shouldn't wonder," Marco thought. "Tell him to call me." And he ended the call.

Tommy picked up his mobile. Sent a message. Just as he was about to press send, Giles' number lit up. "Opening night, dear boy, shall we say July the 4th?"

Tommy laughed. "Independence bloody day," he thought. He loved that movie. "I will speak to Lazlo."

"Six weeks?" He thought to himself. "Shit, can I even pull that off?" He dialled the number.

The long dial tone eventually interrupted by "Tommy, my friend." "Lazlo!" he almost shouted. "I will be needing the merchandise a little sooner than I planned."

Lazlo sighed. Why couldn't the fucking English ever get things right. "No problem my friend, when are you thinking?"

"Six weeks," Tommy said quietly, waiting for the explosion at the other end of the line.
"No problem," Lazlo said calmly.
Tommy was taken by surprise. "You are certain of that?" he questioned. "My client will need the goods for opening night on the 4th of July."
"No problem, Tommy" came the reply. "You will need to set up delivery. And I want you to personally oversee things. I hear Amsterdam went well, so I trust you."
Tommy smiled again. "My turn to say no problem, Lazlo," he said.
"Good. I will wait to hear from you." And the call ended.
Tommy made a fist around his phone. Fucking Giles. As he sat, he felt the anger rise again. Tommy was becoming sick of dancing to Giles' tune. Perhaps in the not-too-distant future, he would see just how 'mustard', Mr Mustard really was. For now, he needed to plan his next delivery. This would have to be perfect. For all the things he hated about Giles, he still wanted in on the business. Time to make a few calls.

Tommy drove fast to the club. His mind racing. Perhaps the next deal was the time to take over. He needed time. To plan. To make sure somehow Giles was involved. He needed to have the fat arrogant bastard out of the way completely, then, and only then could he take over and be all powerful. He smiled. Yes. It was the perfect time. Tommy would no longer be in the shadows. It was his turn. He parked the Aston, strode powerfully into the club and went straight to his office. Poured himself a drink. And took out his phone. He began to put the building blocks in place. It would be his turn.

Anesh spoke to Marco. "Sorry my brother, I was busy," he laughed.
Marco scowled. He didn't need to hear what Anesh had been up to.
"I have The Signalman ready. When will we make it happen?"
"Calm down my brother. We have the perfect cover, but not for a few weeks. Tell The Signalman to wait. He will get a bonus if he can wait for around 5 weeks."
"Five weeks?!" Marco bellowed.
"Yes, my brother." Anesh was calm. He knew Marco could be impatient. And clearly now he had seen Valerie, he was angry for her, never mind enjoying the thought of serving revenge on Giles. For both Valerie, and the way Giles had treated Anesh.
"I have had a message from Lazlo." Anesh went on. "He has had a call from the fat man's sidekick. They want a delivery in a few weeks' time. It will be perfect."

Marco calmed. "OK," he said gently. I will let The Signalman know. I will see you tomorrow my brother."
"I will collect you from the airport."
Marco ended the call. Five weeks. And he was going back to Spain tomorrow. He sent a message. "I have one more night in the UK, but I will be back."
Valerie looked down at her phone. Giles was at the golf club. She had no idea when he would return. She wanted him to fuck her before he left. She replied. "Let me get a hotel."
"OK," was the simple response.
Valerie typed in "Day Hotels" and the hotel she had used only a few days before. She squealed with delight. With a few clicks the hotel was booked. Taking a screenshot, she sent it to Marco.
His response was immediate. "See you there."
Valerie dialled Barry. "Barry darling, I need you to drive me on a little journey."
"Yes Miss Valerie, I'm on my way."
Bless him, Valerie thought to herself. He never asks questions. Never fails me. He is a good man.
She walked up the stairs. Removed her knickers, took off her blouse and skirt. Undoing her bra, she stood naked. Reaching into the wardrobe, she took out the cashmere coat. Long, elegant, with four buttons. Kneeling, she found her boots. Three-inch heels. She had barely worn them. But now was the occasion they suited best. She put the boots on, fastened the coat, and just as the last button had been closed, she heard the Mercedes. She set the alarm. Strode down the path, and climbed into the back of the car.

"Where to Miss Valerie?" Barry enquired.
"Back to the hotel Barry."
"Yes Miss Valerie," he chuckled. Barry drew up at the hotel. He opened the door. Valerie stepped out.
"Enjoy Miss Valerie."
"Oh, I will Barry!"
She walked into the hotel. Glanced around. Marco was at the bar. He looked cool as always: linen shirt, white chinos, loafers. She smiled. He raised his glass.
She walked provocatively towards him. He pulled the stool around. She perched herself on the seat, sat opposite Marco, and crossed her legs as she picked up the glass of wine.
Marco smiled. "I see you are undressed for the occasion," he grinned.
Valerie drained her glass. "I am," she mouthed. "Now take me to bed." And once again she flashed her pussy as she took the key and wandered to the lift.
Marco watched. He liked to watch.
 Valerie beckoned him. He too drained the glass and followed her.
"Seventh floor," she demanded. Marco pushed the button.
They reached room 717. And, for the rest of that afternoon, Valerie was fucked harder and deeper than she had ever been fucked in her life.
When she returned home, Giles was there. He was gazing out of the window. "Where have you been?" he said in a low voice. Angry, and trying to be menacing.
Valerie laughed. "Out," and walked past him.
As she did so, Giles reached out and grabbed her arm.

Valerie spun around. Shocked at his actions. The anger instant in her body and mind.

"I *said where have you been*?" He bellowed. Gripping her arm tighter.

Valerie stood. Silent. Staring into Giles eyes. She paused. Giles loosened his grip.

Valerie shook her arm loose.

"I have been out you arrogant bastard," Valerie spoke calmly.

Giles raised his arm. His fist clenched.

"You are going to hit me?" She mocked. "You, the pervert who likes young girls, watches underage porn, and lets the 18 year old barmaid give him a blow job? And you fucking dare to question me?!"

She moved past Giles. He stood. Rooted to the spot. And in one short sentence he suddenly made Valerie very frightened.

"I own you," he said. Before turning on his heel and making his way to the living room.

Valerie shouted back "Whatever!" And stormed up the stairs, seething with rage. She slammed the bedroom door and was about to throw her mobile, when her words came back. "Listen. Absorb. Process. Then go ape shit if needed!" She decided that her mobile was more important than the rage she felt towards her husband right now. She lay down on the bed. Her eyes closed, and she fell asleep.

Giles took out his mobile. "We have a problem."

Tommy answered immediately. "We do?"

"We have a Michelle and Valerie shaped problem."

Tommy grinned. "I dealt with one problem, leave it to me."

"Let's chat over a round tomorrow dear boy."

"See you around midday." Tommy pushed send, and his mind was already thinking about the best way to deal with both problems.

Detective Sergeant Ken Nicholson.

Michelle waited for the Aston to leave. She didn't have to wait long. Tommy barely spoke to her now. And that was just fine.
Taking out her phone, she sent Valerie "We need to meet," and waited. She made coffee and went into the garden. The peace made her reflect. The last few years had seen her become someone she wasn't. A slut. A whore. Wanting sex as her cocaine. Charlie had changed all that. Yes, she had to admit the sex had been pretty fantastic, but he cared. He felt. He wanted her! And ultimately, they had become lovers who fell in love. She felt the tears fall. But this time, angry tears mixed with the sadness. A depth of feeling of revenge that she had not felt since the children's home all those years ago. She smiled through the tears. As she did so her mobile lit up.
"See you in thirty minutes."
"OK," the simple reply.
Almost on the dot, the doorbell rang. Michelle smiled. "Bloody woman, how does she do it?" She muttered to herself. Opening the door without looking, she was greeted by Barry.
"Hello, Miss Michelle," he said timidly. "Miss Valerie is in the car. She said to collect you."
Michelle looked down. Dressed in her sweats was definitely not a good look!
Barry continued, "No need to worry about what you are wearing Miss, Miss Valerie said just get in!"

Michelle smiled again. "That's just fine, but I bet bloody Valerie won't be in sweats," she thought to herself.
"OK, Barry, let me lock up," and she watched him walk down the drive. Puzzled. Her mind didn't quite know what to make of what was coming next.
Michelle got into the car to find Valerie as immaculate as ever. The pained expression on Michelle's face said it all.
"Oh, stop it!" Valerie laughed. "I am going to wave Marco off back to Spain that's all," and she laughed and pushed Michelle back in her seat playfully.
"Oh!" Michelle said, slightly disappointed. "I thought he had come to plan things?"
"He has," Valerie interjected, "but plans change, and we have the perfect opportunity in a few weeks' time. So it's all in hand. However, that's not what I wanted to see you about." She paused for breath. "Giles attacked me yesterday."
Michelle looked at her in disbelief. "He did what?!"
"Well, he didn't hit me, but he was ready to," she stopped. Faltered slightly, and said, "And I am just a little concerned."
Michelle smiled. She knew it was wrong to, but she couldn't believe this amazingly strong lady was worried!
"So, what exactly are you worried about?"
Valerie paused to gather her thoughts. "He is up to something. And I have an idea, but don't know for definite. However, I fear he is going to go deeper into his sex obsession than he ever has. And it's making him lose control. I have never seen him so animated. I guess he knew I was out shagging, and just for once, it pissed him off, and he lost it."

"So what did you do?"
"I told him if he thought idle threats from a pervert who liked young girls scared me he was very much mistaken. But," she paused, "the truth is, it did. I think he saw Tommy and thought he could do the same. He can't, the stupid old goat, but it did mean that perhaps he has grown some balls. And if he has, Tommy best be careful. As had we." She finished with a flourish.
Michelle was a bit gobsmacked. "You think Giles knew you were shagging?"
Valerie laughed. "I am sure he did. And I wouldn't normally give a fuck. My only saving grace is, Marco has now left the country, and Giles would have no idea who it was anyway. But, something is happening. Something big. Giles definitely is up to something. He has been on about a new club for ages. I think he is close. But this time there is something different. And I don't know what. Despite ALL my influences, I cannot get to the bottom of what's going on. But I have to find out."
Michelle nodded. "So what do we do?"
"Be nice to them." Michelle looked perturbed.
"No, not sex for God's sake! But the doting wife. Get closer. Listen to conversations. We both know about the drugs. The club. Money laundering. This feels different."
"You think Tommy wants me anywhere near him?" Michelle returned.
"Maybe not, but you have to try. Because dramatic or not, your life, or mine, perhaps both, might depend on it."
Valerie finished the conversation. "Drink?"
"Dressed like this?"

"Who gives a shit," Valerie said and stepped out of the car.
Michelle had no idea where they were. But she did as Valerie suggested. A small pub. Out of the way. Good. No one would see her, she thought!
Let's have a drink. And Valerie marched inside.

The nine iron met the ball perfectly. "Fore!" Giles shouted. And watched as the shot from the fairway landed perfectly on the green. "Watch and learn dear boy!" Giles laughed.
"Not bad old man," Tommy smirked. He hit his ball just as cleanly. And it landed not more than fifty feet from his partners.
As they walked along the fairway, Giles began to speak. "I think I know a way we can deal with our problems dear boy," he coughed as he said it. "There might have to be a tragic accident."
"I'm listening," Tommy snarled.
As they walked, neither of them paid any attention to the small dog playing in the trees. Nor the blonde-haired owner. Who took out a small pair of binoculars. Watching both men intently. The crossbow hung by his side. As the dog barked, Giles looked around. But the man and the dog had disappeared. "Bloody dogs," he muttered. But a pair of eyes saw the words.
"You will pay," Brian muttered back. He raised the weapon. Carefully adjusted the sight. Loaded a bolt. And stood. Silent. He could see Giles. And Tommy. He could take the shot. But it would take too long to re-load. He

would wait. He lowered the weapon. And kept out of sight in the trees.
Over the next couple of weeks, the same format played out.
Brian kept observing. Toffee enjoyed the challenge, and, back in Spain, Marco got more and more frustrated.

Callum sent a message to Michelle. "I need to talk to you."
Michelle saw it. Had no idea what to reply. "Why, what's wrong?" Was the pathetic message she sent back.
"I can't deal with it," he returned.
"Do you want to get a coffee and chat?"
"Yes, meet me at the workshop around 10 am would you?"
"OK, I will see you there."
Michelle sent the message and then pondered. She couldn't tell Callum anything that was being planned. She knew his hot head would only ruin anything that Marco and Anesh had in place. However, she needed to do something. Otherwise, that very hot-headedness would make him take matters into his own hands anyway.
She showered. Her mind still unsure which way to take the conversation. But one thing was for sure, Callum needed help somehow. With Tommy out she had all the time in the world. And as she tousled her hair dry, she messaged Valerie.
"I'm going to see Callum," and she briefly explained what he had said.
"Do not tell him anything!" Valerie's reply almost screamed.
"I won't, but what do I tell him?"

"Tell him I know a counsellor that can give him some time if he needs to talk."
"You do?" Michelle smiled. Of course, bloody Valerie did, she knew everyone!
"Yes," came the simple reply.
"OK, thanks." And Michelle got ready to go and meet Charlie's son. In the hope that she may at least be able to keep him calm and perhaps put his mind at ease.
     Michelle pulled into the yard. She smiled. Thinking of the first time she had driven in here all that time ago. Charlie had been standing just there. She felt her mind drift, just briefly. But the inner strength she had found as the time had gone on made her use the energy for positivity now. No longer would she be the meek and mild Michelle. No matter what Tommy expected.
Callum appeared. "Coffee?" He shouted.
She smiled again. Gave a thumbs up, and, as the young man went back inside, she steeled herself for what she thought might be a very difficult conversation. Stepping out of the car, she made her way inside. Looking up at the rickety staircase only made her smile more. *God* Michelle you *tart*, her mind went back to when she had teased Charlie as she walked up the stairs in her mini skirt! Smiling, she reached the office. Callum sat behind his father's desk. Staring out of the window. He looked lonely.
"Hello Callum."
Callum turned. Stood up, and walked around the desk. He opened his arms and wrapped them around Michelle. And sobbed. Michelle was taken by surprise and could do nothing except return the hug. Callum was a strong man.

As she hugged him she felt the toned back, and there was no mistaking the arms that held her were massive. Callum let go as suddenly as he had grabbed her and walked back around the desk.

"I'm sorry," he wiped away the tears on his sleeve. "Sam and I have been talking about the future, and it has just made me miss the old man."

"I miss him every day, Callum, but nothing we can do will bring him back. I loved coming here today, because it reminded me of the first time I met him, and the first time I met you." She paused, "And they are wonderful memories."

The young man smiled. "That bloody dent in your Merc," he grinned. "And the old man not wanting to tell you about me coz he thought it might ruin his chances!" And he laughed out loud. "I haven't done that in a while," he said softly. "I need your help Michelle."

"OK," she looked puzzled. "Why, what can I do?"

"I'm going to ask Sam to marry me"

Michelle smiled as she tried to swallow her coffee. "Good for you," she replied. "But how did all this come about?"

"The truth is Michelle, I keep thinking about dad, and about you and how close you were to making it. And I don't want to wait anymore. If nothing else this has taught me to live for today."

Michelle sat back in her chair. Looking at the young man, she could see Charlie's eyes. She fought back the tears. "Of course I will help you."

"Thank you," he replied. Sam has no family, so I guess it won't make the pages of "OK!" magazine, and he laughed, but I want it to be perfect."

"So do I," she answered.
Just as she did so, a deep voice shouted from the bottom of the stairs "CALLUM SUMMER?"
"Who wants to know?" He answered a little sarcastically.
"Detective Sergeant Ken Nicholson," that's who."
Callum sat up.
"Can I come up?"
"Of course,"
As the policeman walked into the room, he looked at Michelle.
"Well, well, well" he said. "Mrs Shelton."
"Detective Sergeant," she replied sternly.
Michelle turned to Callum. "So, if you could have a look at it as soon as possible I would be grateful." And she stood up to leave.
"I take it you don't need to speak to me?" She questioned the policeman.
"Not at this time," he replied, equally sternly.
Michelle turned on her heel and left. Shutting the door behind her. She made her way back down the stairs. Now a little concerned at what he might want with Callum.
Callum sat back. "How can I help?" he asked.
"You have frequented the club SPICE, I believe."
"Hardly frequented," Callum came back. "More been there a few times"
"I see," The DS replied.
"You see what?" Callum already had his hackles up.
The DS chose not to rise to the question. "Have you ever witnessed any drug taking going on?"
Callum laughed.
"You think it's funny, do you?" The policeman snapped.

"You think any club doesn't have drugs? And he laughed again.
"Listen son," he began.
"No, you listen!" Callum replied angrily. "You lot are fucking useless. Couldn't find a bloody thing to do with my old man's death. So unless you have something useful to say, piss off would you, I'm busy."
The detective stood up. "Your father's death," he began. Callum cut him short again. "Goodbye officer."
Detective Sergeant Nicholson seethed inside. He left without another word and Callum heard his boots clumping down the wooden staircase. He allowed himself a smile. Perhaps that news bulletin was true, maybe there was a new broom in the police cupboard.

    Michelle arrived home. Took out her phone and called Callum. After he had explained the very brief conversation with the police, Michelle called Valerie. And told her the story.
    Valerie laughed.
"What the fuck is so funny?" Michelle spat.
"Giles will just pay him off darling," she replied. "Please don't worry."
"I don't want anything to go wrong."
"It won't, I promise you." And she ended the call.
Michelle was angry, confused, upset, and also joyous over the news about Callum and Sam.
She opened the laptop.
"Cheap flights to Spain."
Smiling, she said to herself. "I'm going to my villa." Her hands flew over the keyboard. Within a few minutes, she

had booked the flight, and she went to the fridge, poured herself a large glass of pinot, and sat back down. She had never felt more in control of herself. Even if deep down, she wasn't in control of very much right now. But she figured a week away, some Spanish sun, and the chance to forget it all would be most welcome. Besides, she wanted to see her gay husband again! And she grinned. Then realised she had only booked one ticket. Quickly she opened the laptop again. And booked Valerie a seat. Content now, she closed the laptop, and flicked on the T.V. looking up at the clock, Tommy would be hours yet. She sank back into the sofa. Took a large gulp of wine. And settled herself for an afternoon of nothing.

Detective Sergeant Nicholson was beginning to get a feel for the small village. Everyone kept themselves to themselves. No one gave anything away. And they most certainly didn't trust anyone new.
He had been surprised to see Michelle with Callum, but right now couldn't concern himself with that. He had been brought in since around the time Charlie Summer had died, to try to put a stop, or at least slow down, the amount of drugs in and around the local towns. Having come from the big city, he was both dubious that there really was a problem, and, even if there was, he wasn't quite sure what he was going to do about it.
He sat motionless for a moment in the car, gathering his thoughts. Why did a little place like this have a nightclub so close? Why on earth did everything seem so squeaky clean? Except perhaps the nightclub owner. He had only met him briefly, but had an instant dislike for Tommy

Shelton. Normally a man who liked to understand then judge, on this occasion he simply didn't like him.
Time would tell if he was a good judge of character. But for now, he would observe, record, and build what case he could. It was no secret that it was just another piece of government bullshit, but it was his job. So, he would do it to the best of his ability.
His mobile rang. SHIT! It was the Chief.
"Get back to the station, would you, I want to welcome you properly and have a catch-up dear boy" and the call ended.
"Dear boy!" He exclaimed in his head. "Who the fuck says dear boy?"
He smiled to himself. Put the car in gear, and did as he had been asked. Made his way back to the station.

Giles finished the round one shot ahead of Tommy. As usual the wager was in place, and Tommy duly paid up. "Well done dear boy," came the reply as Tommy handed over the cash. "Now," Giles paused, "How do you fancy a little trip out?" and he winked theatrically, "to see how my new venture is progressing."
Tommy smiled. With only around three weeks until Giles grand opening, Tommy hoped it was almost finished, never mind progressing.
"Sure old man."
"Good, good. Rosy darling, could you spare a few minutes to check out the new place with myself and my dear Tommy here?"
Rosy smiled. Not quite a blush, but a naughty glint in her eye.

"Gigi!" She shouted, "Could you come back from your break now sweetheart?"
"On my way Rosy!"
Rosy smiled. "She is a good girl," she whispered.
Giles, Tommy and Rosy climbed into the Range Rover.
"When did you get this old man?" Tommy asked.
"Oh, a little time ago, just fancied a change dear boy!"
Tommy smirked. "Just wanted to show off even more," he mumbled.
Rosy said nothing. Years of experience had taught her to see nothing, hear everything and use only what needed to be used to keep yourself safe.
They drove for around forty minutes. A small country lane. Empty, nothing around.
"Fucking hell Giles, this really is the middle of nowhere!" Tommy exclaimed.
"Best place dear boy," Giles replied, as he swung the car through the gateway. "Keep all the riff raff out eh!"
They parked in a stone car park. Small, perhaps with only room for 30 or so cars. Tommy stepped out. And was greeted by a small semi-circular almost wall of glass, set into the ground. "Is that it?" he said indignantly.
"Just wait dear boy," Giles brushed him aside. "Just wait."
Giles dug around in his pocket.
He found the fob. Held it to the door lock, and with a small click, the black glass door opened, and as it did so, and Giles stepped inside he smiled. Paused slightly and put his hand on a small panel to the left.
A soft female voice spoke. "Welcome Giles."

He turned to Tommy. Smiled, and said, "Impressive dear boy!" As he stepped a little further in to allow Rosy and Tommy inside.
Tommy smiled. "Impressive indeed."
Giles boomed, "Lights!" And one by one as if to light a path, the overhead lights came on. Dimly, nothing too bright or garish. Tommy took a deep breath. This was indeed impressive. Dark panels. Interspersed with small LED bulbs like stars in the night sky. The floor almost a runway guiding you into the deeper recesses of the club. The temperature cool.
"No need for aircon really dear boy," Giles said informatively, "but to keep the air pure I thought it best. State of the art you know."
Rosy smiled. "Come to the bar," she said and walked provocatively along the runway.
Tommy duly followed. Coming to a door simply labelled 'the cloakroom'. Rosy stopped, turned on her red heel, and said, "Self-explanatory, however, it's all digital. Lockers, safes, everything anyone would need in order to be completely happy that their belongings are both safe and hidden from anyone."
She marched on. After a couple of twists and turns, the runway opened out into a lounge. Big enough for maybe 50 people. Lavishly furnished. Beautiful handmade sofas, chaise longue, and tables and chairs. Lighting was provided by LED strips. Again dim, nothing bright. The whole place oozed class and expense.
Rosy smiled as Tommy took it all in.

The bar area was equally impressive. Everything immaculate. No beer pumps. Bottles only.
Tommy looked around. "Where is the CCTV?"
"Everywhere dear boy."
"So how the hell do you propose to get all your punters to do anything other than have a drink if they know they are being filmed?" Tommy laughed.
Giles smiled. "Because my dear boy, once they leave the bar, the cameras are nowhere to be seen."
Tommy looked puzzled.
"No security?"
"I didn't say that, did I?"
"Show dear Tommy here to our relaxation areas," and he wandered off to the bar.
"Follow me," Rosy beckoned. Only then did Tommy take in that the room was a perfect circle. Black walls. Again, with the same lighting as the entrance hall.
"There are 5 rooms in total," Rosy explained like a tour guide, "we won't take them all in, but I am sure you will get the general gist," and she toddled off. She touched a slightly lighter patch in the wall. The small plate lit up briefly, and with the same click as the front door, a panel in the wall opened. Tommy followed, and the panel closed instantly, causing Tommy to jump.
"Don't panic darlin," Rosy quipped, "this is just a dress rehearsal, you get nothing," and she smiled.
Tommy grimaced. "Thank God for that!" he thought.
Rosy looked him up and down as the lift (for that is what turned out to be behind the panel), went down very briefly.

"I would eat you alive," Rosy grinned, "but my boss wouldn't like that," as she finished the sentence the door opened. This is 'The Boudoir', she said, opening her arm as if to introduce the room.
Tommy stepped inside.
Again, the room was stunningly furnished. A central, and massive, bed. Lighting, discreet. A place to change. "Over there is the bathroom," Rosy smiled, "we want our guests to be fresh after all," and she fluttered her eyelids.
"Goes without saying," Tommy responded. "So, what do they get?"
"Whatever they want. No pain, no poo, no pee." It's a sex club, not a fucking toilet."
Tommy smiled. "Don't tell me, classy!"
"ABSO-FUCKING- LUTLEY!" Rosy snapped. "Shall we?" And she touched the internal panel again. The door opened as before, and they were soon back in the lift.
"So you see, Giles has spent a lot of money. Got a lot invested in here. And he wants to make sure it's a success."
"Oh I am sure it will be," Tommy grinned. "And do I get a membership?" He laughed.
"You best speak to the boss."
Tommy couldn't help but be angry. Here we fucking go again, his mind said, as the lift opened, and they were back in the bar.
"SO DEAR BOY!" Giles bellowed. "What do you think?"
"Very nice! I still don't see how on earth you will get the hoi polloi here and let them do what they want without them being seen or having their picture taken?"

"Leave that to me," Giles responded. "I have a couple of secret weapons."
Tommy rolled his eyes.
"Chiefly, I have Helen," Giles carried on. "A fiery red headed Scots girl who takes no shit from anybody." Giles looked wistfully into the distance. "Any nasty business in here will be dealt with by her."
"A fucking girl?" Tommy laughed.
"I wouldn't laugh too loudly, dear boy, she doesn't take kindly to being laughed at."
"Oh, is that so old man," and Tommy laughed again. Forcing himself. "Ha ha fucking ha!"
As he did so, a small red headed woman appeared behind Tommy. With one action, she chopped the back of his neck, and he felt faint. As he fell to the floor Helen turned him onto his back, sat astride his chest, and took out the knife. Tommy shook his head, came to, and opened his eyes wide to a six-inch-long blade under his nose.
"You laugh at me again," the voice had a strong Scottish accent, "and next time it won't just be a shave you get." Tommy looked down to see his whiskers on the edge of the knife blade. "Alright you made your point!"
She climbed off his chest.
"Good to see you two getting on so well," Giles chuckled. "You really must relax a little more my dear Tommy."
"Fucking relax?" Tommy shrilled. "You have an underground whorehouse protected by Braveheart's fucking wife and you tell me to relax?"

"Exactly dear boy, can't you see, it's all in hand? You just get that delivery here, and then we will clean up any loose ends."

"Helen darling, thank you so much for the demonstration, I am sure Tommy now fully understands my club is in very capable hands!"

Helen turned and left. As she walked past Tommy she muttered, "Wanker!"

Tommy stood up, ready to retaliate.

Helen turned back. "Don't you fucking dare," she breathed. The knife was already in her hand. She left without another word.

"Time to calm down dear boy, let's get back to the golf club, have a drink or two, and then have a chat about the opening night."

The three of them left in silence. Rosy climbed into the back of the Range Rover, and Giles pulled away.

Tommy felt even less in control than he ever had before.

Nikki turns killer?

With three weeks to go until the grand opening, Rosy had been busy finalising the girls. Never an easy task, but Giles wanted to make sure he had everything perfect for the big day.
Tommy had spoken to Lazlo again. The aircraft was arranged, and Harvey's kid would do the collection. Tommy had the car sorted, he just needed to make sure Harvey's boy didn't fuck up. He had done well to get the information to help Tommy get rid of Charlie Summer, but collecting a boot full of drugs was another thing. Still Aaron was scared enough that he would do just as Tommy said.
Nikki wanted to get out. Tommy had beaten her, fucked her mouth so hard she passed out, and now he seemed totally disinterested in her. Even though they still fucked, she felt her time was short, and she had to escape.
Callum was feeling good. Michelle had been so happy for him with the news he wanted to propose to Sam, and Michelle needed to help him. Not that there would be much to the wedding.
In fact, as the plane touched down in Spain, Michelle said to Valerie, "It would be great if they got married out here."
"Who is getting married?"
"Oh God! I'm sorry, I thought I had told you, Callum wants to marry Sam. He said that since Charlie died, he

realised he needs to make her his wife and grab life by the balls."

"Sensible lad," Valerie returned.

Anesh met them at the gate. "DAHHHLINGS" he said in his best theatre voice. "How lovely to see you again!" He embraced the women one by one.

They drove quickly to the villa. As they swung through the gates, Ruth waved shyly and smiled.

And the unmistakable voice of Marco shouted, "The water is lovely ladies."

Valerie looked at Michelle.

"You are not going to fuck in my pool," she laughed.

"I wouldn't dream of it dahhhhling," her friend laughed. Now, where is that delicious cock?! And she almost ran around the side of the house.

Anesh laughed.

Michelle looked at him. "Thank you, Anesh," she said deeply.

"Don't thank me until it's done," he replied. And he walked to the back of the house.

Ruth stood silent. "Are you OK, Ruth?" Michelle enquired.

"My grandmother is not very well," she replied with tears in her eyes.

"You should go to see her," Michelle felt for the young girl.

"But it is my day to be here," Ruth replied.

"Go!" Michelle raised her voice, "You only have one family."

"Thank you!" Ruth's tears ran down her face as fast as she ran out to her little Peugeot. "I will come back tomorrow," and with that she was gone.

Michelle smiled. "You only get one family," she muttered quietly. As she rounded the corner she grinned. Valerie was already naked and in the pool with an equally naked Marco.

"Will you both behave!" She laughed and went inside to find Anesh. He was sitting at the table, with a glass of wine, and one already poured for Michelle.

"There you are dahhling, "leave those two to it I say," and he laughed in his theatrical way.

"Yes, I think you are right." Michelle smiled. "How are you, Anesh?"

"I am very OK, daaaahling, in fact, I think both myself and my brother Marco have found a new lease of life whilst enjoying you and Valerie. And Marco is definitely enjoying Valerie!" He laughed and leant back on his chair.

Michelle laughed, but quickly became serious. "Will it work Anesh?"

"It will work." Anesh snapped back to the cold individual he could be. "I had never cared what happened to Giles, and, if I am honest, I still don't. But I do care about Valerie, she cares about you. And, if I can get my revenge on Giles, whilst being 'clean', then I will take the opportunity. Marco loves it. He never wanted to leave our dark past, but I persuaded him. He has always kept closer contact with our friends than I have. And, just for once, it will be useful."

Michelle didn't know what to do or say.

"I assure you, we have the best man. And it's about time Giles and Tommy learnt that they are not unstoppable. They are not invincible." And his smile terrified Michelle. "Let's go and see what those two are doing."

"I'm not sure I want to," Michelle laughed. And grabbed both the bottle and her glass as Anesh followed. With her hands over her eyes, she stepped out into the garden. Valerie and Marco were sitting, now clad each in a robe, and chatting.
"Bring two more glasses would you please!" Marco shouted,
Valerie followed, "And two more bottles!"
The four friends sat close. Enjoying the warm sun and laughter.

Giles slammed his fist on the desk. His face red as he held the phone to his ear. "What do you mean it won't be ready?!" He bellowed.
Rosy walked in just as he looked ready to explode.
"Calm down," she mouthed, "it will be fine."
"I am sure it will be you naughty minx," he laughed as Rosy bent over and flashed her stocking tops. Giles smacked her playfully on the arse.
"Good, good, dear boy, you see, now you are thinking!" And he beamed. "I look forward to having them here this week," and he ended the call.
"Now my dear Rosy," he grinned, "Where are we with the girls?"
Rosy turned. "We have currently 20 ladies all of whom I have personally interviewed and I'm confident they all understand what is needed."
"Good, good," he muttered. "Do I get to meet them?" He chuckled.
"All in good time. You naughty man!" And she smiled before leaving the office.

Tommy picked up his mobile. "Lazlo my friend," he sounded in a remarkably good mood. "How are you?"
"I am good, my friend," he replied. "I wanted to check you have everything in place for the delivery."
"It is all in hand," Tommy returned.
"And you will be there to personally oversee things?"
"I wasn't planning on it, no. I have my courier ready, and he will bring the cash."
The phone went silent. Tommy waited patiently.
"OK," Lazlo replied. "But I don't want any mistakes."
"There won't be any mistakes." Tommy growled menacingly. "I took care of Amsterdam, didn't I?"
"You did, Lazlo paused, but it's a very different matter trying to beat the English coast guard, just ask all those poor bastards in small boats!"
Tommy quietly fumed.
"I will make sure nothing goes wrong," and he ended the call.
He drove slowly to his club. There was no way he wanted to be anywhere near the drop. However, £250k of his money was involved. Could he really trust Aaron with it? Of course he could, the boy knew if he did anything wrong Tommy would have his dad killed. And he had already lost his mother. Harvey would have to make sure the boy did good.
He strode into the club. As he did so Allan Mustard appeared. Tommy smiled. Perhaps this could be his first test.
"Just the man," he said, "come to my office, and bring Harvey."
"Yes boss."

"And don't you forget it," he smiled at the younger man. Allan smiled back. "Oh, I don't think you will let me," and he turned to go back to the club.
Tommy opened his office door. Nikki sat on his desk. He sighed. She looked at him.
"I want out," she said. And stood up to leave.
He stood in the doorway. "You are going nowhere," he said quietly.
"You won't fucking stop me," she snarled.
Tommy laughed. "Course I won't," he chuckled. "You are going to be a big brave girl and deal with me all by yourself," and he walked towards her.
Nikki screamed at him. "You don't give a fuck about me, or anyone, you bastard!" Her eyes filled with tears. "I have done nothing but be there for you, let you use me, and now you have had enough of me you think you can just treat me like some piece of shit?"
"What the fuck are you gonna do about it anyway?" Tommy laughed in her face.
As he got closer to her, she reached behind her.
"Does Daddy want to know what I will do?" She laughed.
Tommy looked puzzled. Suddenly the panic on his face said it all. He felt the cold hard round silencer barrel pressed into his stomach. "I will fucking kill you," she snapped. Her eyes wild.
"What the fuck have you been taking?" Tommy shouted.
"Whatever I fucking want," Nikki spat. And pushed him away. "Now who is in control, you bastard?" She screamed again.

Allan Mustard found Harvey sitting in the back bar. A little morose. Knowing that his son would be collecting the shipment of drugs bound for the new club.
"Tommy wants to see us."
"Whatever," and Harvey got off the stool and slowly walked towards Tommy's office.
Nikki waved the gun at Tommy as he stumbled back. "I fucking hate you," she said, and her fingers tightened on the trigger. The bang was loud. Much louder than Nikki expected. And she shot backwards across the office, ending up on her arse and with her legs splayed and the gun hit her in the chest.
Tommy fell. Clutching his stomach. Harvey and Allan ran. Hard.
Nikki looked at Tommy. Saw the blood and suddenly became super focussed. She stood up, faltering as she did, but standing now she made for the door. As she opened it she heard Harvey shout "Tommy!" As he rounded the corner.
Oddly calm now, she stood. Legs apart and raised the gun. Pulled the trigger and fell onto her arse again. But it was enough to slow the two men. Standing again, she began to run. All the time the gun never left her hand. Reaching the back door of the club, she smashed her shoulder hard against it and threw it open. She ran to the bright red MX5 Tommy had bought her, climbed in and started the engine. Reversing hard she turned the wheel and slammed the front of the little sports car into Tommy's Aston Martin. She panicked. The noise was much louder than she expected, and she stamped on the brakes. As she did so, a foot came through the driver's window and

hit her square on the jaw. She slumped across the car, the gun fell from her hand and in one swift movement a slim hand opened the door and turned the car off and took the keys out of the ignition.
Allan Mustard stood holding the keys, as Harvey knelt next to Tommy. The blood coming through his shirt had slowed.
Tommy sat up. "Have you got that cunt?" He said calmly. Harvey smiled.
"Yes, Colonel Mustard has her."
"Get her the fuck back in here," Tommy's voice rose.
"Will do boss. You OK?"
"I'm fine. She couldn't shoot for shit, thank Christ! The bullet just grazed me. Cunt must have opened the drawer."
Harvey decided not to challenge whether the drawer had actually been locked. He helped Tommy to his feet.
"I will go get some water and a couple of towels," he said.
"Good man. And get me a fucking drink," Tommy laughed.
As he did so, Allan stood in the doorway, with Nikki slumped over his shoulder. "What should I do with her boss?" He questioned.
"Put her in her office, lock the door, and give me the key."
"Yes, boss," and he left.
Tommy quietly fumed. He should have seen this coming. But he didn't. What the fuck was he going to do with her now?
Harvey arrived. "Get your shirt off," he said in a very matter of fact manner.
"Shut the door."

Harvey did as he was told. Tommy removed his shirt. Harvey smiled. "Christ is that it?" And he allowed himself a little chuckle.

"Don't start with all that war hero bollocks," Tommy laughed. "Saw a bloke with his bollocks blown off… blah blah blah!" And he looked Harvey in the eye.

"It's just a scratch," Harvey smiled, "and a bloke with his bollocks blown off was nothing Tommy, it's when your mate standing two feet from you loses his head you begin to question things." And his head fell slightly.

Tommy had no real idea what Harvey had seen or experienced. He just knew that the man who had served him well over the years had gone through his own traumas that would pale into insignificance against anything Tommy had felt.

Harvey opened the rum, swigged some, then poured it onto the wound.

Tommy almost screamed. "Fuck that!" He wailed.

"Oh shut up man!" Harvey returned. "It cleans it," and he looked closer. "It really is just a scratch Tommy, you will be fine in a few days."

Tommy took the bottle. Took a deep swig and said, "Thanks mate." He looked at Harvey.

"No problem boss," he smiled back. "Let me bandage you up, and get you a shirt." He paused. "She hit the Aston," he said softly.

Tommy was about to explode when Harvey said, "Calm down, your blood pressure is already through the roof, if you want that fucking thing to stop bleeding, calm down, the car will mend."

Tommy sat quiet. "OK," he said and took another swing of rum. "I will look later."
"What do you want me to do with her?" Harvey asked.
"I don't fucking know yet, I didn't see this coming."
"Neither did I boss." And he handed Tommy a clean shirt. "I will wait for your instructions," and he quietly closed the door.
Tommy sat silent. What the fuck had happened? He needed to get rid of Nikki. But this close to the club opening? This close to the deal? He had other things to think about. Never mind his bloody wife and Valerie. As he now poured another drink, his mind was unsettled. He picked up the gun, which Allan had returned to him. Two shots fired. Plenty left. He breathed a huge sigh. "She could have fucking killed me," he said to himself. Took a large slug of rum, picked up the gun, and walked out of his office. The side of his stomach was smarting a little, but his mind was very focussed. It was time to teach her a lesson.

    Nikki woke to a massive pounding in her head. She tried to get up, and quickly realised she was bound to the chair. Hands behind her back, her feet tied at the ankles. As she tried to scream in temper the gag silenced her. She looked around her office. Tears of anger and frustration fell. Why hadn't she killed him then and there. The drugs were wearing off too. Her face was bruised, and she felt sick. With her hands tied and no way of attracting attention she could do little except sit quiet and wait for whatever was in store for her.

Fuck, fuck, fuck! Her mind became angry again. Fucking Charlie Summer! This was all his fault. If he hadn't kicked her out she would never have ended up here. Her fingers tried to make a fist, but the ropes were too tight around her wrists. She sighed, tilted her head back, and resigned herself to what was coming.

Tommy entered the room. Closed the blinds. Nikki swallowed hard.

"You best swallow some more," Tommy said menacingly.

Ruth.

Michelle kissed Anesh lightly on the cheek. Marco slid into the front seat of the Bentley, and the two friends waved as they left the villa.
Michelle closed the door. She sighed as Valerie walked into the hall, holding a glass. "Vino?" She asked.
"Please," as she followed Valerie into the lounge.
"I don't want to go back," Michelle said firmly.
"I know you don't, and once Tommy is out of the way you won't need to. But right now, if you just disappear, and he does come looking, you are vulnerable, and as lovely as Anesh is, he won't always be here. Let him and Marco do what needs to be done. Come here with me, or alone even to escape Tommy. But right now, you must go back to the UK, so everything appears normal."
Michelle shook her head. She knew Valerie was right, but she felt more and more at home here. And she certainly didn't want to go back to Tommy and her life. As she looked around the villa, her mind went back to Charlie. The feelings. The love. She smiled.
"So," Valerie said sharply. Let's get our glad rags on and wait for the boys."
"You go," Michelle said softly. "I actually just want to chill tonight."
"Your gay husband won't be happy," Valerie laughed as she made her way to the shower.
"He won't," Michelle paused "but he will understand."
"Yes," Valerie said softly. "I think he will."

Michelle went to the fridge. She looked around the magnificent kitchen. "He will pay Charlie," she whispered. "He will fucking pay," and she refilled her glass and stepped outside. The evening was stunningly warm. She slipped out of her robe, put her glass on the small table, and dived into the pool. The cooling water welcome on her body. She swam, quite hard, the frustration ebbing away with every stroke.

Valerie enjoyed the shower. The powerful pump allowed the water to massage her head. In her mind, she could feel clearer, think more clearly, and inevitably, her mind wandered to Marco. She knew only what he had told her about himself, as well as any information she had been able to find out. As the shower pounded her head, she thought about Giles. Tommy. And Marco. Her eyes widened as she realised she liked Marco's company. He wasn't handsome. But she laughed. She enjoyed how he made her feel. And she realised that perhaps she wanted just a little more than his massive cock. She laughed, shook her head, "nah," she muttered, "I just want his cock," and she soaped herself and let the water cleanse her.

She came down around an hour later. Michelle was still sitting in the warm evening air. She heard the gates open and the Bentley pulled in.

"Are you sure?" Valerie asked.

"I'm sure. You go and enjoy; I just want a little quiet time."

"OK! Be safe and I might see you later, I might not!" And she laughed as she skipped through the house and closed the front door.

Anesh opened the door of the Bentley. "And Michelle?" He questioned.
"She just wants a little quiet time with her thoughts and the villa," Valerie answered.
"Is she OK?"
"She is fine Anesh; I think she is better than I have seen her in a very long time."
"Well then daaahhhling" he laughed, "Let's go eat and have a good time."
He climbed into the driver's seat.
"Thank you, Anesh," Valerie said softly. He took her hand, kissed it softly, then pressed hard on the accelerator, and swung the car out of the gates and away down the road.
"For you dahhhhling, anything!" He laughed, and they sped away and towards Marco.

  Michelle smiled. Her mind went back to happier times. She looked up into the sky. Clear. The light beginning to fade. As she did so, she heard the front gate open, and a car pulled in. She quickly opened her phone. It must be someone she knew, as they had entered the gate code so must be a trusted friend. As the screen opened revealing the security cameras, she was surprised to see Ruth's little Peugeot back into the driveway. Michelle stood up and made her way to the front door. Behind it she could hear Ruth hunting through her bag for keys. Her manner got more and more frustrated as she clearly couldn't find them. Michelle opened the door to find Ruth crying and upset.
"What's wrong?" she asked sympathetically.

Ruth looked into her eyes. "My grandmother has died." And her eyes fell into floods of tears.
Michelle gathered the young woman into her arms, pulled her inside the house, and guided her to the living room.
"Do you want coffee?" Michelle enquired. "Or brandy?"
"B b b b brandy, por favour" Ruth muttered.
Michelle went over to the cabinet. Took out the glass decanter and poured two measures into beautiful crystal glasses.
"Here you go," she said, handing the glass to Ruth.
"I am sorry I came here," Ruth began, as Michelle passed a tissue and Ruth wiped her eyes. "Thank you, Michelle," she smiled.
"It's OK, you know you can come here if you need to, but why are you not with your mother?"
"My mother is very angry," Ruth explained. "She hit me when I said that it was sad but my grandmother was very old and maybe it was time for her to rest."
"That's OK," she said softly. "Your mother is just sad that she has lost her mother."
"I know," Ruth sobbed gently. "But I have lost my grandmother too." And the tears fell again.
Michelle said nothing. She simply cradled the young woman and let the emotions of the day come out. She could see Ruth was exhausted. "Do you want something to eat?" Michelle asked.
Ruth shook her head. "I would like another brandy."
"Of course," Michelle said. She took both glasses, and refilled them. Ruth was calmer now. Michelle said, "Would you like to take a shower?"

"Yes please," was the reply. "But I have no clothes to change into."
"Don't worry, I am sure I have something you can use. There is a robe in the bathroom. Go and shower and make yourself comfortable."
Ruth did as she was told. Michelle fussed around and tidied. Then smiled to herself. "Christ! This is her bloody job!" She laughed to herself.
It seemed like only seconds later Ruth reappeared. Her hair wet. Her face slightly red, from both the hot shower, and the tears. Michelle handed her another brandy. "Have you texted your mother?"
Ruth shook her head.
"Don't you think you should?"
"My mother told me to get out, so right now Michelle I would rather be away from her if that's OK."
"Of course it is, you do what you feel is best."
She led Ruth out into the garden. The sun setting now, darkness falling. An awkward silence developed. Ruth asked, "Are you married?"
Michelle laughed. "It's complicated."
Ruth smiled. "Marco and Anesh looked after me and my mother when my father was killed. My father used to work for Marco."
"At the restaurant?"
"Not always," Ruth let her eyes fall.
"It's OK, we all have a past."
Ruth smiled.
"How old are you Ruth?"
"I'm 32."

"You look fabulous," Michelle was envious. This woman looked half her age. She hadn't counted on her being older than 25. "Do you want to be a maid for the rest of your life?"

"No Michelle, I don't, but Marco looks after me well. And sometimes I meet nice people like you."

Michelle blushed. "You don't know me," she laughed.

"No, I don't," Ruth answered. "But I see a pain behind your eyes when you look around here, and also a determination that you are going to be OK."

"You are a good judge of people Ruth."

Ruth came and sat next to Michelle. "I hope so," Ruth said softly.

"So, Michelle enquired, "do you have a boyfriend?"

"No," came the short answer.

"A girlfriend?" Michelle laughed.

"I haven't had anyone."

Michelle choked on her brandy. "You haven't?"

Ruth blushed. "No, "she said, "I have never found the person I wanted to."

"You are beautiful," Michelle said.

"I am plain. And the maid," she replied. "Ordinary, and no one wants ordinary, and I never wanted anyone. Or at least I never wanted anyone enough. So I just didn't."

Michelle held Ruth's hand. "I Am sure you will find the right man," she replied.

Ruth answered. "Or girl."

Michelle looked surprised again. "You would prefer a girl?"

"For my first time, yes" Ruth went red. "I have always been so scared of a man being rough with me, and I am not rough."

Michelle smiled. "I am sure whoever the girl is, she will be perfect for you."

"I hope so," Ruth blushed.

Michelle brushed her hair from her face. She looked deep into Ruth's dark brown eyes. Michelle froze inside briefly. They leant forward. She kissed Ruth softly. Their mouths touching. Lips electric. Both of their bodies fizzed at the touch. Michelle had never initiated anything with a woman before, not even in the children's home. Her mind went back to Rita. She kissed Ruth harder. Felt her nipples stiffen. She pulled Ruth in closer. Not really knowing what or why she was doing this, but she knew she wanted this delicate woman to enjoy her first experience, not rough, and not to be scared like Michelle had been. She reached for Ruth's robe and found the belt. Pulling at it gently exposed Ruth's smooth skin. Michelle wanted to touch her. Softly her fingers began to explore. Ruth shuddered. She was already beginning to lose herself in the pleasure.

Michelle touched her nipples. Ruth's body stiffened. The only time she had ever been touched was by herself. She responded by moaning slightly as Michelle pulled at her breasts. Michelle was lost in herself. She had not thought about sex with a man or a woman since Charlie. Her mind suddenly stopped. Charlie. Shit. She couldn't do this. She pulled away from Ruth.

"What have I done wrong?" The young woman asked.

Michelle held her hands. "You have done nothing wrong Ruth. Nothing at all, but it's complicated, and I'm sorry. I shouldn't have started anything."
Ruth burst into tears. "I have offended you," she wept.
"You have done no such thing!" Michelle snapped a little too harshly perhaps. "But I lost my lover in a car accident a year ago, and no one has touched me since. I'm just not ready."
Ruth stopped crying. "You said you were married?"
"I said it's complicated," she laughed.
Ruth laughed too. "We all have a past," she said.
"We do," Michelle returned. She stood up. And removed her robe. Walking softly to the pool. She stepped into the water. Not ashamed to be naked, she looked back at Ruth. Ruth stood. Undid her robe. And followed. The two women swam in the warm water. The moonlight bathing the pool. They would have sex that night. Ruth would be free to feel confident. Michelle would know that she could still enjoy sex, if not love.
When they rose in the morning, Ruth dressed and slipped out of the house silently. Smiling. Knowing she definitely wanted to be with a woman now. But also knowing it would not be Michelle.
Michelle was in a quandary. She felt like she had cheated Charlie. But she knew what Ruth was going through. And at 32, no woman needed to go through that. She would never be gay. But she was comfortable in her own skin that fucking a woman wasn't a crime to be hung over.
As she laughed, the gates to the villa opened. And the stunning blue Bentley arrived. "Coffee dahhling," Anesh shouted, and waved his arms in the air.

Valerie looked suitably worse for wear.
Michelle opened the door. "You look like shit," she said to her friend.
"That's good, coz I feel like shit too!" And she ran to the bathroom.
"Anesh" Michelle shouted as she went to the kitchen, "What the hell have you done to my friend?!"
"Daaahlinng," he replied, "I haven't done anything," he paused, "Marco however, may have done rather a lot."
Michelle laughed. "Does that include sex, or just booze?"

"I think it includes both," he laughed. "Are you all packed?"
"Almost," Michelle said. "I really don't want to leave, but Valerie says I must."
"It's for the best for now."
"I know, but I don't want to. Here is where I belong."
"You will have plenty of time to come back Michelle, and when you do I can make all the necessary arrangements to make sure it is as painless as it can be."
"You are my perfect gay husband," she laughed.
"And you are my perfect straight wife," he smiled.
"Thank you for looking after Ruth last night."
"How did you know?" Michelle looked shocked.
"Dahhhling," he paused, "I know everything! And besides, she called me. Her mother was worried. Ruth had already told me she was coming to see you. She needed you."
"I think I needed her too."
Valerie arrived. "Coffee… please," she gasped. "I'm fucked."
"You slut," Michelle laughed.

"Sugar, please!" Valerie begged.
"Here," Michelle thrust the cup at her. Valerie drank it greedily.
"I'm going to shower," she said shakily.
An hour later, the friends were packed, dressed, and in the Bentley on the way to the airport.

Giles meanwhile was beside himself. "Where is my fucking wife!" He shouted to no one in particular.
Tommy had not told Giles about the incident with Nikki. He didn't need anything to ruin Giles' big reveal, much less the drug deal.
He decided that Nikki needed some time off. So, he told the Coleman to take her back to her flat. Lock her inside. And under no circumstances was she allowed to leave. If she tried… kill her.
There were only three weeks until opening. Giles was furious. And Tommy's wound had not got much better.

As the plane touched down, Michelle and Valerie smiled. Two weeks. And their whole world would change.
Valerie looked at her friend. "It's our fucking turn," she whispered.
"It's our fucking turn," Michelle mouthed in return.
Barry was there waiting. The two women couldn't contain their happiness. "My beautiful Barry," Valerie shouted. Barry went red. He never liked being in the spotlight. As they walked to the car, Barry spoke softly. "I think there is trouble Miss Valerie."
"Trouble Barry?" Valerie said.
"Mr Giles is in a very bad mood, and Mr Tommy has not been himself," Barry spoke quietly.

"How do you know all this?"
"You tell me to keep watch, well, I don't always have a nap Miss Valerie," he said.
"Good man Barry, I always knew I could rely on you." And she grinned. He was old. He was harmless, but he wasn't quite as daft as people thought.
They drove back in silence.
Barry dropped Michelle home. Then carried on to Valerie's.
"Where is Giles?" Valerie asked.
"He is at home Miss Valerie," Barry replied.
This was not going to go well, Valerie imagined. Packing and leaving without a word to Giles had not been her best plan. But fuck it. She had had enough now. In a few weeks Giles would be no more.
She opened the door.
"WHERE THE FUCK HAVE YOU BEEN?!" Giles screamed in her face.
"Wherever the fuck I want," Valerie said calmly.
His fist came from nowhere. It landed perfectly on her jaw. Valerie blacked out instantly. And Giles came in his trousers. He felt his cock harden, and the power surge through his veins. He may have been fat. And a coward. But this time he had shown her. He walked back to his office. "I fucking own you! He screamed. "I fucking own you, bitch!"
Valerie came to after a few minutes. Her head hurt. Her jaw hurt. And she had no fucking idea what was going on with her husband anymore. She had always been in control. But suddenly there had been a power shift. And she was scared.

She went to bed. She needed to sleep off the hangover, the sex, and most of all, needed her head clear to decide what her next move was.
Whatever it was, she would make damn sure it was final. She took out her mobile.
"Don't let me down my friend."
Anesh smiled. "I won't."
Anesh sent a simple text. "We must not fail my brother."
A simple reply. "The Signalman has never let me down."
Anesh smiled.

Nikki's dead!

Callum woke in a sweat. Every night it was almost the same. Despite the time that had passed, he couldn't get rid of the image of his father's death. He looked at the woman lying next to him. One way or another, he needed to sort himself. For her sake. For his sake too. But try as he might, he couldn't shake the image of his father. He had asked Sam to marry him. But he couldn't let her take him on like this. Somehow, he must either get to the bottom of his father's death, or let it go, and make a future with her. But right now, laying in a cold sweat, neither of those things seemed a great option.
He text his brother in the U.S.A. "I need your help." He knew he wouldn't reply. The time difference meant his brother would be sound asleep.
So when the phone pinged. "What's up bro?" Callum was surprised.
"What are you doing up?"
"I can't sleep, the old man is playing on my mind."
"I can't either."
"Go see a therapist man, I am!"
"Does it help?"
"I have no idea, only been once!"
"Haha, so what made you do that?"
"I ended my last three girlfriends because I was becoming a freak. So I had to do something."
"Yeah, I hear ya."
Callum paused.
"You OK?"

"I'm OK, man. It's just gonna take time."
"Raymond," Callum paused, "I'm gonna ask Sam to marry me."
"Wooooohooooo," came the excited message on the phone. "About time man, but good for you. I am guessing she doesn't know yet?" Raymond laughed.
"She doesn't, Callum paused. "I need to sort myself out first."
"If she loves you like I think she does man, you just need to tell her. She will be there for you."
"What about you Raymond?"
"I'm cool bro, we do things different out here!" And he laughed. "Besides, at $500 an hour, my shrink better work huh?"
"Yeah, I guess."
"Stop being so hard on yourself man, ask the girl, get your life back, and enjoy it."
"I will. Thanks bro."
"Anytime man. Now, I'm gonna try to go back to sleep. Chill. Speak to you soon."
"Cool." And Callum ended the text. Maybe his brother was right. He turned to look at Sam. She woke as he did so.
"Good morning gorgeous," he beamed.
"You are cheerful," she replied.
"Sam," Callum said sternly. "We need to talk."
"Oh shit!" Came the slightly shaky reply. "What have I done?"
Callum smiled. "You have done nothing except make me fall in love with you, and I want it to be forever."
Sam sat up with a start. "Callum Summer," she said loudly. "Are you taking the piss?"

Callum smiled. "I have never been more serious." "Sam, will you marry me?"

Sam was dumbfounded. She sat open mouthed. Callum looked deep into her eyes. "I saw my father happier than he had ever been, and it was taken from him. I'm NOT going to let that happen to me," and he took her hand softly and kissed it.

"YES, YES, YES!" She screamed... and she threw her arms around the young man and burst into tears.

Callum didn't quite know what to do, he certainly had not expected that reaction. He looked at Sam. She smiled, and he lowered his head to kiss her. As he did so, she threw back the covers and opened her legs. "Fuck me Callum," she said in a husky voice.

Callum smiled. He admired her body. She had pale skin, and he gently knelt between her legs. Pushed her back onto the bed. And softly nibbled her thighs. She squealed. And grabbed his head and demanded. "Eat me." Callum did as he was told. Softly he raised his tongue and licked along her pussy. She moaned softly as he tasted her. His tongue flicking across her lips and finding her clitoris. She was already sexually charged and he enjoyed feeling how wet she was. Sliding a finger inside her as he licked her harder, she moaned louder. "Don't stop," she demanded, "I'm going to come!"

Callum obeyed. He greedily worshipped her by now, soaked pussy. Licking and biting and sucking until Sam could hold back no longer. She grabbed his head. "Bite me!" She shrieked. And as Callum did her orgasm exploded. Her body shook violently, and she shut her eyes and gave a muffled scream. Callum began to use his

tongue again. "Stop!" She said loudly, "I can't take anymore right now!"
Callum smiled. He looked at her lovingly. "I love you." And jumped off the bed. "Coffee?"
Sam smiled. "Yes please."
Callum whistled as he went downstairs. Today was going to be a good day.

Tommy had taken most of Nikki's clothes. He made sure she had a meal. But the supply of drugs had stopped. Her body was craving them. She screamed every now and again to no one. She even bit her arms just to feel. The frustration of her situation made her mind lose itself. Her body needed the cocaine. Her mind needed to escape. The toxic combination meant Nikki slowly slipped into oblivion in her own mind. Charlie fucking Summer. The anger built once more. She stood up. Went to the bathroom. Turning on the light she looked in the mirror. The tears streamed down her face. She raised her fists. And hit the mirror as hard as she could. The glass smashed. Shards of razor-sharp glass scattered over the basin and floor. The instant pain in her hands made her even more angry. She looked down. And smiled. Grabbing a fairly large piece of mirrored glass, she deftly ran the razor sharp glass down her arm to her wrist. The blood appeared immediately. She did the same for the other wrist. Once again, the thick red liquid flowed. Nikki quickly felt faint. Falling forward, her head smashed against the bath as she collapsed. She blacked out almost instantly.

The Coleman sat outside. His duty was to Tommy. But to be honest, he didn't care much for being a babysitter. It had only been a few days. But he was bored beyond belief. He began scrolling through his phone. As he did so it rang. "Take her somewhere remote and dump her," and the line went dead.

Allan smiled. "Yes boss," he mouthed gently. And opened the door of the car. He would do just as Tommy asked. But not before he had at least had the chance to fuck her. It has been a long time for him. He checked the inside pocket of his jacket. Just enough cocaine for her to beg, he was sure. He made his way up the steps, slid the key into the lock, and stepped inside.

The flat was cold; dark, and silent. The Coleman's natural instinct was to be on alert. Something didn't feel right. He turned on the light but could see nothing and no one in the small living room. The flat was completely silent. He moved towards the kitchen and pushed the door open, his hands ready at any moment in case there was a surprise waiting for him. Moving further along the hall he came to the bedroom and pushed it open but again it was empty. When he finally reached the bathroom, he pushed open the door but there was a resistance. Pushing a little harder he could feel something preventing the door opening. He used all of his might and gave the door a massive shove. As he fell into the bathroom there was Nikki laying in a pool of blood. He took out his mobile phone. "Boss, we have a problem."

This was the last thing that Tommy needed, yet in some respects it had saved him from doing the dirty work, and he could easily cover it up by simply saying that she had been depressed, he had given her some time off, but had no idea that she would kill herself. He told the Coleman to call an ambulance and act like nothing had happened. Putting the phone down he dialled Giles' number. "Hello dear boy, what can I do for you?" Came the cheerful greeting.

"Nikki's dead," Tommy replied and proceeded to explain. Giles was secretly rather pleased. Though she had definitely been a perfect little slut she had also been in the way, and perhaps now Tommy could direct his energies back into their business ventures without distraction.

"I'm sure you can make the necessary arrangements dear boy," he said and hung up. Sitting back in his chair he smiled to himself. With only weeks left until the club was open, finally feeling like he was in control again. Giles felt very pleased with himself indeed.

Rosy was putting the finishing touches to the bar area. Helen had checked all of the girls' changing rooms to ensure that there was in her words 'no funny business', and the six private rooms were all immaculate. 'The Warren' was pretty much ready for business. Rosy had personally interviewed all of the girls, to ensure they knew exactly what was expected of them and in return for their silence, they would be extremely well rewarded. She allowed herself a little smile. Though the years had caught up with her she knew how to run this business and even though she was in her 60s she still enjoyed the thrill and power that having a man either between her thighs or she between his gave her. She wanted to make sure that everything would be perfect, and Gigi would be part of that.

The Coleman returned to Tommy's Club and immediately went and found his boss. "Everything OK?" Tommy asked. "All sorted boss, there will have to be an inquest as there always is but they were pretty confident that this was nothing more than a suicide."
"Well, it was." "Even if perhaps I did help a little bit," and he allowed himself a menacing smile. "Now," Tommy snapped, "since you've seemed to be capable of many things, I need you to run an errand for me in a couple of weeks. There is a very exclusive package of merchandise landing from Spain that I need collecting and I need somebody I can trust. I will provide the transport and I will ensure that everything goes without a hitch, I just need to make sure you are there to make the collection."
"OK, boss, whatever you say just let me know."
"Oh, I will old son, I will."

Valerie phoned Michelle. "I don't like this," she said bluntly. "I have never seen Giles so angry or animated. In fact, it's not even that, it's like he has suddenly become brave, and that frightens the hell out of me!"

Michelle listened. She too had a fair share of trauma with Tommy though for some reason he seemed to have calmed a little lately. Perhaps he just had other things on his mind.

Just what was making Giles so jumpy?

"I honestly can't tell you how much I need that man out of my life, I'm going to call Marco."

Michelle listened but didn't offer much in return. She too wanted her husband out of the way but this was a world she was not familiar with and all she could do was hang her hopes on the promise of her gay husband Anesh, and his good friend. "Just be patient." "We both know that Anesh and Marco have all of this in hand and we just need to leave it to them, I am certain they will not let us down."

Ken.

The DS had had just about enough. Almost every door had been slammed in his face. So he decided he would take the matter into his own hands and go and visit Tommy's club, 'Spice' for himself. After all, he didn't care who's feathers he ruffled, it was his job. As he swung into the car park, he couldn't help but feel that he was on the right track. The club looked dark and brooding, yet it was obvious even in the daylight that neat green neon signs would look spectacular against the black background. He banged on the door. And pressed the intercom at the same time. Tommy pushed the intercom. "We are closed!" he snapped.
"Well then I suggest you open," the DS answered back. Tommy answered the intercom once again. "Are you fucking deaf? We are closed."
The DS replied, "Are you fucking deaf, it's the police."
Tommy sat bolt upright. He quickly picked up a radio "Harvey, what the fuck are the old bill doing here?"
Harvey replied, "I have no fucking idea."
Tommy roared back at him "Well I suggest you go and fucking find out, and make sure everything is clean as a whistle."
Harvey quickly related the messages to the Coleman and the other members of staff. It wasn't unusual to find the police knocking on the door. It happened every now

and again and of course every time they came to the club it was as clean as a whistle. Tommy ensured that whatever drugs were on the premises almost certainly could never be found. False walls and trap doors may have been a thing of the past, but they were very much a reality in Tommy's world. Harvey opened the door, and the detective showed his warrant card.

"What can we do for you, officer?" Harvey replied cheerfully.

"I would like to see Thomas Shelton please."

Harvey grinned "Oh you mean Tommy the boss."

"Yes, I mean Tommy the boss."

"No problem officer, I'll just go and get him."

"If you don't mind, I'll make my own way," and he looked down at Harvey.

Harvey looked back up and smiled "No problem at all, I will lead the way," and beckoned the policeman to follow him. The Coleman watched the policeman with suspicious eyes as Harvey got to Tommy's office, he knocked on the door.

"Come in," Tommy said harshly.

"DS Nicholson to see you."

"I didn't know I had any appointments booked."

Harvey smiled, "You didn't boss, but we are always here to help an officer of the law. Are we not?"

"Of course," Tommy said with a grin, "come in forgive me!" And he smiled as he showed him in.

Harvey closed the door and almost burst with laughter. The Coleman was waiting for him.

"What the fuck is so funny?" he enquired.

"Seeing Tommy squirm with a copper in front of him," Harvey laughed.
Allan joined in the laughter.
Tommy couldn't have felt less like laughing. "So, Mr Shelton," the DS began.
Tommy shifted uncomfortably in his chair. "How can I help you officer?" he smiled, really a grimace.
The chat that afternoon was informal. The policeman explained that there was a new government drive to clean up the rural areas, so every nightclub owner was having a chat just really to see that they were keeping everything in order. Tommy felt a little more reassured as he showed the policemen to the door. The DS left with a parting gesture, "Keep it clean Mr Shelton or I will find you."
Tommy grimaced again and as he shut the door took out his mobile phone dialling Giles.
"Hello dear boy, what can I do for you?"
Tommy winced. How could the bloody old bastard always be cheerful.
"We may have a problem," he muttered.
"We never have problems here, only opportunities," and Giles' belly laughed at his own joke.
Tommy said, "Well this opportunity is called Detective Sergeant Nicholson. So I suggest you better use your persuasive charms and get rid of him."
"What seems to be the issue dear boy, you know there will always be policemen after all."
"Apparently there is a government-wide crackdown on drugs in rural areas and he seems to think that nightclubs might be a source of them. This one isn't your

average village copper. He's smarter than I like, so, have your little chat with the chief super and let's see if we can't find him some traffic duties to do." He ended the call angry.

Giles smiled, he already had the chief super in his pocket, in particular he was very interested in Giles' new club, so Giles didn't see any issues with a slightly rogue detective being brought in and he was pretty sure that the chief super would soon sort everything.

"Now Gigi," he said, "why don't we have one more little practice. I definitely want you to look after everybody in my club." His lecherous grin did nothing for Gigi's mood. For while she had dreamt of being a porn star, she wasn't entirely sure this was the way to do it.

Everything was finally in place. Giles had worked very hard; the bribes, the corruption, had been relatively easy when you have the money that Giles has. You can just throw it around and people will do what you ask, but now that the grand opening was only a short step away, everybody was getting nervous, Giles in particular. Knowing his wife had been screwing somebody else though he had absolutely no idea who, and though he actually didn't care, it hurt his pride and he was very very disappointed that if anybody found out outside of his circle, they might be able to use it as a lever against him. The one thing Giles *never* wanted was any bad press. Valerie was still in shock from Giles behaviour towards her, after all she had always thought of him as a slightly weak and frightened man with way too much money, but when he struck her a week or so ago, she realised that somewhere in there was some fight and that perhaps she would have to play things a little more carefully then she imagined.

Michelle too was worried, Tommy was parading around like a peacock in full flourish, though she had little idea why and was scared to ask. All she was certain of is that it wasn't good. She had tried her utmost to find out, but it seemed everyone, including Harvey, was remaining very tight lipped, and not about to reveal anything.

Things changed slightly in her mind when she read a small piece on the internet about a woman who had killed herself in a small flat. The doctor said that the cause of death was suicide brought on by withdrawal of cocaine, her name was Nikki.

Michelle shivered, looked over her shoulder and muttered to herself, "I guess I am next." Tommy was becoming far more powerful than even she had imagined when he first opened that club and she had begun to sing there.

I fucking own you!

Tommy took the call from Lazlo, "No problem," he muttered. "I will be sending one of my best men, just make sure everything is covered."
Lazlo smiled as he replied. "Don't worry my friend, I am sure everything is covered. I will have the package delivered in two days' time, just make sure your man will be there. The usual airfield and make sure there are no mistakes. Bring the money and do not let me down. I have told the pilot if anything looks unusual, he is not to land.
"Lazlo my friend," Tommy paused thoughtfully, "when have I ever let you down?"
"There is a first time for everything, Mr Tommy," he snapped. "I will make sure everything is in place at my end and in a couple of days you will have your merchandise Mr Tommy, I hope your new customers enjoy."
Tommy ended the call feeling pleased with himself. A new club, a new venture, more money, more power, though he had to admit this time Giles had stolen a march on him, and once again he didn't like it. He cut two perfect white lines of cocaine, snorted hard and felt himself absorb the drug. His eyes widened and he suddenly realised that with Nikki dead, no longer did he have on tap sex. She may have been a cheap slut but whenever he wanted a fuck she was there. He needed a new cheap slut. As he felt the power coursing through his veins, he decided

that it was time for his wife to show him some affection, and he marched out of the Den. Shouted, "Michelle!" And waited for an answer. He listened intently and could hear water running. "Perfect, I will fuck her in the shower," he said to himself, and made his way upstairs. By the time he reached the top he was naked, his cock hard as he opened the bathroom door.

Michelle had not heard him coming and had no chance to defend herself as he roughly walked into the shower, grabbed her and fingered her hard from behind. She screamed as the water cascaded over her head and she began gasping and drinking far too much of the hot water as she choked. Tommy bent her further forward and forced his hard cock inside Michelle. She hung on to the wall as Tommy fucked her hard from behind.

"I fucking own you!" He screamed, as he fucked her harder, and within a few minutes his orgasm was over. "Know your place," he said as his cock slid out of her. He pushed her roughly against the wall.

Thankfully her hands were still outstretched so she managed to save herself. She straightened herself up, turned around and swung a fist at him.

He grabbed it instinctively and said to her, "Your time will come."

"Just like their time came?" Michelle asked sarcastically. "Which one, Charlie or Nikki? Tommy smiled. "Well, let's see, how about whichever fucking one you want," he said as he washed his cock in the water before stepping out, wrapping a towel around himself and leaving the bathroom. Like a lion that had finally finished with its prey,

he went into his bedroom, lay down and closed his eyes. Michelle was seething. She wanted to kill him. She wrapped herself in her dressing gown and crept downstairs taking the kitchen knife off of the wall. She padded softly back upstairs and went to Tommy's bedroom door. Little did she know as she tried the handle that the door was locked. Banging loudly on it in frustration, she swore at her husband and stuck the knife in the door, before returning to her own room. She cried herself to sleep.
The next morning, the Coleman reported to Tommy's office. "Come in and shut the door," Tommy said abruptly. The Coleman did as he was told.
Sitting down in front of Tommy he simply answered, "Yes, boss"
Tommy threw him the keys. "There is an Audi out the front, an RS4, if you have any trouble put your foot down and get away. You are only collecting a small package, it will be enough to fit in the back of the estate car. You leave tonight. Pick up time is 2 am and do not fuck this up."
"I won't fuck this up boss I assure you."
"Make fucking sure you don't. Now get out of here, get down there and wait."
Allan Mustard did as he was told, slowly picked the keys up and walked out of the office. He made his way towards the car park. Sitting there was the most immaculate black Audi RS4 Estate. The young man smiled, Tommy had a certain style even if you really didn't like him.
Harvey watched from the window knowing it should have been his boy doing the job. However, he was secretly

pleased that Aaron was well away from it all. Harvey knew Tommy didn't really like him and that suited Harvey just fine. With any luck, all of this shit would be out of the way soon and Harvey could go back to what sort of resembled a normal life. He knew in his own mind he was getting older; he definitely wasn't quite as sharp as he used to be and his son had little prospect of following in his footsteps. This left Harvey rather frustrated and disappointed at times. He stood at the window and saluted. "I wish you well Mr Coleman," and he turned to go back into the club.

Allan Mustard started the car. It was barely three pm what the fuck was he going to do for almost twelve hours. To a location in the middle of nowhere where hopefully a small aircraft was going to land with some very high quality drugs in it. He hadn't even managed to fuck that cheap slut before she had taken her own life. Frustrated, angry and feeling a little worthless he put his foot hard on the accelerator, the car sprang forward, and he decided that the fastest of drives would be a way to get rid of his anger. He looked in the back seat just to make sure the briefcase was there and breathed a sigh of relief. "No point going to pick something up if you can't pay for it," he said to himself.

Lazlo Kiss sent a text to Anesh and to Marco. "The deal is still on for tonight."
Anesh replied "Well done, I guess we let The Signalman take it from here. I will make sure all goes to plan, hopefully retribution will be sweet and swift. And he ended the call.

Harvey phoned Allan Mustard. "Slow down you soppy bastard, you're supposed to be inconspicuous."
"Don't fucking tell me what to do," came the reply.
"I will tell you what I fucking like you jumped up little prick, I have been doing this a long time, and the one thing you learn is never to attract attention to yourself. So slow down, put the heated seats on, the music on, chill out and do your fucking job."
The Coleman ended the call abruptly. He knew in his heart of hearts that Harvey was right but his frustration at being a babysitter, then finding Nikki dead before he could fuck her, and now being used as a courier was not his idea of fun. Still. He did as Harvey said, and gently made his way whilst inside he was still angry.
Harvey smiled. He had been that angry young man. He was too old for all that shit now, and used his brain more than his brawn. Dealing with Tommy's problems had become tiresome, and he really needed a way out. He had been foolish enough to be in debt to Tommy Shelton however, and that was not a great place to be. He cursed himself. And made his way back to the office.

    Giles was at home. He sat back in his leather armchair in his study and looked around. Life couldn't get much better than this. The only fly in the ointment was his wife and that fact she had so blatantly been screwing someone and couldn't care less. Giles didn't mind her fucking someone else, but she could at least be discreet. He pondered.

Tommy's injury was finally healing. He sat in his office, looked around the club, and smiled. As soon as he was fighting fit and Giles' new club had opened successfully, he would plan a tragic accident for his wife. He was sick of her now, and how much she knew. He took a deep swig of rum, and smiled.

Valerie looked in the mirror. Finally, the bruising was fading. She looked at her face in the mirror, it made her angry. Giles had never touched her before. And she was not about to put up with it now. Marco had better make sure this was final. She smiled, happy at the thought that Giles would finally get what he deserved. And as she pondered, she realised she cared not one jot about him anymore.

Michelle pottered. She hated it. The quiet. She wandered around the immaculate house. Almost at a loss. Thoughts of Charlie spinning around in her head. Callum, Sam. She smiled. The wedding! Oh! How she wanted to be a part of this. She sent a text to Valerie. "How are you?"
"I'm OK," came the immediate reply.
"Good. I'm nervous."
"Of?"
"Things going wrong."
"Will you stop, woman!" Valerie replied. "You have forgotten my rules. Evaluate, process, Then do whatever is needed LOL."
"I know! But I need it to happen, I have realised how much I hate him."

Valerie smiled softly to herself. "I understand better than you know," she sent back. "Now relax, and just let Marco and Anesh do what they do."
"OK."
Michelle felt no better but had little choice but to do as Valerie suggested.

The Signalman started the battered Land Rover. Toffee sat beside him. He patted his small companion's head. Signed, "Let's go!" And made off. He didn't do anything fast. For The Signalman, brains now were his speed. The plan was in place. He knew the time of the drop, and the location. As he left, he gazed back at the boat. "See you soon," old girl, he thought, and pulled out. It would be a long journey. Noisy, though he cared not one bit. Toffee curled up next to his master, and they made their way to the middle of nowhere to wait for the plane to arrive.

Allan Mustard was already at the closest village to the drop site. He had used the power and speed of the Audi to ensure he got there swiftly. Sitting in the small village pub, he ordered food and sat patiently.
As he did so, his mobile lit up. "All OK?"
"Yes boss."
"Good, bring it back safely."
"No problem boss."
As he did so, the barmaid came over.
Blonde. Short skirt, low cut top. She leant forward, and smiling asked, "Is everything OK?"
He couldn't help looking at her tits. "Oh yes," he grinned childishly.

"Well if you need anything else, just let me know," she said provocatively. "Are you here for the night?"
Mr Mustard seemed blind to why she might ask that. "I have some night work to do, so no, not here for the night, just a few hours."
He could feel his face go slightly red as she leant on the table next to him, her skirt riding up a little.
"Oh, what do you do?"
The Coleman suddenly panicked. "Oh," he faltered, "er this and that," he mumbled. Harvey's words rattled around in his head. "Be inconspicuous." Bollocks! He said to himself.
"Well," she said softly, "If you need anything," and she walked off towards the bar.
He couldn't stop looking at her legs. She picked up a glass, and the plates and cutlery from a table across from him. As the fork fell, she stopped to retrieve it, and the Coleman was left under no illusions as to the colour of her (very small) thong. He grinned, felt a twinge in his cock, and wanted to fuck her. He had planned to fuck Nikki, and, if the truth be told, he wasn't exactly experienced when it came to sex. Not naive either. But he had only fucked 5 women in his life. And he wanted number six this afternoon.
The barmaid turned to him, smiled, and winked as she retrieved the fork. "I will come back," she mouthed.
The Coleman grinned. He had plenty of time. And in a few hours, he would be gone and she would never see him again. What could go wrong?
When she returned, he said, "Do you have anywhere I could perhaps freshen up? It's been a long drive."

She smiled sweetly. "We do have a couple of rooms available," she said knowingly. "I could do you a special rate, as you are not staying all night," and again she tottered off to clean the bar area.

He looked around the pub. There were, he guessed, a couple of locals in the main bar, but other than that, he was the only person in the place. As he looked down the corridor, he saw her beckon him.

Finishing his water, he made his way towards her.

She stopped at the bottom of the stairs.

"Don't you have other customers to look after?" he asked.

"We close at 6 for a couple of hours," she smiled. "As you can see it's pretty dead."

He checked his watch, it was 5.45.

She gave him a key. "Go up, Room 5."

And she wandered off to the bar. "Time gentlemen please!" She said in a loud voice. The two locals drained their glass, as the Coleman turned the key in the lock. He opened the door to a small, yet beautifully presented room. Ducking into the room due to the low doorway, he looked around. The small high set window gave a great view, but he wasn't interested in that. He pulled the curtains over, and took off his shoes and jacket. Laying down on the bed, he put his hands under his head. And closed his eyes. Not realising how tired he was, the peace and silence meant he was soon sleeping.

He didn't hear the door open, or lock again.

Mary the barmaid stood at the end of the bed. She slowly stripped. Naked now, except for her hold ups, she approached the bed. As she did so, he woke with a start.

"Well hello sleeping beauty," she smiled.
The Coleman took just a few seconds to focus.
As he did so, Mary's hands tugged at the button on his jeans. He didn't try to stop her. She unzipped his fly.
"Now," she paused. "What would Sir like?" And she smiled as she took his semi stiff cock out of his trousers.
"Everything," he said softly.
Mary proceeded to undress him. "First though," she stopped. "I need you to shower," she said succinctly. "You may be a very good-looking man, and I am going to fuck you, but I do have certain standards." And she kissed the tip of his cock. "So go shower, and I am all yours."
The Coleman did as he was told, smiling all the way. Finally, he would at least be able to relieve his sexual frustrations and he didn't really understand why this woman wanted to fuck him, but he certainly wasn't going to say no.
As he showered, Mary was on her phone. She sent the text, "He is here, how long do I keep him?"
The reply came back "I am about an hour away, make sure he is still there."
"No problem, I am sure I can keep him busy for an hour," and she finished the message with a laughing face.
And the equally laughing face reply from The Signalman "I am bloody sure you can!"
The Coleman came out of the shower, his naked fit body glistening, and even though Mary had done this many times before, she couldn't help but be impressed by the man's physique.

Dressed in nothing more than hold ups, she smiled and said, "Come here big boy, let's see what you've got for me."

She stretched her hands out, and caressed his cock as it began to stiffen.

"Now make sure you don't come too quickly," she said sarcastically "I want to enjoy myself."

He looked down at her. "I want to enjoy myself too, so I guess we're on the same page," and he smiled at her as she took his cock in her mouth. The Coleman closed his eyes and let out a little moan of ecstasy.

As he began to fuck her mouth deeper, an hour away an old, battered Land Rover was making its way towards the pub. The Signalman turned to his small dog. Knowing exactly what the Coleman was experiencing he smiled, patted his furry friend on the head and thought to himself, "Lucky bastard, once upon a time it would have been me!" And he laughed at the little dog. Toffee looked up at his owner and almost seemed to be smiling back. The two of them had spent many years together and though Toffee was almost 12 now, he still had all the life and soul of a puppy. Something his master loved him even more for. The Signalman, to be honest, was terrified that if anything happened to Toffee, the sudden realisation he would be alone was not the greatest thought. He had, after all, been in a lonely world for most of his life. He shook his head, as if to clear his mind. "Pull yourself together you have a job to do," and he pressed the accelerator a little harder, though the tired old diesel engine had very little else to give.

Mary climbed on top of the Coleman. His cock was actually a decent size and for once, fucking him wouldn't be a chore. Good looking and with a good body, for once in her life this job was turning out to be okay and she would be paid well for it.

"Anesh my brother!" Marco said in his deep voice, "Everything is going to plan. The Signalman is about an hour away from the pickup and Lazlo has assured me that everything is in place. All he wants to make sure is he either gets his drugs or his money!" And he gave a deep guttural laugh.
Anesh smiled as he listened to the words. "Do not worry my brother, I will make sure that he is well-rewarded, and it will be time to teach those two English bastards a lesson, for both my friends, Valerie and Michelle, but also for me. And when all of this is over, I will make sure that Valerie comes back out here with Michelle and we give them the best time ever, for they will finally be free."
"Yes," Marco smiled. "I must admit I would definitely like to see Valerie again. I have never met another woman quite like her, she can even take almost all of my cock!"
"Be careful Marco, it sounds like you are falling for her. And you never fall for anyone," Anesh laughed.
"I like her. Let's leave it there, shall we?"
"Let's leave it there my brother, I will speak to you once the package has been delivered and collected."
"You will, I will speak to Lazlo now."
Everything was set. One thing that was for sure was that neither Giles nor Tommy suspected anything about a double cross. And that was just the way it needed to be.

The Coleman was too blinded by the needs of his cock to actually realise that this was a set up. And as the woman sitting on top of him gently rode his cock he had nothing else on his mind except coming inside her. For Mary this would be the best ten grand payday she had had in a long time. She didn't mind being used as a whore but just occasionally she managed to enjoy it.

Tommy phoned Giles, "We are all set old man."
"Good, good, dear boy, I knew I could rely on you. Now, once the club is open and everything is settled, we need to make a plan to try to get rid of our other problems. But for now, let's just enjoy what we are doing, have a drink, have a round or two and look forward to plenty more money, lots more sin and debauchery, and to becoming even more powerful than we already are."
Tommy smiled. If things went the way he wanted he would soon be all powerful, however that meant eliminating three problems, and at least one of those would be bloody difficult. He already knew the stubbornness of Valerie and was starting to realise that her influence was rubbing off on Michelle. He would have to be very careful just exactly how to make those problems go away.

    Valerie and Michelle wanted nothing to do with anything that was going on. Even though they knew exactly what the plans were now, they wanted to be out of the way, so the best thing for them this evening was a spa. That way they could legitimately say they were not even around.

As they sat opposite each other in the sauna Michelle spoke first. "I will be glad to get him out of the way, I never thought I would say this about my husband, but I don't give a flying fuck what happens to him. He has killed Charlie, and definitely had a hand in that slut Nikki's death. He is a vile, evil individual and I have no idea how I let it go so far."

Valerie smiled "There is an old saying, absolute power corrupts absolutely. And to be honest I think that's where Giles is. I have no idea where this violent streak has come from, but clearly, he is sliding out of control. The problem for us Michelle is that we know too much, and whilst I'm sure they can't risk anything happening to either of us, we also can't go to the police." She paused. Her mind thoughtful. "The only way to deal with them is to fight fire with fire, and that's exactly what I intend to do. It's why I employed Marco to get rid of them."

"OK, so what happens then, what happens when Giles and Tommy are out of the way, what do we do?"

"We play the sweet innocent wife, and we know nothing. We just assumed that their husband was a hard-working individual who provided for his beloved wife."

"And you think people will believe that?"

"Of course they will fucking believe it!" Nobody believes you were a whore for the last two years, but you were!" And she laughed.

Michelle's face went red, and it wasn't just from the steam of the sauna. "Yeah okay bitch," she laughed. "You have made your point, so are you saying that we take over?"

Valerie grinned an evil grin. "I'm saying that we ride the storm and see what the outcome is when it's all settled down. Inevitably the police will be involved, and we will have to make bloody sure that they are convinced we know nothing, otherwise all of this will be for nothing."
"So what's the plan Valerie, what do you have in your head?"
"I plan for us to take over. If Tommy and Giles think they know me, and Giles thinks that one smack on the jaw is going to change my mind they haven't got a fucking clue. And now I have you by my side it's time to show those fucking idiots who really is the boss."
The venom in Valerie's voice took Michelle by surprise. "Where has all of this come from?" she asked.
"When Jamie died, I see now, my world kind of fell apart, for no other reason than I had a glimpse of being happy. I chose not to take it and to carry on the life that I already had. Partly because of him telling me to but also partly because I was too scared, even though I would have had a great life with Jamie. Clearly that isn't the case anymore, so the only thing I can do is fight Giles and believe me Michelle, I will."

Allan Mustard moaned loudly and grabbed Mary's arse as his cock exploded inside her. Incredibly for her, she managed to orgasm almost at the same time. Something she had never experienced. Her body shuddered. And the orgasm swept over her.
As she lay down on top of him, the battered Land Rover pulled into the village. Allan Mustard smiled and kissed the top of her forehead.

He sat up, his cock still inside her but she quickly climbed off of him.

"Don't you be getting too familiar now. I need to go and open the pub," she looked at the clock it was a quarter to eight.

He looked a little disheartened but simply said, "Okay." He watched her as she began to get dressed and smiled. She actually was pretty fit for her age, he felt quite pleased with himself and decided that he would close his eyes and enjoy being fucked for the first time in a long time.

She came out of the bathroom fully dressed. "I guess my public awaits," she smiled. "I'll see you later," and she quietly closed the door and crept down the stairs. As she did so The Signalman stood at the front door. She opened it discreetly and then went round to the side of the pub, the door used as the main entrance to the bar. Swinging the door open she smiled, "The bar is now open!" And went back and stood behind it.

The Signalman grinned and pointed to the IPA tap. His hands made an extended signal and he mouthed "Pint." He pointed to the dog, and Mary laughed.

"Pint too?" She mouthed back.

Brian laughed. "Water," he mouthed. Mary put her thumb up, and went into the kitchen area behind the bar. She came back with a small bowl of water for the dog. Brian looked at her and pointed upwards. Mary nodded, "Yes, that's where he is," she said.

The Signalman gave her a thumbs up, as Mary made the symbol to indicate that Allan Mustard was

about to go to sleep. Brian took out his phone and sent a brief text. "I am here, all is going to plan."
He got the simple reply, "Well done my brother."
Brian took a big swig of his pint and settled down to wait and ensure that the Coleman was asleep.
Mary went back to her duties, as a couple of the locals came in and ordered their drinks. She had done her bit. The Signalman stood up and laid an envelope on the bar. Making a symbol of a circle and winking his eye. She smiled. This was easy money and for the first time in a long time she had enjoyed obtaining it. The Signalman sat quietly with his small dog at his side. He could feel the blood coursing through his veins. He hadn't actually enjoyed himself in a long time, and coming out of retirement was definitely appealing to him.
As more and more of the locals came in, The Signalman pointed upstairs. Mary nodded, and held up her hand to indicate room number five. The Signalman stuck up his thumb and looked down at Toffee. Nodding towards the stairs he made his way up. When he reached the top of the stairs and looked along the landing, he quickly found the room. He tested the door, and found it was unlocked. As he went in Allan Mustard stirred slightly, but The Signalman was not phased. He simply took the loaded handkerchief out of his pocket, deftly he crept up to the sleeping man before covering his nose and mouth. As he did so Allan Mustard woke with a start, but it was already too late. The Sevoflurane and The Signalman were too powerful for a man barely awake, and the drug didn't take long to have its effect.

Suddenly Allan Mustard was back asleep again. The Signalman turned him onto his side. Not wanting him dead, he made sure the young man's airways stayed open whilst he was unconscious. He took the handcuffs out of his pocket, and put one pair of each around his wrists. Pulling his arms back, he clipped each cuff to the bed. He then used Mary's dressing gown to tie the young man's feet to the bed so there was no way he would escape. By now the clock had gone midnight and Brian searched the young man's jacket until he found the keys to the Audi. Mary came upstairs, the locals had finally left. She mouthed to the signal man, "Is everything okay?"
He grinned and put up his thumb.
She indicated she was going to bed, but that she would give him the key to the pub. He was to make sure he locked the door, and she disappeared off to her room.

    Brian was still slightly pissed off. She was a good looking woman and he too had not had sex in a long time! However, this was one night when he needed to concentrate on the job at hand. He looked down at toffee, nodded his head, and they made their way out to the car park to find the car.

He pressed the key fob, the door opened, and he let Toffee climb in before settling in the driver's seat. Pressing the starter button, the engine roared into life. Despite being deaf, Brian could feel the power of the car. He laughed to himself and thought about his battered Land Rover. Putting the car into gear, he set off.

    He had been driving for about 30 minutes or so when his sat nav alerted him that he was in the right

place. He found the almost hidden gate, opened it and carefully drove the Audi along the path.
Having to almost drive along on instinct, as he had chosen to turn off all the lights. Thankfully it was a bright evening, and the moon did its best to light his passage. After another 10 minutes or so he was literally in the middle of nowhere, the black Audi glistening in the moonlight. He looked at the clock, it was now approaching 1:00 am. Leaving the car running and switching on the heated seats he reclined the backrest, set his alarm to vibrate on his phone and settled down to wait for his delivery.

What the fuck went wrong?

2am. Almost to the second, the pilot appeared; he had made this run a few times. Always difficult, but he prided himself on how skilfully he avoided being tracked.

Engine switched off, he silently glided towards the open field. He could see the black Audi, shiny despite the dark.

As softly as he possibly could, he let the aircraft touch down.

The Signalman put a finger across his mouth as he looked at his dog. It was almost as if the dog understood, and, as the plane came to a stop, he opened the door and let the small dog out. Toffee sprinted across the grass towards the plane. Silent, yet ready. He did not rush. His days of running and rushing around were gone now.

The pilot opened the side door of the aircraft as Brian approached. He said nothing, but pointed to the large box. Brian smiled, and pointed to the briefcase. He opened the tailgate of the Audi, and made a gesture to indicate he wanted help to carry the package to the car. The pilot took hold of the briefcase and threw it inside the plane. Then walked around and took hold of one side of the box. The Signalman did the same, and they carried the box to his car, sliding it into the rear of the car and pressing the button to close the hatch.

The pilot made his way back to the plane, but not before a handshake. Both men looked each other in the eye, Brian mouthed, "Good luck," and the pilot got in and closed the door. This was always the most dangerous part. Starting the engine and the runway before take-off. But all was silent as he pushed the button and the propeller began to turn. Speed was of the essence. He thrust the plane forward, and in what seemed like seconds, the aircraft was gone.

    The Signalman made a fake salute and turned back towards the car. His faithful dog Toffee following behind. He was always cautious and still didn't turn the lights on, on the Audi, even though everything had gone smoothly, and his cargo was safe. Forty-five minutes later he was back and parked next to the battered Land Rover. He beckoned Toffee into the cab, and told him to stay on guard before he crept back to the pub. He let himself in and crept up the stairs to room five. When he opened the door, Allan Mustard was still passed out.

    Just as he was about to go to Mary's room she appeared. He looked at her. He signed to tell her that he would have to put the young man downstairs and that one way or another Mary was going to end up with a bruise and a few glasses broken in the pub. As he finished the sentence he hit her squarely in the eye. She fell backwards, and the anger instantly rose in her.
"You bastard!" She screamed. As she stood up, her fists flailing, he grabbed her arm and thrust another small brown envelope into her hand.
"Here is another £10,000," it said on it. "Now be a good girl and do as I tell you."

    Brian undid the handcuffs, untied the Coleman's feet, and picked him up. Slumped over his shoulder, Brian walked down the stairs quickly. When he got to the bar area, he dropped the young man into a chair, as he needed to make sure that other things were in place. When he reached the bar, he simply threw a few glasses on the floor here and there, and wrenched the till from the wall.

Opening the side door, he quietly placed the till in the Land Rover before coming back to pick up Allan Mustard. He walked around to where he had parked the Audi, and, using the key fob, he opened it and threw the young man into the boot complete with his keys. Just for good measure he took out a small bat from the Land Rover and hit Allan Mustard clean on the temple. The sound was just like a coconut dropping on the floor and there was an instant 'egg' appearing on the young man's head. The Signalman turned and started to walk back to the Land Rover. However, he hadn't gone more than a few steps when he turned back, and, bending down he picked up a small rock and threw it hard straight through the back window of the Audi showering Allan Mustard in glass. He got into the Land Rover laughing. As he looked up, Mary stood at the doorway shaking her fist and her head. He sarcastically blew her a kiss, started the rattly old vehicle and left.

As soon as the Land Rover was out of sight Mary dialled 999. She already had the story fairly clear in her head, and just for good measure threw a couple of bottles onto the floor so they smashed. As the village was so rural it took at least 25 minutes for the police to arrive. After statements, the police were fairly convinced this was nothing more than an opportune robbery. Mary had clearly forgotten to lock the side

door, the thief had come in, smashed the place up and as she came down after hearing the noise, he had hit her before stealing all of the takings. She didn't mention the Audi or Allan Mustard. The police left, Mary smiled and then suddenly realised she had the problem of when Allan Mustard would wake up. She didn't have too long to wait before he came charging into the pub angry, with the headache from hell and wanting answers.
Mary was sitting with a scotch, looking around her smashed up pub and nursing a black eye.
Allan Mustard staggered through the door. "What the fuck did you do to me bitch?"
That was all the motivation she needed. She snapped, leapt out of the chair, lunged towards him, punched him squarely, and as hard as she could, in exactly the same place as The Signalman had left his damage.
Allan Mustard flew into a rage. He karate chopped her on the back of the neck, and she passed out instantly. Falling to the floor, his rage knowing no bounds he swung his right foot but just before he made contact, he realised this was not the way to avenge anything. He stopped. Took the glass of Scotch, sat down and wondered how the fuck he was going to tell Tommy that he had no drugs and no money. Somebody must have been waiting for him, and he was certain this bitch knew something about it, but right now, and after what he had shared with her earlier all he could find in his heart was a little sympathy. If this woman really was involved she took a hell of a pasting for the price.

The battered Land Rover trundled on, The Signalman was pleased with his work. Taking the occasional swig from a hip flask, he smiled. Everything had gone perfectly.

Allan Mustard found his mobile. Was there really any point calling Tommy at 5:00 am? He guessed so. He found his number and dialled.

As he did so Mary woke again, however, this time she looked at him whimpered and tears fell from her face.

Allan Mustard put his finger to his lips. "Be quiet," he said. "I have something to do."

"FUCK OFF!" she said to him and walked behind the bar to get another Scotch.

As she did so Tommy picked up. "What the fuck do you want?"

"I've been ambushed."

"Are you taking the piss?" Tommy exploded. "You have to be taking the piss! I thought you were fucking Mustard, mustard!" He bellowed.

Allan Mustard was worried. He was expecting Tommy to go ape shit, yet there was a calmness in his voice suggested that one way or another, Tommy's retribution may not be anything that Allan Mustard wanted to experience. Either that, or he thought he was telling him bullshit.

"OK, you stupid cunt tell me."

Allan Mustard didn't really know what to say. "I fucked the barmaid, went to sleep, and I was still sleeping when someone put something over my mouth, I don't know what drug it had in it, all I can tell you is I was out cold."

"So what the fuck did they do?"
"They took the drugs. Tommy, they took everything. Right now I have a black eye and a lump on my head the size of an orange, a fucking headache from hell and no fucking way of knowing who it is what it was or why it is, so I suggest you do some fucking investigating."
Tommy exploded "Who the fuck are you to talk to me like that, you cunt? Your life will not be worth fucking living. Don't even think of returning back here, do not come anywhere near me or I swear I will kill you!" And he put the phone down.
Allan Mustard looked at Mary. "Who the fuck was it?"
"Who the fuck was what? You jumped up little shit."
"Who the fuck hit me?!"
"Probably the same fellow that hit me you wanker, you think I want to look like this for fun, and I am happy that my pub is smashed to pieces?!"
Allan Mustard didn't know what to think. Certainly the state of her face made her look a damn sight less pretty than she had been when she was riding his cock. He had no idea quite what to believe or not.
"Shut up," he said. "I need time to think." But the truth was he had no idea what to think. All he was certain of was that this was planned. There was no way this was some amateur burglar but how the fuck could he prove it? He sank the Scotch hard, and walked out of the pub. He walked around to the Audi, and, seeing the smashed back window just made him question a little bit more. One way or another he had to get back to Tommy, back to town and face what the fuck was going to happen to him. He jumped into the car. As he pulled out of the pub and

floored the Audi back to the club his mind was racing; his head in agony, and his temper and blood boiling.

Tommy had no idea what to do or think. Somebody had double crossed him but who the fuck would? Especially knowing him, knowing Giles, who would be brave enough to take him on? Just as he was about to call Giles an anonymous number appeared on his phone, and delivered a very simple message.
"I have your package."
Tommy was apoplectic with anger. He didn't know what to say. He wanted to go apeshit. In his mind who the fuck would do this was all that kept going through his head.
"Who the fuck is this?"
"Oh, you don't get to find out that easily you prick, you have made enough people suffer, so now I'm going to teach you that you are going to suffer for a while. I will contact you when I'm ready.
Tommy threw his phone across the office. It shattered against the wall and he had absolutely no idea what to do with himself. However, he quickly realised it was quite foolish to have thrown his phone. After all, how the fuck was he going to contact him otherwise. He walked over to retrieve the phone.
Thankfully the damage wasn't too bad, and he could put it back together.
He sent a text to Giles, "We have another fucking problem."
He knew damn well there would be no reply for hours, so sat back in his chair, put his feet on the desk side, closed eyes and fell asleep.

Many hours later the plane landed back in Spain, the pilot exhausted, his precious cargo safe.

Lazlo Kiss was there to meet him. Smiling as Juan stepped out of the plane and handed the briefcase over. "You have done well my friend," he commented, before passing an envelope full of cash to the pilot.

Juan smiled, "We have known each other a long time. I won't make a habit of doing this shit as there is too much risk now, but I did it because it's you. I hope it was worth it my friend," and he made his way towards the Porsche glinting in the sunshine.

"Take care my friend." Lazlo smiled as he went over and got in his BMW 7 series. In an instant both vehicles were gone.

Lazlo sent a text as he drove. "All is in place my brother and the money is safe, I will see you at Marco's later this evening."

Anesh smiled. So far everything was working to plan, and let's be honest who didn't love a good double cross. He could only imagine how Tommy and Giles would be feeling! He was about to text Michelle but thought better of it. He would wait until things were perfect.

He text Marco. "Cash delivery this evening."

Marco replied, "Well done my brother."

"Do not say anything yet to the girls, I want them to keep out of it as much as possible."

"You are the brains my brother, I will leave that to you, besides, I am fairly comfortable that Tommy and Giles will by now be going apeshit."

Truth be told neither Tommy nor Giles were going ape shit. However, Tommy did have the unenviable task of letting Giles know that all his big plans for the opening evening of his new club may well be in jeopardy and right now he had no idea or why this had happened. He had woken up uncomfortable, angry and still with his feet on the desk in the office. Blinking, he looked around, picked up his mobile and sent a brief text to Giles. "We need to talk, we have a problem."

Giles replied, "Of course dear boy, did you want a round or two?"

"Yes, a round would be very good right now, give me an hour."

"Anything for you dear boy, though an hour will be cutting it fine perhaps we will just do nine?"

"No problem, give me an hour to get myself sorted out."

"See you then dear boy."

Clearly Giles had absolutely no bloody idea about what had happened, so it was nothing to do with him. He couldn't call Lazlo, after all Lazlo had been as good as his word and got the aircraft there with the package. If he wanted to double cross Tommy, he would have kept the money and the drugs.

Tommy's mind was in a whirl. There was nobody close enough or bright enough to do this.

He felt the anger building. His fists clenched, and decided he needed to go take a shower and try to calm down before giving the news to Giles.

The hot water pounded down on his head. It was a welcome relief and felt good as he turned the shower to maximum, his mind unable to think clearly as the anger continued to wash around him.

Toffee jumped back onto the boat and made straight for bed. Jumping onto The Signalman's bed he looked up his master. Brian nodded, it had been a long evening, and even longer drive and he now needed to rest. He threw all three mobiles onto the side just as he was about to go to sleep one of them lit up a simple message.
"Who the fuck are you?"
Brian smiled to himself before sending back an equally simple text.
"Your worst fucking nightmare."
He felt very pleased with himself as he lay his head down to sleep. Toffee crawled up on the end of the bed, the first part of their job having been completed successfully.
Tommy swung the Aston into the golf club. Nothing really phased him. He had seen a lot in his life.
He had always wanted to be the best, but his very persona, slightly angry as it had been almost since he was a child, had held him back until now.

Your worst nightmare.

He saw Giles' Range Rover and even though it was a cliché, his stomach turned over and he got instinctively a little nervous.

"Don't be so ridiculous you fucking idiot," he said to himself, but he knew in his heart of hearts that the old man was about to go ballistic.

As they made their way out to the first tee and, making sure there was no one else around, Giles said "So what's the problem dear boy?"

"The problem is Giles, that you want your big party to happen and your new club to be launched but right now I don't have any icing to put on your very expensive cake." He finished the sentence just as Giles struck the ball, sliced it and watched it disappear into the bunker.

Rooted to the spot Giles' face went red and Tommy thought he was going to have a heart attack.

"What the fucking hell do you mean?" Giles barked when he eventually calmed down enough to be able to speak.

Tommy related the story of what happened to the Coleman.

"Are you taking the piss?"

"I am telling you it was set up."

"So, are you saying we have no merchandise to offer our clients?"

"This is where it gets a bit trickier." Tommy nervously smiled, and he held up his mobile, and showed a few brief texts that had come from the unknown number.

"So what the fuck does this idiot want?"

Tommy held the phone up again. "How the fuck do I know Giles, read the fucking phone."

Giles clenched his fists. Tommy could see the rage in Giles face, and as Giles turned towards Tommy and without thinking he raised his fist, and swung it hard. Tommy was too quick for him and moved his head, meaning Giles punched nothing but thin air.

"I will let you have that one old man. But if you try to hit me again you are really going to wish you had not."

Giles looked Tommy in the eye. "Well someone has to take fucking control don't they? It would appear you can't."

It was Tommy's turn to get angry. His fists clenched, but he was breathing deeply to keep himself calm.

Giles screamed in Tommy's face, "*So what the fuck do we do now?!*"

"We wait Giles, we wait," and he hit the ball perfectly sending it soaring towards the Green on the short par 3.

Giles wasn't in the mood to wait, but because he had often kept himself away from the drugs and not wanted to know exactly how everything worked, he just enjoyed the profits, there was very little else he could do.

Not that that calmed his mood at all. His face grew redder and his temper just got worse and worse as they walked the course.

"*I don't wish to fucking wait! I wish for my club to be open and my clients tell to have the fucking merchandise I have paid for,*" he lifted the club up.

Tommy was puzzled; he had never seen Giles in this state before, in fact, for once the roles had been reversed, and it was Tommy who was the calm one. He could only afford the luxury of being so because he knew deep down whoever this was, had clearly planned it very carefully, but that must have meant somewhere he had inside information. Suddenly his brain clicked. Was this Colonel fucking Mustard just having one over on him?

He said nothing to Giles other than, "Shut the fuck up old man, until we know who it is and what they want there is very little we can do. I have had ears out and eyes out all over the place. No one knows a thing, whoever this is, I believe it's nothing to do with drugs, but more to just let us know they are onto us. So you best remember who you pissed off, because for me it's impossible, I have a list longer than your arm. But if they are out to get you that's a whole different story."

As he said the words his brain clicked again. What about his wife? Michelle now knew that he was responsible for Charlie's death, or at least she thought she knew. Could it be anything to do with her? He began to doubt almost everything and everyone around him. The one thing he didn't doubt was Giles. Just seeing the rage the man was in was enough to tell Tommy there was no double cross going on certainly with his business partner.
"So you expect me to open my club and have nothing exclusive to offer them!" He snapped.
"Relax old man," Tommy said lazily, "whoever this is they are bound to make a mistake, everybody does."
"Including you, you fucking idiot."
Tommy reacted instantly. He raised the club high in the air and brought it down as fast as he could. It missed Giles face by millimetres. So much so, that he felt the wind go past him. The club thudded into the green.
"You will fucking pay for that!" Giles almost screamed.

"If you speak to me like that once more old man, you will pay for it in the worst possible way."

Tommy wrenched the club out of the ground taking a huge divot with him and began to walk back to the clubhouse.

Giles raged, "Where the fuck do you think you're going?"

"Fuck off!"

Neither of them noticed the small figure in the woods. Smiling quietly to himself. The pot was definitely boiling, and it would not take much for it to spill over onto the stove. He had both of them just where he wanted. This time he did not allow Toffee to run free. He kept him tight by his side, he had just wanted to check on progress and ensure everything was going nicely. As he made his way back to the battered Land Rover he began to carefully refine the plan which had been in his head for a few days. In fact, ever since he had taken Giles merchandise.

Brian had never cared for drugs, had little interest in what was in the box but also couldn't quite work out why Giles was so animated. He decided that maybe the box deserved closer investigation and he would do just that. Toffee climbed into the Land Rover. Brian followed and made his way back to the boat. Having lived the life of a recluse, it was no problem for him to disappear into the background, living on a boat. No one looked for him and he was completely off the grid. Which is just the way he liked his life right now.

Giles was beside himself. He too had his best men on the case. Geoff had been in and around drugs forever, but he had heard nothing. There was no word on the street.

Eugene would have loved nothing more than to shoot somebody, but right at this moment, he had nobody to shoot at. Whoever had pulled this off had become a ghost and disappeared. It only added to the frustrations. Giles made his way back to the clubhouse no longer in the mood to play golf, he wanted to find Tommy. As he got back and got out of the golf cart, he heard the Aston Martin start up and roar out of the club.

"Bollocks!" It was the only word he could use and he stormed into the club and back to his office.

This had not gone unnoticed with Rosy, only this time she was pretty sure that a blowjob and a flash of her smile was not going to calm down things. However a blow job and a smile from Gigi just might. For all of Rosy's expertise, Giles liked them young. Rosy sighed.

"Oh well, old girl," she said to herself, "perhaps you need to look for some younger flesh!" And she laughed as she went and found the young girl.

Gigi was busy tidying the bar, serving, and generally doing all the things a pretty barmaid would. Flirting with the customers, showing a little too much cleavage and flashing her beautiful smile to anyone she thought would take notice.

"Gigi darling I need you to go and see Giles."
"Do I really have to?" she questioned.

"Yes, my darling you do. However, you need to understand he's in a very bad mood and I don't quite know why, so the first thing you need to do is find out. The second thing you need to do is flash that smile, take your knickers off, bend over in front of him and just for a little while help the old bastard forget all these troubles. Because otherwise, everything is going to turn to hell in a handcart and I'm too old to put up with that shit. I want it all to run smoothly, so run along there's a good girl, put the old man out of his misery and I will take care of things here."

    Gigi sighed. There were no rules to her becoming a pornstar. There were no rules to her being paid so well, but having to fuck Giles was something else again. He smelt. He was fat. He wasn't good looking, and his cock was not big enough to satisfy. Frustrated, she slammed down the ice bucket and stormed off towards Giles' office. As she went to walk past Rosy, the older lady grabbed her arm.

"Just remember who you work for!" She snapped angrily. "And remember what you want to be. Sometimes you have to take the shit before you get to the champagne darling."

Rosy thrust a glass of champagne in her hand. "Now drink that very quickly, I will refill it, and go and keep the old man happy."

Gigi did as she was told. Downed the glass of champagne as fast as she could, she knew for no other reason that it would give her a little bit of Dutch courage, which, to be honest, she could do with right now.

    Rosy beckoned her towards the back of the bar, put her hands under her skirt and removed Gigi's knickers.

"Hold ups! There's a good girl," Rosie smiled. "Now do your thing."

Rosy took off her shoes.

"And put these on," she said and kicked them towards Gigi. Four-inch-high black patent leather stilettos.
Gigi smiled. She wasn't used to heels but for the short walk to Giles office she would be just fine.
She pulled her hold ups a little higher, which gave her just enough flesh exposed above the top of them to ensure that they were 'boiling over' slightly, and it was a look she loved.
"Okay," she said, as bravely as she could.
Rosy laughed. She imagined Gigi had a slightly fuzzy head from the champagne. Rosy watched as she disappeared towards Giles' office hitching her skirt up even higher as she got closer. She knocked on the door. Giles raged, "Who the fuck is it?"
"It's Gigi," she replied, "I thought you could do with a drink."
Giles almost immediately mellowed. "Oh yes, my dear, come in, and yes, I could definitely do with a drink."
Gigi brought in the bottle of champagne and two glasses. Hers already full. She stood at the doorway, sipped it slightly and walked over to his desk. As she got to the desk and placed both glasses and the bottle on the table, she lifted her leg and rested one foot on the chair. Giles immediately looked down to her pussy. He considered the hold ups and the fact that she had no underwear on.
"You are a naughty girl," he smiled.
He took the glass of champagne and sipped it gently.
"I can be, now why don't you make yourself comfortable?"

Giles leant back in his chair as she knelt down and undid his belt. Giles put his hands on her head. "Hasn't Rosie taught you anything?"

She said, "It's not polite to force a lady, and I know exactly what I'm doing."
She took a big gulp of champagne and knelt and put Giles cock in her mouth. The cold fizzy bubbles made Giles jump unexpectedly. He had never had this sensation before. His head fell back against the chair.
"Oh my goodness! Young lady, you know exactly what you are doing," and he looked down as she began to suck his cock. Leaning back a little further for no other reason than to make his stomach look as slim as possible, and for once he could almost see his cock, well perhaps just the tip.
Whenever Gigi's head moved, she wanked him, and carefully watched his face.
"Now close your eyes like a good boy," she said.

Giles did as he was told. She stood up, hitched up her skirt, turned around and gently sat on his hard cock. Giles put his hands on her arse.
"I am in control," she said, "though you are more than welcome to play with my arse," and she gently began to ride him. Whether it was the events of the day and all of the frustrations coming out in him he had no idea, but all he knew was that for the first time in a long time this felt good. Her tight little pussy gripping him as she fucked him and Giles head began to spin far too quickly in a sea of ecstasy.

Gigi knew she was performing well. The old man's cock hadn't been this hard probably since she had known him. She too was enjoying herself though she was pretty sure that was down to the champagne and Giles' finger slowly sliding up her arse. As he pushed further she too began to feel horny and far from it being a job, she was enjoying the fuck. She had no idea of the CCTV camera in Giles office nor that he would watch it back, and wank himself over her again and again as he has done to every other girl that had worked there. She hadn't been there very long when Giles announced he was going to come. That was one thing Gigi would never allow, so she got off and took his cock in her hand, wanking him faster and using her thumb on the underside of the head teasing and caressing. She spat on his cock head and it wasn't too long before her hand was covered in hot sticky semen and Giles was crying out. She was pleased she had made him orgasm. But frustrated she hadn't come. Especially as she had actually been enjoying herself. Just as he had finished Gigi took a big mouth full of champagne, went down on his cock, spat some of it over him, stood up, pulled down her skirt and said, "I hope everything is okay."

Giles in his moment of ecstasy spilled out, "Everything would be okay if that fucking idiot Tommy hadn't fucked up my delivery."
"Oh, I'm sorry, I had no idea."
"Nor does anyone else and I suggest you keep that to yourself lady."
He looked down at his wet crotch and smiled that was the best blowjob and fuck he had had in years.
He looked her in the eye.
"You will go far young lady, I will make sure of it."

"I hope so Mr Williams," and she smiled sweetly, adjusted her skirt, and closed the door.

Giles reached for his handkerchief. Dried himself where necessary and got himself dressed. He looked at the clock, decided he had had enough and was going to go home. He could do nothing now except trust Tommy so all he could do was wait.

Tommy arrived home and was calm though his mind was in a state of unrest. He didn't believe his wife, he didn't believe Valerie, he didn't believe Lazlo, he didn't believe Giles, in fact he felt right now there was absolutely nobody he could trust. He opened the front door and could hear the TV on.
Perhaps Michelle needed to understand exactly who she was dealing with. He walked into the room to find both Valerie and Michelle sitting there watching TV smiling sweetly at each other as if butter wouldn't melt in their mouth.
"I'm going to the Den," he snapped reached for a bottle of rum and was just about to reach the door and leave when Valerie asked,
"What the fuck is up with my husband?"
"How the fuck should I know what's wrong with the stupid old bastard?" Tommy hissed as he left the room.

Valerie didn't believe a word of it. Whatever was going on was pretty secret but much deeper than either of them were letting on. She poured another glass of wine, muttered, "Fuck you Tommy you have no idea what's coming!" And sat back on the sofa.

Tommy was furious there had been no contact from whoever had stolen his drugs. He was baffled as to why Giles was so stressed over it, Nikki was dead, his wife clearly knew something about it but he didn't know what, and it felt like far from being in total control, he was slowly losing his grip on everything.

Michelle looked at her friend. "How the bloody hell did we end up here?"

Valerie looked at her and smiled. "I guess, my dear Michelle, if you end up getting involved with a villain, you would always end up here somehow, it just depends which side of the fence you want to sit on."

Michelle suddenly burst into tears. "I never wanted this life, you know. And I didn't really realise it until I met Charlie. When I came to England all those years ago, I was just a kid with an attitude. I thought Tommy was the best thing that had happened to me. Now look at me. I can't wait to get rid of him. But what about you Valerie you haven't had the life I have?"

"Haven't I?" she questioned. "Perhaps not in the same way as you but I can assure you I never wanted this life either. I may have had a better upbringing, and Giles when I first met him certainly wasn't the man that he is now. Though I can assure you if I had known my life was going to turn out like this I would never have said yes at that bloody party.

"So what was Giles like when you met him?"

"He was a bit like Tommy in some ways. Less aggressive for sure but still super ambitious. His parents had money so Giles had money. So whilst he didn't have the tough upbringing that either you or Tommy have had, that didn't make him any less aggressive when it came to business. He was always out for the next deal, always wanted to be the best and I quickly understood that he didn't suffer fools gladly, though at the time it was really only how he treated his employees, and if they didn't want to do what he wanted them to, he almost fired them on the spot."

"Very Alan Sugar," Michelle said as she laughed.

Valerie continued, "I never really fancied him, but we got on and he made me laugh. Sex was always a chore mainly because he'd never been slim and his sex drive clearly only really went towards young girls, however, I understood very quickly that this very nice lifestyle would always come at some sort of price, and if Giles wanking himself off to a 16 year old getting fucked on a park bench on a porn film was what got him off I didn't really care. That sounds appalling but the truth is I didn't really have much ambition and though I may appear very strong now, at the beginning of our relationship I was completely the opposite. All I wanted was a nice quiet life and really that's what Giles gave me. I didn't have to do anything, I didn't have to lift a finger, everything was on a plate for me. What a weak woman I was."

"So how did you become so strong?"

"It was only really when Giles and Tommy began to have their business relationship. I quickly realised that Tommy was nothing to do with Giles as a friend, and that socially, other than golf they wouldn't have known each other, so they had to be something else. That's when I decided that I was going to make some very powerful friends and find out exactly what was going on.

That's how I could check out Charlie so easily. However, for a time Giles always seemed to be one step ahead of me. He had always been powerful even when he was young because as I said, his family had money and as we both know money always talks. But when I met Jamie I realised that what I actually needed was to feel loved and wanted and desired. Giles could throw all the cars and jewellery at me but as I reflected, I understood that he had never really loved me. I fitted him, I could keep my mouth shut, I learnt not to be upset if you got rid of an employee and I learned to accept if he was screwing his secretary. How weak am I? It made me sad and made me angry with myself. Neither of those things are a good combination so I decided fuck you and I would become the strong woman I am right now. Not even Tommy scares me, though I must admit Giles' behaviour in the last few weeks has frightened me a little. I've never known him aggressive. He's always been that passive pussycat, but the worm has definitely turned and for whatever reason Giles is most definitely on edge."
Michelle looked up. "Valerie I'm just a little scared."
"My friend, you have nothing to be scared of. It's about time that these two men got what they deserved."
And they settled back to watch the rest of the film and make idle chit chat.

I want to make you a deal.

Tommy poured a large glass of rum and kept staring at his phone. He hated the situation. He could feel the anger rise inside him and his blood began to boil.
He picked his phone up and screamed at it "Why won't you fucking ring!" He was just about to throw it at the wall when it lit up.
"I have a deal for you."
"I don't make deals with anyone," he replied.
"That's fine."
Tommy waited for another reply. However, it was not forthcoming. He knew in his mind that he shouldn't have been so aggressive 'fuck!' He shouted in his head. He always was hot headed and never quite managed to find the balance of calm whenever the situation called for it. He sat down and beat his fist on the desk. As he did so the phone lit up again.
"Do I have your attention now?"
Tommy took another swig of rum, took a deep breath and replied, "Okay, you have my attention."
"Good, then let's be sensible about this shall we? I have something you want back. And you are going to pay me for it."
"Who the fuck do you think you are?!" Tommy replied, the anger rising once again almost instantly.
"It doesn't matter who I am, the question really is do you want your stuff or not? I will send you instructions over

the next couple of days. You will follow them to the letter or everything I have will go to the police."
Tommy panicked.
"I will be in touch." And the phone went dark.
Tommy screenshot the messages and sent them to Giles.
Giles opened the screen. He read the brief exchange, put his rather fat sausage fingers to his forehead and then dialled Tommy's number.
"What the fuck are we going to do?"
"What the fuck do you want me to do? I don't know who he or she is, and right now I can't find out who he or she is. If you want this fucking stuff back so badly and I can't understand why, it's just a bit of gear, then I guess we have little choice but to do what he or she says."
"She? You think it could be a woman?"
"It could be your fucking wife Giles, how the hell would you know."
This stopped Giles in his tracks. He suddenly became very aware of the change in Valerie's behaviour.
Could there be any truth in what Tommy had just said?
"The reason I want that stuff back," Giles replied, "is there are diamonds in that box. A small gift for some of the ladies. And they cost me a lot of money."
"But I thought you knew nothing about the deal?"
"I don't know anything about the drugs, that was your department. It just had to be the best quality. I don't want any of my customers being disappointed. but I already knew Lazlo from Amsterdam. "Even if I didn't

get my hands dirty, that's your job, you work for me remember."

Tommy was seething with rage.
"We are partners Giles. I don't work for anybody."
"Well, you fucking do now! And I'm telling you don't fuck this up again," and he ended the call.

As he did so the pain in his chest became almost unbearable. He collapsed backwards in a genuine state of panic. The incident lasted less than 2 seconds and suddenly he felt okay again but probably for the first time in his life he looked down at the brandy glass, the cigar, and just for one moment, questioned himself.

The next day it dawned bright and clear. The Signalman woke to Toffee laying by his side. Today would be the day he would send the demands. He had a great night's sleep and was feeling good about his job. He didn't need the money, and certainly with the lifestyle he had he had no real need for any money, just enough to take him to the pub now and again with his little dog. It was the perfect cover, but in truth it was also the perfect lifestyle. He had only agreed to this because he was doing this for a friend, nothing more. He rubbed his eyes. 5:30 am, perfect, that should be the perfect time to piss Tommy off royally.

He inserted another SIM card. He had hundreds of them.

Sent the message, "I want to meet." He knew damn well there wouldn't be a reply for a good time yet, so made himself a coffee, opened the back door of the boat in order to let Toffee out, then sat back in his big armchair feeling very pleased with himself.

Brian picked up one of his other phones and sent another simple message, "Tomorrow night my friend." He didn't expect a reply from that number either.

He looked across to the small bench and smiled when he saw the super powerful crossbow sitting there. It had been a long time but he was pleased with how his practising had gone.

Said to himself, "I guess once you have it you never lose it, and despite the ravages of time, you how to handle the weapon better than anybody else." He smiled. It was true. He did.

His phone lit up.

"I am counting on you, my brother. There are some people that are very special to me that need this to happen."

He text back. "I have never let you down."

Marco smiled. "You have never let me down my brother, good luck and let me know when everything is settled."

"I will do my friend, enjoy your day, keep smiling and I will speak to you soon."

Brian settled back on the sofa. All of the plans would hopefully come together. He had spent a week working out exactly where, exactly how. The only thing he was unsure of was how quickly he could get the second bolt into the crossbow. This worried him slightly. Every other time he had to eliminate anybody it had been a single individual. If it had been multiple, he had never used the crossbow. Still, he smiled to himself, they're stupid. That fat bastard Giles wouldn't be able to get out of the car fast enough, so he was pretty confident that everything would be fine.

His secret phone lit up.

"What do you want?"

"I want what every mercenary bastard wants. To steals your drug money you fucking idiot!"

Tommy was furious. Who the fucking hell was this guy?

Whoever he was, he was extremely confident and what worried Tommy most was there was no fear. He could tell that just from the brief messages this was a confident individual who certainly wasn't scared of him. Well, he fucking well ought to be scared.

"I will send you coordinates. You and the fat man will come. If neither of you show up, no deal. If only one of you shows up, no deal. If you bring anyone else, I will kill you."

He sent a series of numbers. The map coordinates.

Tommy was absolutely dumbfounded. He had not seen this coming. And was certainly not prepared for it and was even less prepared for the final text.

"See you tomorrow at midnight don't be late!"

Tommy didn't like it one bit but he didn't really have a choice. He phoned Giles and explained the situation and the demands.

Giles was having none of it. "Don't be so fucking stupid, can't you see this is a setup?"

"What do you expect us to do? Go to the police? I'm sure your chief super would love to hear all about you wanting to collect your drugs and illegal diamonds. That would sound great down on the golf course wouldn't it old man."

"Now, now, dear boy we both know there are limits even to what I can achieve with the officers of the law. But, why the pair of us? Why not just you? Why not just me?"

"If I knew the answer to that old man, I would probably be able to get the stuff back without worrying about meeting anybody."

"I want you to go and check out where this place is, I want to know just how much danger we are going to be putting ourselves in before I go anywhere."

"You have no fucking choice old man, if you want those diamonds back you will have to do as he says, it's that simple. Besides, I will make sure I take at least one gun and I suggest you do the same."

"How do you know there won't be an army of them?"

"Call it a gut feeling. This guy is a professional whoever he is and whatever he is, he has done this before, my guess is he is out for his own ends. It might have something to do with Lazlo, but I can't prove that. He is a man on his own. There are two of us and we will both have guns, he won't stand a fucking chance."

Giles suddenly was overcome with bravado. "Do you think we can take him?"

"Of course we can fucking take him! How long do you think I've been doing this Giles? I may get other people to do the dirty work for me now, but it doesn't mean I can't do it, it means I choose not to. This time it's different, this time it's personal, so I will take great pleasure in teaching this fucking idiot a lesson and we will be rid of him once and for all, just like I got rid of that idiot Charlie and that fucking coke sniffing whore Nikki!"

Giles felt trapped suddenly. He realised that his whole empire could come crashing down around his knees, or that he could be putting himself in very real danger, but he had come so far along the road there was no turning back now. He had already promised some of his high-class clientele the finest merchandise, and that included the diamonds, so now whatever path he took, he had to make sure at least that he was there to deliver. However, with less than a week to go until the club was open, he too could see that ultimately there was little choice.

"We will take my car," he said. "But in the meantime, either you send your man or I will send Geoff to check this place out."

"What are you going to check out exactly Giles? Have you not seen the coordinates? It's the middle of fucking nowhere! You don't think he's gonna pop along to a coffee shop and invite us in do you?"

Giles was furious. "Who the fuck do you think you're talking to, I want to know it's safe!"

"Well it won't be fucking safe will it, we are meeting a guy to collect drugs and diamonds and pay him off, for fuck's sake will you get real, surely you've paid people off before?"

"Yes, but they have been lawyers, solicitors, barristers, even the police, anybody to get my own way with the buildings and get anything through that I wanted. But I've never met a killer."

"Oh you most certainly have Giles. When you first met me," and he belly laughed.

Giles didn't see the funny side of this at all. He felt backed into a corner, trapped, but had no way out. With over half a million pounds invested, despite all of the dangers he was not a man to walk away from that sort of money.
"Just do as your fucking told," he said to Tommy
"If you speak to me like that once more old man, I'll fucking kill you myself," Tommy said and he ended the call.

He had already checked out Google Maps, put in the coordinates and basically, they were to meet at the entrance to a wood. There was no actual footage, but all the area was green on the map. Tommy guessed that somewhere there would be a track or clearing, and he too was a little nervous about what he might find waiting there. But he too had come this far and he had no intention of letting whoever this was get away with it. This was his manor, he ran the place and nobody was gonna take that away from him. He unlocked the filing cabinet next to his desk and took out two pistols. Dropping the magazines out of each of them he ensured that they were both fully loaded and carefully clicked the safety catch to make sure that everything was working just fine. Even Giles would be able to operate one for these. He sat at his desk and pointed the gun at the imaginary assailant on the wall.
"Bang! You're dead!" And grinned to himself. It had been a long time since he had had to do the dirty work himself and he was relishing the challenge.

At the club Rosy had everything in place. Everything was working like a charm, all of the girls were ready and she was confident that Gigi would be able to look after everyone. They had a select list of minor dignitaries, minor celebrities and even the chief super coming. It would have to be very discreet, but she had run clubs in Paris and Barcelona, so for her this was easy. And she had her little Scottish tiger Helen should anything go wrong with any of the clients. She had experienced more than her fair share of heavy-handed men getting out of hand. Back in her prime she would probably have handled them herself, but now she was quite content to let her little Scottish firecracker deal with any problems. She smiled to herself, despite all she had been through in her life including recovering from cancer, she was determined to give everyone the best show she knew how. With a confidence in her ability stretching back nearly 40 years, she too had had a very poor life, and turned to sex at a young age. It had paid very well and was now the only life she knew, and if she was honest she still
enjoyed it. Perhaps not going down on Giles, even she had limits! But as a madam and a sex goddess she was more than happy to take on that mantle.

      She would make sure everyone had a good time. She had the finest quality alcohol; wines, and spirits, that sometimes ran into thousands of pounds per bottle, as well as the finest drugs that money could buy. She knew this place would be a success underground, underhand, and under the radar.

It was perfect for the high and mighty of this world to enjoy a little relaxation with no questions asked, just the way she liked it.

Tommy had had the Audi repaired. He found the Coleman and told him, "Go and check out these coordinates." He wanted to know everything about it and he only had a couple of hours to do it.

"It's a two hour fucking drive just from here." The Coleman answered angrily.

"Then you had best get a fucking move on hadn't you, and if you fuck this one up I will kill you myself."

Allan Mustard couldn't really answer to that, having fucked up the initial shipment and delivery, he knew that he didn't really have an argument.

Rather sheepishly he took the keys. "I will send you a report," and he disappeared.

Tommy picked up his phone and sent Giles a message. "I have the Coleman on his way to check it out."

"You just make sure you're still awake at midnight tomorrow old man. It's a two-hour drive. I don't want you sleeping all the way."

The Signalman carefully checked the battered Land Rover over. Oil, water, tyres. The old girl had never let him down but that's really because he looked after her. He had owned the bloody thing for over 20 years and, whilst he could afford whatever Ferrari he wanted, he liked the simple life. And the truth was, there was no need to display the wealth he had. He whistled to Toffee who jumped off the boat and ran towards the Land Rover. With the door open, the dog jumped inside and sat patiently on the passenger seat. Brian went back into the boat, picked up a huge leather satchel, and carefully placed the crossbow inside. With separate compartments for several bolts all fully sharpened, and ready to do some serious damage, he locked the boat, locked the gate behind him and climbed into the Land Rover. It may have been a two-hour drive in an Audi RS4 but it was at least a four-hour drive in an old Land Rover. He would stay in a nearby village and be ready and refreshed for what was to come tomorrow. As he pulled out, he couldn't help feeling a twinge of nerves. But this was more than outweighed by the excitement running through his veins. He looked at Toffee and smiled. Patted his furry friend on the head, and began his journey.

Broken ribs.

Callum kissed Sam goodbye. His life seemed really good right now, a baby on the way, a wedding on the way, and despite the loss of his father which still troubled him, certainly sleeping and mentally, he couldn't shake the picture of his dad crashing his car, but overall life was good for him. The business was thriving. He had a woman who loved him dearly, a brother who he was finally becoming more acquainted with, and he smiled. He felt warm inside as he made his way to work. He would take the back roads today. The BMW needed some exercise. He enjoyed driving it fast. It taxed his abilities a little bit and always made you feel slightly on edge. He loved that. The feeling that you were never quite in control of the car, that it always had a trick up its sleeve and you had to outsmart it.

Sam closed the door in a similarly buoyant mood. She really believed that this was the man that had been put on this earth for her, and now, with the baby on the way and being able to look forward to a wedding, she couldn't be happier. She went into the kitchen. There was no way they could tell anybody yet, the only person who knew anything was Michelle. She was super grateful that she had been so happy for them and now, wanted just to make sure that everything was perfect. Sam had absolutely no idea of any of the dark side of Charlie's death and Callum wanted to keep it that way. He had mentioned nothing to her of his suspicions of that fateful day. Callum knew the back roads just as well as his father ever had done, in fact probably better as he had always been slightly naughty when he was younger and certainly used one or two of his dad's cars without his dad's knowledge! Driving fast and learning the roads. He was almost too casual as he flung the BMW around the corners at speeds that most people would have been terrified of, but the day was clear the road was dry and the car was performing well. Sam walked out into the garden. It was a beautiful place. The cottage was so old, so typically traditionally English with its thatched roof and stable doors it was a picture postcard piece of heaven. She sent her future husband a simple text, "I love you Callum."

Callum looked down at his phone and smiled.

The Audi hit the back of the BMW hard, spinning the car around out of control completely. It smashed into the one telegraph pole that was in the vicinity. The driver's door immediately folded, the airbags exploded and the car came to a shuddering halt.

Allan Mustard had no idea what had happened. The Audi careered across the road. It smashed through the gateway and deployed all of its airbags. The Coleman had not been wearing his seatbelt and despite the airbags his head cracked hard against the door, sending him instantly unconscious.

The silence immediately after the crash was deafening. Callum opened his eyes. The airbag had gone off in his face, but with the BMW being that much older it had none of the side impact protection. The door was pressed hard into the seat. Callum yelped as he tried to move. His ribs in pain. He reached for the door handle, and despite the severe damage, the strength of the BMW won out, and the door sprang open.

Callum slumped to the ground. His eyes were wild, but the pain in his side limited his movement.

He saw the Audi across the road. The fire in his belly helped him overcome the pain. He rose to his feet and marched across towards the stricken Audi.

Allan Mustard was out cold. He had managed to hit his head, it had rendered him totally out.

As Callum reached the car and wrenched open the door, the anger exploded. He punched the Coleman so hard in the face his finger broke. And the clean crisp crack told him that, even if the guy in the seat did wake, he would be hurting pretty badly.

He took out his mobile. Dialled 999.

"Police and ambulance," he breathed, before slumping to the ground.

He explained his location, and what had happened. His breathing getting shallower as he talked. Until finally he could speak no more. In the distance he heard sirens. And for once, was glad of the noise. He needed help now.

Allan Mustard did not move. The head knock had been enough. The punch from the big built Callum had been enough to fracture his jaw.

As the ambulance arrived, so did the Ford Focus ST. Out stepped Detective Sergeant Nicholson. Callum's heart sank. His head said "That fucking copper," as he looked up.

"I will be needing a word with you son," he smiled.

"I am sure you will," Callum replied

The ambulance crew attended to Callum. A quick examination determined broken ribs, but an x ray would be needed. However, the concern for Allan Mustard was greater. He still had not woken. And nothing the crew could do would make him. Fearing he could slip further into unconsciousness, and with the limitations of the ambulance and getting another to the scene quickly, Detective Sergeant Nicholson offered to drive Callum.
"I will make sure the local officers keep the scene safe." He assured the young man.
    Callum had little choice. He was in too much pain to argue. With that, and a few words on his radio, they began speeding towards the hospital. As the DS drove, careful not to make Callum's injuries any worse, he chatted.
"So, what happened?"
"The fucking prick didn't stop at the crossroad. Smashed straight into the side of the M3 and spun me across the road into the pole." Callum took a deep breath.
"Take it easy, " the DS said slowly.
Callum did as he was told. He sat quietly.
They arrived at the hospital. The DS helped Callum into a wheelchair. And pushed him inside.
Callum smiled. His dad would have been laughing. Suddenly the tears flowed. His dad. Sam. The baby. Shit! He needed to let them know. As they walked to reception, the ambulance crew arrived. Allan Mustard was still out cold on the stretcher.
    The ambulance crew didn't stop. Marched straight through and disappeared behind a curtain. Callum's anger

boiled over again, and he tried to get up. The pain stopped him.

Ken touched his shoulder. "Sit down son," he said gently. "You have enough to worry about," and he pushed Callum into a cubicle as instructed by the nurse.
He turned. "Oh," he paused. "I will be back later, but I thought you should know, the Audi is registered to one Tommy Shelton."
And with that the DS was gone.
Callum shuddered. Took out his phone. And dialled Sam.

Tommy was at home. Detective Sergeant Nicholson took a chance and drove to his house. He pulled into the driveway. The Aston Martin resplendent. The Mercedes he didn't immediately recognise. He knocked on the door. Michelle opened it. She froze slightly at the sight of the policeman. "Is your husband home?" He enquired.
"Just a minute," Michelle said softly. She turned. Walked back into the house. The DS took his chance and stepped inside, closing the door quietly.
Tommy marched out of the den. "What the fuck is it now?" He bellowed.
"Do you own an Audi?" The DS said calmly.
"What if I do?"
"Answer the question Mr Shelton" he paused. Registration number RS04SPC"
"Yes," Tommy said arrogantly.
"And can you tell me where it is right now?"
"How the hell should I know?"
The detective held up a photo. The car was destroyed.

"What the fucking hell happened?" Tommy shouted.
"It's been involved in a collision."
"No fucking shit Sherlock," Tommy said with real venom. "What prick did this?"
The anger in his eyes alarmed Ken.
"According to the other party involved," the DS paused "your prick of a driver did." He stared deep into Tommys eyes.
Tommy felt his fists clench.
"I dare you," the DS whispered, as he moved toward the door. "We will be in touch," he smirked. And left as quickly as he had come in.

    Michelle smiled. Tommy looked at her. His fist raised. He swung his arm back. Michelle dodged the oncoming blow. She instinctively picked up the scissors. Raised them. "I dare you!" She snarled.
"Fuck you!" Tommy replied as he left the house.

    What the fuck else could go wrong? And why the fuck had he employed that prick Mustard? Tommy was angry as he dialled Giles.
"Tommy, dear boy."
"Don't fucking dear boy me," came the reply. "Just get on the fucking phone and get rid of this prick copper."
Tommy explained all.
Giles laughed. "You must be very proud," he said as he put the phone down.
Tommy seethed. He wanted to go to the scene. But figured it would be crawling with police.
The hospital then. Yes, the hospital. The fucking prick Mustard needed getting rid of. He pushed harder on the

throttle. Gave the Aston its head. And arrived loudly at the hospital within twenty minutes.

Storming inside he looked around. As he marched to the desk he demanded "Where is Allan Mustard?"

The nurse spoke quietly. "If you continue to use that tone, I will call security."

Tommy wanted to explode. But he bit his tongue. The one thing he needed to do was make sure the Coleman had kept his mouth shut. He had no idea that Allan Mustard was still unconscious.

"Sorry," he said apologetically. "Just want to know he is OK."

The nurse calmed. "He is still unconscious right now. Take a seat and I will see what I can find out."

Tommy sat patiently. At least two hours passed. Suddenly Tommy realised he needed to get to Giles. Time was running out for the drive to the meeting point.

Just as he stood up, Callum appeared. His bruised ribs now bandaged. He walked slowly through the waiting room. Sam waited patiently across the room. Callum's eyes met Tommy's, and he smiled.

Tommy snapped. Lunged towards Callum. He tripped. Fell against the waiting room chairs and collapsed in a heap. Callum smiled again, flipped his middle finger and was gone before Tommy could even get up.

As he rose to his feet two security guards approached him. He was about to hit out. Then looked at his watch. "I'm fucking going!" he shouted. And stormed out.

Allan Mustard never regained consciousness…

Sam slapped Callum hard. "What the fuck were you thinking?!" She screamed as she drove. The tears of both anger and relief fell from her face.

"It wasn't my bloody fault," Callum protested. "The prick hit me!"

They drove home in silence. Callum knew he needed to slow down.

Sam knew it wasn't his fault.

The Rendezvous.

Tommy now needed to get to Giles, it seemed right now that his whole world was falling apart. He needed to get the drugs and diamonds back and get himself back on track. Somewhere in this mix either his wife or that prick Callum Summer was involved, he was sure, but he couldn't think about that right now. He texts Giles as he got in the car. "We are going to have to move old man."
"I am ready when you are dear boy, just make sure you have the tools to protect us from any danger."
Tommy opened the glove box of the Aston Martin and sure enough there were the two Beretta Pistols which he would take along just for insurance purposes.
"Where should I meet you?"
"I will be at the club dear boy let's go from there shall we?"
Tommy didn't reply again, he put his foot down, smashed his fist into the steering wheel and screamed "fuck!" As loudly as he could. How on earth had he got here? One minute he was in control of everything. Now, very slowly, he felt like he was losing his mind. He swung into the golf club around 15 minutes later. It was now past nine pm. The journey would take at least two hours and he was very conscious that he wasn't as prepared as he would like to have been. He parked the Aston, swept into the club and made straight for Giles' office.
Rosy was standing outside. "Hello Tommy," she smiled. Tommy nodded at the old man's door. "In there is he?"

She nodded back and Tommy stormed in.
Concealed in his jacket were the two pistols. He walked in and shut the door, took them both out of each inner pocket and stood in front of Giles pointing them at him. Jokingly said, "Put your hands in the air."
Giles looked up for a moment and had just a flash of fear across his face.
"So dear boy. What happened this time?"
"Nothing but an accident Giles, that prick Mustard didn't know the roads, wasn't paying attention and smashed straight into the side of that fucking arsehole Callum Summer."
"And where is Mr Mustard now?"
"Probably on his way to the morgue. It seems that the motorbike crash not only did his leg in, but there was definitely brain damage too. So, when he crashed the car, and after his whack on the head a couple of weeks ago, it was enough to kill him."
Giles smashed his fist down on the desk. "This has gotten far too messy. I am sick and tired of it. Once upon a time I could rely on you."
Tommy grabbed Giles by the lapels. "I fucking told you, you speak to me like that again and I will knock you out," and he swung his fist. Just before it connected, Tommy pulled it back. "And when this is over," he said, "if you speak to me like that again I will fucking kill you."
    "I suggest you concentrate. I'm getting back what is mine right now!" Giles then calmly marched out of the office.
    Tommy followed. The anger was palpable.

"I will drive," he said to Giles and climbed into the driver's seat before Giles could even argue.

To be honest Giles didn't mind. Secretly, he hated driving but always enjoyed the glamour of getting out of a fancy car. It went back to his very privileged childhood. His father always had a Rolls Royce, and Giles had always relished the feeling of everyone noticing him whenever they went out. It had always made him feel powerful. A feeling he had enjoyed. And still did. His father had always told him, with power comes control. Giles enjoyed control. As he sank back into the Range Rover, suddenly his eyes became wide. He realised the one person he could no longer control was his wife.

He would deal with her when he got back.

Tommy started the car. He had a tinge of nerves, but he was sick of this. Time to put everything to bed once and for all. He pressed the accelerator. The huge car leapt forward.

Giles clicked the heated seat. And was asleep almost as soon as they left.

Tommy muttered. "Stupid old fart," and pressed on. Not long into the journey his mobile lit up.

"Hope you are on your way."

"Oh, believe me I am on my way!" Tommy answered angrily.

"I know you both are. Tell the fat man he will need to sleep so he can keep his strength up."

Tommy's brain couldn't quite understand. "How the fuck do you know we are both on our way?"

"I just fucking know," was the short response.

"Fuck you!" Tommy shouted. Giles stirred and grunted. "You can fucking shut up too!" Tommy growled. It began to rain. Horrible, weak, fine rain. "Christ! This just gets better," Tommy muttered.

     The Signalman drank down the last of his pint. The weather wasn't great now. But that only added to it for him. He piled himself and Toffee into the Land Rover. It was about a thirty-minute drive for him. Fine rain. And a dark night with a bit of wind, and very little moonlight. Perfect.
He had everything he needed. Including the box, Giles was so desperate to get back. He laughed to himself.
     He drove slowly now. The weather closing in a little more made the gateway hard to see. Eventually he pulled off the road. A small tree lined track. A gate about 500 yards deep in. The trees unkempt. Blowing hard in the wind. It was a desolate spot. And on a night like this, exactly what he needed. The Signalman opened the gate. Drove the Land Rover inside. Carefully he closed the gate again. Parking the Land Rover just to one side, almost into the trees, making sure it could not be seen at all as you pulled into the track. He then climbed into the back of it and began to prepare. The excitement in his stomach he now couldn't contain. Though he couldn't hear himself, he was pleased. A feeling inside that he was about to do something good. Not that he thought killing was good. But he did love retribution on those who deserved it. That always made him feel good inside. He patted Toffee hard and ruffled his neck. He took out the projector. The crossbow. And the most powerful torches

money could buy. He always felt a bit sad liking his torch. But it really was like having flood lights on when it was on its most powerful setting. He clicked the button. The Land Rover lit up as if the moon had been dropped inside it. Toffee shied away. The amazing light was too much for his old eyes. The Signalman smiled. He mouthed a 'sorry' to his furry friend and cut the light.

Giles snored. Loudly. Tommy drove in silence. He was actually impressed with the car. And for some reason felt more confident. This evening, he would show Giles just who was boss. And who knows, perhaps the stupid old bastard would even use the bloody gun. Tommy smiled. As if.

Michelle got a text from Callum. "I don't know what's going on, but my car has been smashed to pieces today by a prick driving for Tommy."

Michelle dialled his number.

"Hi Michelle." he said slightly breathlessly.

"Are you OK?"

Callum explained what had happened earlier that day. Michelle listened intently. She could feel her gut twisting, and wanted nothing more than to tell all. Her mind prevented it. She needed him to know nothing. The less anyone was involved the better.

"If Tommy had any fucking thing to do with it, I will kill him!" Callum said slowly. The pain in his ribs meant he was in pain just talking.

"I don't know whether he did or not, but please, just concentrate on you, Sam, and the baby," she paused.

"Tommy isn't worth it." She swallowed hard as the words came out. There was a steely determination in her, but she refused to let it spill out and affect anything right now. Doting demure wife. "Yes sir, no sir, three bags full sir." She was more than happy to play that role. After all, unknowingly she had been doing that for years.

Callum knew that Michelle was right. But he also couldn't shake off his father's death, and the man he felt was responsible in some way shape or form. He ended the call with Michelle and slumped onto the sofa, exhausted.

Sam sat with him. Kissed him gently on the forehead and said, "Go shower Callum Summer, you stink!" She laughed.

Callum smiled. "I'm going," he said. Wearily he climbed the stairs. It was now getting late and his body was beginning to tell him he needed rest. As the shower ran and he tried to get undressed, over a hundred miles away, a black Range Rover was speeding down country lanes to its destination. Trouble was that its destination was pretty much unknown.

Tommy was bothered. There had been no communication, in fact, nothing at all to even let Tommy know that the deal was still on. The rain continued. The night was almost completely black. Tommy drove on.

The Signalman decided now would be a good time to communicate, and sent a simple text.
"Don't be late."
Tommy saw the phone light up. He shouted to the sleeping Giles.
"Answer that fucking phone."
Giles woke with a start. "Wha- what dear boy?"
"ANSWER THAT BLOODY PHONE!" Tommy shouted at the top of his voice.

Giles looked at the screen. Instantly his hackles rose.
"Who the fuck do you think you are?"
"What did you send?" Tommy enquired. Giles showed him the screen.
"You fucking prick!" Tommy roared. "We don't fucking know who he is, and he isn't about to give us his address and inside fucking leg size is he?!"
The phone buzzed again.
"That's not very polite now, is it, fat man?" came the reply.
Giles froze. Looked at Tommy. "How the fuck does he know I am replying?"
Tommy laughed. "Coz," he stopped, thought for a moment, then decided he was right, "I have already had that speech."
Giles calmed. "Yes," he said sheepishly. "I suppose you have."
Giles replied again. "We are on time."
"Good, I will see you in an hour or so."
Giles turned to Tommy. "How can he be so confident?"
Tommy shrugged his shoulders. "It's like he is just proving a point. He thinks he is in total control. Well, I'm going to show him just exactly who is in control."

Valerie text Michelle. "It's time to take control."
Michelle smiled. "It certainly is."
Her mind clear. The memories of Charlie are all too vivid. It helped drive her to cope with Tommy. He had it all. And it was time for him to pay.
Valerie felt the same. A swell of both anger and passion. She had loved Jamie. And though Giles had nothing to do

with his death, Michelle, Anesh and Marco... Oh gosh Marco! How she loved his cock!, Had made her see that Giles too was out of control. She had had enough of living a lie. "It's my turn," she said in her mind. "It's my fucking turn."

      Tommy turned left. Just as the satnav had told him to. The rain had not eased. If anything, it was raining harder now. Giles became apprehensive. A completely black landscape. No means of escape. And at the mercy of God knows who. He gripped the Beretta a little more tightly.

Tommy needed to concentrate. With the wipers on fast, the rain beginning to lash down, and his mind racing, he must focus. He shook his head like a dog as if to try to clear his mind.

And the voice on the satnav said... "Your destination is on the right." Tommy swallowed hard. It was now or never.

"You ready old man?" Tommy said in a low menacing tone.

"I'm ready dear boy," Giles returned.

His overly posh accent grated Tommy more than it ever had for some reason. Tommy was on edge.

Giles oddly wasn't. After all of the build-up, he simply thought of it as an adventure. And, like a small child, couldn't stop himself grinning.

"What the fuck are you smiling at?"

"Exciting isn't it, dear boy," he laughed.

Tommy looked in disbelief. "Are you fucking mad?"

"Never done this sort of thing before," and he took out the pistol.

"Now be careful old man," Tommy instructed. "We don't want that going off just now do we?"

Giles looked at Tommy. Was about to raise the pistol in jest but thought better of it. He lowered it again, and, just as he was about to speak, the sat nav spoke.
"You have arrived."
Tommy slowed the Range to halt. "Where the fuck have we arrived?" he said out loud.
Giles tapped his ear, and pointed. "There, dear boy," he said. "Just over there, there is a clearing."
Tommy looked to his right. Sure enough he saw it. He drove past the entrance. Put the car in reverse. And carefully using the Range Rovers excellent mirrors and camera, expertly began to reverse down into the small lane.
"Why backwards?"
"Because old man," Tommy paused, Christ! He was hard work sometimes. "If we need to get the fuck out of here, I want to able to drive forward doing it!" His voice rose to almost a squeak. Tommy was nervous.
He continued down the lane. The cameras worked perfectly despite the dark. Suddenly it picked out the box that had been stolen from Tommys Audi! Tommy stopped sharply, as the sensors started screaming inside the car for avoidance.
He stopped the car and reached for the door handle. As he did so, his mobile lit up.
"Not so fast."
Tommy froze. Said to Giles. "He is here."
Giles' face went white. "Where?"
"Are you taking the piss old man? How the fuck do I know?" And he thrust the phone at Giles. "But he is here!"

Giles gulped. Suddenly it was real. He looked behind him. As he did so, he could have sworn he saw a figure.
"There!" He shouted.
"Where?" Tommy now had the pistol in his hand.
He looked in his rear view mirror. There, standing in the middle of the lane, in the pissing rain, was Charlie Summer.
Tommy rubbed both eyes with his fists, and opened them again. Like a cartoon character who thought things would be different when he opened them again. But nothing had changed. How the fuck was Charlie Summer there? Tommy felt the goose bumps on his arm. "But you are dead," he whispered. "Dead!" He bellowed. And went to open the door.
As he did so, the brightest light appeared in front of them. So bright neither could see anything. Tommy shielded his eyes, but could see nothing.
Giles had his eyes closed. The piercing white light against the darkness rendered them both almost blind. Giles had his head pressed hard against the headrest. As he began to raise his arm to shield his eyes from the piercing light, the crossbow bolt went through the windscreen. It didn't deviate from its course and hit Giles perfectly in the centre of the forehead. Smashing into his skull, it hit the back of the headrest. Giles was killed instantly. His head pinned to the car.
Tommy reached again for the door handle. Total panic in his eyes. He couldn't see the assailant anywhere. The bright light still made him disorientated, he found the door handle, wrenched it open, and fell out of the car. As he hit the floor, he knew right then he had made a

mistake. The size ten climbing boot hit him square in the face. Tommy blacked out. A perfect kick to the temple rendered him unconscious. The second crossbow bolt smashed into Tommy's skull. His body quivered. Then stopped moving.

    The Signalman smiled. Carefully hit the switch in his hand, and the lane was plunged into darkness once more. Toffee sat at the end of the lane, watching intently. But there was no one and nothing around on this miserable night. The Signalman calmly picked up the box. He opened it, and tipped the entire contents over the inside of the range rover. He poured the world's finest cocaine over Tommy's limp and lifeless body. And smiled as he saw Giles' terrified expression on his face. He saw the diamonds. They were unexpected, and he wanted one. So he took one; two, no let's have three. They would just top up his fee nicely.

    He loaded two huge spotlights, the crossbow, and the projector back into the Land Rover. The Range Rover blocked his path. But he had already planned to go out through the other side of the field. Having carefully checked maps and diagrams, he knew this place was used for 'green laning', and knew that his tracks would soon be covered. As he loaded all of the equipment, he beckoned to Toffee. The little dog came scurrying along. Eager to please his master, he stopped and growled, and made to bite Tommy. The Signalman laughed. Toffee ran towards the Land Rover and jumped in. He sent one last message. "Goodnight!" It landed on Tommy's mobile. He threw his phone into the field. When the police scanned Tommy's and called the number they would hear it ring. He smiled to himself. As he drove slowly across the field, the rain became more intense. The perfect night. The perfect storm. It took him over an hour to find the road. He couldn't believe his luck. The gate had not even been closed! The old Land Rover hit the tarmac, and began its journey back. The Signalman patted Toffee and turned the heater up. The rain lashed down. And he sent one text. "It's done."

Michelle didn't care anymore. She had grown tired of living in fear. And would now never have to. She only wished she had stabbed him when she had the chance. But now, if all had gone to plan, her meek and mild manner would be the perfect antidote for removing all suspicions.

Valerie had not even had to arrange any money. Anesh had done all of this on trust. She smiled. Giles had been correct. Power gives you control. She felt powerful. At 1 am, she settled down to sleep.

Valerie was wide awake. She was waiting to hear from Marco. The night dragged on. She looked at her phone. Clicked on internet browser. History. There was that bloody website. Her mind briefly reflected on the awful time she had using it. Then her mind switched to Marco. She had little doubt he was screwing everything in sight. But he had made her feel like Jamie had. Alive! She enjoyed that feeling. She enjoyed his enormous cock too. A grin appeared on her face. She went back to the first time he fucked her. She just had not been able to take it all. God! He was huge! As her mind wandered, she could feel the tingle in her stomach, and the wetness in her pussy. She lay down a little further. As her mind played, so did her fingers. She dropped the phone, and relied on her mind. Marco's massive cock. Trying to get him in her mouth. She undid her robe. Opened the drawer, and took out a huge dildo. Right now, she needed Marco. Her mind, and the rubber cock would have to suffice. She bent forward, lowered her head, and slowly pushed the toy inside her. She gasped as it went in. It almost felt bigger than he did. Fucking herself harder now, her mind concentrated on Marco.

As she continued to play, she thought about Giles. The anger built in her. Suddenly she was shaking. Angry. Fucking her pussy as deep as she could, but with anger as her emotion. She had never felt this way, but she knew her body was about to explode. The orgasm came out of nowhere. Her body convulsed and contorted as the most powerful orgasm she had ever experienced swept over her. Her eyes closed, her breath became short, and she completely lost herself. She found tears running down her face. Somehow a massive outpouring of emotions: sex, anger, despair. Everything mixed into one, had caused both her mind and body to almost literally explode. Only then did she realise that her pussy had gushed its juices all over the bed. Everything was soaked. She had never experienced 'squirting', and she wasn't sure she enjoyed it. But she knew she had not been able to control it either. As she began to come down from the orgasm, her phone lit up.

"It's done."

Valerie smiled. Couldn't have timed it better if she had tried. She scooped all of the bed clothes up. Went downstairs, loaded them into the washing machine, and made her way to the lounge. She switched on the TV. Sat on the sofa, and felt the relief. She leant back, and within minutes, was asleep.

DEAD!

It was 7am. The rains from last night had finally stopped. The storm had not been especially violent, but it had certainly been enough to make The Signalman's journey slow going. He had crawled into bed around 6am. Toffee had joined him, and they were asleep almost before their head hit the pillow.

The assembled motley crew of vehicles consisting of old Land Rovers: cut up Range Rovers, Jeeps, and even the odd Suzuki Jimny, finished their breakfast at "The Lamb" and started to head out to their favourite spot to do some off roading.
The villagers hated it, but there was little they could do. The farmer who owned the fields earned nicely out of the green laners, and had no plans to stop them unless they kept leaving the bloody gates open. And the landlady of the Lamb didn't mind at all. Twenty breakfasts at 9.99 each was a very good start to a Sunday morning!
The first vehicle turned into the field around 7.30. Slowly, the 12 battered off road vehicles all entered, and the occupants of the last one closed the gate.
The lead car driver then got out. "Right, you all know the rules." Stick to the paths and tracks. There is a nice section to the south that goes through deep woodland and has some sharp slopes. But be careful. It rained hard last night, and there may be some traps, or deep puddles!" He laughed. "For the unwary!" He stopped, then continued. "We will go straight through to the Deacon, then use the gate on that side to exit, and carry on into

the village for lunch. You all have radios, so let's just make sure they all work before we set off. If anyone gets into trouble, you know the code word."
There was a nod of agreement from all. They clambered back into the cars and disappeared off.
There were three distinct paths, all of which ended up at the Deacon. There was only one issue. When they got to the Deacon this morning, they would be greeted by rather more than they had bargained for. As the off-road club slowly made their way along their respective paths, both Valerie and Michelle were sleeping soundly. Callum had had an awful night's sleep. His bruised ribs rendered him in pain and uncomfortable.
The Signalman and Toffee were sound asleep.
Marco and Anesh had just opened a bottle of red. "To us!"
Marco smiled. "To us my brother."
"That fat bastard had it coming."
It was just before 12 midday that the V8 cut down Range Rover arrived at the gate. The owner Dave smiled. Muttered to himself, "Thank Christ the gate is shut!" Before stopping down and making his way over. As he did so he saw the black Range Rover about 50 yards the other side of the gate.
Bloody marvellous he thought, some posh twat dog walker has decided to leave their posh bloody car in our way. He shouted, "Hey!" But no reply. "Bollocks!" He muttered. Drove the car out of the gate, but didn't bother to close it. There would be others. As he got a little closer, he saw the steam from the exhausts. The car was running. Excellent, Dave said to himself, they can bloody move.

He pulled up closer to the car. Nothing moved. He pressed the horn. He had fitted a loud 'train' style horn. It was loud enough to wake the dead he had joked to his wife.
Except it wasn't. Neither of the bodies in or around the Range Rover moved. Dave began to get frustrated. "Can you move?" He shouted. The frustration in his voice showed. Still nothing.
Dave switched off his car. Got out, and marched towards the much newer car. As he walked to the driver's side, he stopped in his tracks. The driver's door was open. A body lying on the ground. He walked closer. Peering inside he saw Giles. Pinned by the head to his seat. The crossbow bolt still sticking out of his head. Dave turned. And threw up. As he did so, tears ran from his face. His passenger, and wife Jackie stepped out.
"What the hell is wrong?"
"Call the police!" Dave screamed. "Dead." And he retched again.
The other off roaders arrived before the police. Unbelievably, the local police had trouble finding the place. Once a local car had turned up, it was clear they couldn't deal with the situation. Frantic calls were made on radios, lots of swearing and even one officer fainting. You couldn't have made it up. No one actually bothered to check anything. At least it meant the crime scene was preserved.
  An ambulance arrived.
  "Waste of bloody time that is," Dave muttered, having regained some composure after talking to the police.

The crew of the vehicle made their way toward the Range
Rover. They checked on Giles. The simple head shake would have told anyone in the outside world all they needed to know.

The crew knelt down next to Tommy's lifeless body. Suddenly there was frantic activity. "He's alive!"

Dave breathed. "Shit! He's alive?"
His wife Jackie told him to calm down.
But Dave suddenly was filled with regret. He kept saying over and over, "I had no idea, I had no idea."

The paramedics had machines and lines inserted into and onto Tommy's body within minutes. Despite all he had sustained, the angry bulldog fight in him, and the fact that the crossbow bolt had entered his head slightly to the left meant whilst he most certainly wasn't in the best of health, he was, remarkably, alive. The ambulance crew took Tommy's body and put him in the ambulance. Whilst waiting for the air ambulance was considered, all agreed that, if he had survived this far, chances were, he would last the journey to the hospital by road.

Ken arrived on the scene around 2 hours after it was called in. The scene of crime officers by now had the place cordoned off. The off roaders had been sent on their way, statements taken, and all had been told not to go anywhere without informing police, though in truth, they were about as far removed from suspects as the pope. He surveyed the scene before telephoning the Chief.

The conversation was brief, uncomfortable, and at the end of it, Detective Sergeant Nicholson didn't quite know what to make of it all.

A respected member of the community, and a small-time pretend gangster, murdered, or at least one of them, and a car full of drugs and diamonds. Suddenly this little village didn't seem quite so sleepy after all. Perhaps he would have something to get his teeth into. Question was: Where did he start? It was a racing certainty Tommy Shelton wouldn't be talking anytime soon, if he survived at all. How the hell had he survived? The scene of crime boys would be here for some time yet. Of that he was certain. Whoever had done this was a professional. He was pretty certain of that too. Remote spot. Very little chance of witnesses. No CCTV. almost nothing to go on. Christ! Even the weather had been kind to the assailant. However they got there would almost certainly have been erased by last night's rain. He got back into his car and scratched his head. The wives he supposed. That would at least be a place to start. He decided he would take a look around before he left. But did not hold out much hope of finding anything.
As he got out of the car one of the SOCO team walked past.
"Anything to tell?"
"A big fat zero so far," came the dejected reply.
Ken had figured as much. "Thanks."
The coroner arrived. Took away Giles' body.
Little point in asking the cause of death, but he would wait for the autopsy report anyway. However, with a twelve-inch-long piece of steel sticking out of his head,

even Ken could work out that Giles died due to a crossbow bolt. Under his breath he muttered, "buggered that interior up too," and he smiled to himself. As he carefully walked around the site, he couldn't help but feel there was something deeper. He had been a copper for a long time, and his gut was rarely wrong. What connected Giles and Tommy? Why the drugs? Why the uncut diamonds?

He was bloody sure it was going to take a long time to get to the bottom of things. He started the car and made his way back. Pretty sure in the knowledge that his battles were just beginning.

The Signalman sent a message. "It's done."
Marco replied. "You missed one."
"What the fuck?"
"You missed one," again. "Tommy Shelton survived."
"Impossible!"
"I am fucking telling you he is alive. Barely, but he is."
"So what's the deal with payment?"
"You get half, I told you my brother, finish the job."
The Signalman couldn't believe it. He didn't bother to reply.

Callum couldn't go to work. The pain in his ribs was too much. He decided to drive in anyway and put a sign up to let anyone know he was off for a few days. He would call all of his customers and do the same. Rest, the docs kept saying, and Sam wouldn't shut up too!

He knew he would be OK. But he also knew he had others to think about now. It made him feel warm inside. Callum didn't need the money, or even need to work.

Thanks to his dad he would never worry about money again, but also, much like his dad, he loved what he did, and never tired of helping people and fixing things that had others beaten. He was a tenacious little sod when he needed to be, and he loved it. Just as his father had. But, for this week at least, Summer Auto's would be keeping its doors closed. Whether he liked it or not. He would have to rest up.

DS Nicholson arrived back at H.Q. Immediately the Chief Super demanded his presence. "DS Nicholson!" He bellowed "I demand to know what is going on."
Ken couldn't believe what he was hearing. He had never seen the chief super so animated although if he was honest, he had barely seen the chief super at all. So why the hell was he suddenly demanding to know what had happened?
"I would appreciate it if you didn't use that tone with me Sir."
The chief super was incensed. "I will use whatever tone I need to, in order to find out what has gone on, and what has happened to my dear friend and golfing buddy Giles Williams."
The DS smiled. So that's what it was about. The old pals act, golfing buddies, gin and tonic brigade, what, what and all that bullshit, the very things that Ken couldn't stand. He understood there had to be a hierarchy, but he just couldn't stand it as some people thought they were above the law or certainly better than it.

"Well Sir," he began to reply, carefully choosing his words. "At present all that has been established is that two men were involved in an incident in a remote location involving a vehicle registered to one Giles Williams. The vehicle contained substantial amounts of illegal drugs and uncut diamonds which we suspect were brought into the UK illegally."

The chief super sat down. His face said it all. Absolutely dumbfounded he nonetheless carried on, "Well I won't hear a word of it. Giles is a fine upstanding fellow and there must be some mistake, or this other fellow must have got Giles involved somehow."

"Well Sir, I think we need to gather all the evidence before we come to any conclusions, don't you?"

The chief super glared at Ken, yet he also knew that he had to be careful. After all, he too could be implemented if there was anything untoward with Giles, he certainly had done him a few favours in the past and turned the odd blind eye, even if it was just parking offences. Giles and the chief super went back a long way. And the chief super may have to be very careful with some of the things he had done or been associated with certainly in his younger days. However, first and foremost, he was an officer of the law and long-term friendship notwithstanding, he would always uphold the law. Having been a policeman since he was in his teens, it was all he had known, and to be honest, probably the only career he had ever wanted.

He looked up at DS Nicholson. "You need to find whoever did this, and make sure they are punished for it. I will not stand for this in my community."

The DS decided he would pick his battles and simply said to his commanding officer, "I will do my best Sir," and turned on his heel and left.

The chief super reached for the top drawer of his desk, took out the small hip flask, and probably for the first time in his career actually realised he needed a drink. Leaning back in his chair he took a big mouthful of scotch. Said to himself "Giles old man, what the fuck have you done?"

DS Nicholson decided that the best place to start would be with Valerie Williams. He had expressly given orders that neither of the wives be told what had happened. He wanted to do it personally and he knew deep down there was only one reason for this. He had always been a great one to read body language. It wouldn't, however, be the first case he had ever worked on where the sweet and innocent wife had been behind something very sinister indeed.

Valerie was at home.

The DS pulled up outside the magnificent gates and rang the intercom. He gave his name, and the gates swung open, and for the first time he was greeted by the Williams' magnificent house. He drew his breath in deeply. "I say old boy," he muttered to himself, "you certainly have plenty in the bank. I wonder if all that came from drugs and diamonds?" He questioned in his mind.

He was just about to knock on the door when it was swung open and there stood Valerie Williams. "How can I help you DS Nicholson?"

"I wonder if I could come in madam?"
"Please call me Valerie, there's no need to be so formal"
"Certainly."
"Come in, she beckoned "Could I get you a coffee?"
"Coffee would be great." He wanted to buy himself enough time just to have a discreet look around. Valerie went off to the kitchen and he began to admire the amazing house. He looked around and could see photos of the couple in various countries on holiday invariably with a drink in their hand, always smiling and looking altogether the perfect couple. He noted there were no children or at least none that he could see pictures of, and made a mental note to ask, though at this time that certainly didn't have any relevance to what had happened to Giles last night, or so it seemed.
"Make yourself at home!" Valerie shouted. "You go along the corridor and take the second room on the left, I will bring the coffee in there."

    Initially impressions for the DS were good. As far as he was concerned, certainly at face value, Valerie knew nothing about what happened to husband. However, he questioned why, if Giles had not come home last night, Valerie wouldn't be wondering where he was.
Valerie arrived with the coffee, placed the tray down on the small coffee table. He smiled. She had brought biscuits as well. He wasn't entirely sure this was going to be the smoothest sailing, in particular as Valerie seemed so calm and ordinary.
"So, Detective Sergeant," she asked again, "What can I do for you?"
Ken shifted uncomfortably as he looked her in the eye.

"I'm afraid I have some rather bad news," he said bluntly. "Could you tell me if your husband is around."
"No, I'm afraid he's not, he didn't come home last night."
"Is that something that he would normally do?"
"It depends really," she said very matter of factly. "Generally if he's gone out for a drink with Tommy or played a few rounds, and then had some whisky, there are occasions when he will sleep at his office."
"Does he let you know?"
"Sometimes he lets me know, and sometimes he's too drunk, but I don't really worry about it, why?"
"I'm afraid I have to tell you that we believe we have found a gentleman matching the description of your husband who was pronounced dead at a crime scene earlier this morning"
Valerie stopped in her tracks.
"Are you sure it's Giles?" She asked, her breath a little shorter, already.
"We have a vehicle which is registered to him, and the passenger of that vehicle was a man fitting your husband's description."
Valerie put her coffee cup down and a tear fell from her eye.
"Was it an accident?" she questioned.
"No, Mrs Williams. We believe right now that your husband has been murdered."
Valerie began to struggle for breath. Close to hyperventilating, she began to breathe deeply, seven, eight, nine times, he lost count as the tears fell from her eyes. She slowly began to compose herself.

"What on earth do you mean?" she said, reaching for the box of tissues and wiping her eyes.
"We don't know too many details yet, but I can assure you that we are treating the investigation as murder."
Valerie burst into tears. Ken slowly sipped his coffee.
"I am terribly sorry for your loss Mrs Williams, is there anybody you would like me to call."
Valerie shook her head.
"Are you up for answering a few questions?" He asked as she dabbed at her eyes.
She nodded gently.
"Only if you are sure," he said.
"I'm sure," she said softly. "I will do all I can to help you find whoever did this."
The DS took out his notebook and began to ask Valerie a series of questions. Valerie answered them calmly, with the occasional sniffle and occasionally having to either blow her nose or wipe her eyes.
All the time he asked the questions he kept his eyes fixed firmly on her expression.
"One last question for now Mrs Williams," he asked. "Do you have any idea of anybody who would want to hurt your husband?"
Valerie paused. "I am sure there are many people, detective, who are jealous of us. Our happy life, indeed, our very luxurious life and the fact that my husband has worked very hard to get it all, so I would imagine there are a lot of people that are jealous of Giles."
"Jealous enough to kill?"

"Hmmm, can't think of one." She paused. "However, I do know that he and Tommy Shelton have had a few run-ins just lately."
The DS smiled and then immediately felt angry at himself. He had almost given his own game away.
"Thank you for your help Mrs Williams, please let me know if you need me to call anyone or you would like an officer present. I will see myself out."
He placed his cup down and left. If this woman wasn't grieving and was faking her surprise at what he had just told her, she was a bloody good actress, he certainly couldn't see if she was lying.
He decided that the best port of call now was to Mrs Michelle Shelton. Let's see what she had to say.
Valerie collected her phone and sent a very brief text.
"Police on the way, time to put that actress face on and tell them exactly what they want to hear."
She got a one-word reply.
"OK."
The DS pulled into the driveway. Michelle's Mercedes was there again. The house was smaller than Valerie's, but it was still impressive, and certainly a far cry from anything he had ever owned in London. He rang the bell. Michelle opened the door.
"Mrs Shelton," he said.
"You know bloody well it is. What do you want?"
He was slightly taken aback, he didn't realise she could be so abrupt, she always looked so demure.
"This is about Tommy, do you have any idea where he is?

"I have no bloody idea, I haven't seen him since yesterday."
"Can I come in?"
"Sure," Michelle said abruptly and walked inside. "Do you want coffee?" She said, a little more mellow this time.
"Coffee would be great,"
"Make your way into the lounge, the door on the left."
How ridiculous, the DS thought, almost the same speech, but I guess if the lounge is on the left it would be. He shook his head, perhaps he was being far too cynical. He went into the immaculate living room beautifully furnished. But all he could think of was that it felt cold. Michelle came in. There were no biscuits this time but certainly a very good cup of coffee. She sat opposite him, the tracksuit didn't cover much and he couldn't help but admire her body. Shaking his head again he told himself to get a grip.
"Is it unusual for your husband not to come home Mrs Shelton?"
"No, it's not unusual at all!" She snapped. "He's probably fucking one of the tarts at his Club."
The DS leaned forward.
"So your marriage had problems?"
Michelle answered abruptly, "Not at all, I have got used to Tommy and his ways over the years." She stood up, "Why what's he done now?"
"I would appreciate if you would sit down Mrs Shelton."
Michelle sat down as he asked.
"So, what has he done now?" she asked again.
"We believe your husband has had an attempt made on his life."

Michelle flinched. Her mind racing. Fuck he isn't dead! Either the DS didn't see it or didn't want to see it. Michelle's voice faltered
"An attempt on his life?" She breathed. "Is he okay?"
"I am afraid he is in hospital at present. His injuries are currently listed as life-threatening."
Michelle sank back in the chair, her mind racing. He was supposed to be dead; she hadn't planned on this.
"Can I see him?"
"Currently I would suggest that's not a great idea. But I will leave you my card and let you know when it is safer. Do you have any idea who might want to harm your husband?"
"Christ!" She sat back. "I could give you a list as long as your arm. Tommy has never been very good at public relations, and has made many enemies over the years."
"Enough enemies that might want to kill him?"
"I can't answer that, I know I'd like to kill him some bloody days."
The DS watched her body language but once again, he certainly couldn't see a chink in her armour, and believed that the woman had no idea what had happened. The only thing that puzzled him was why she was slightly less upset than Valerie. Only then did he noticed a tear fall from her eye.
"Is there anybody I can call? Anybody you would like present, or I can get an officer to you if you need?"
"No, thank you. "I always worried that Tommy would upset somebody but I never actually believed anybody would want to kill him."
The DS finished his coffee.

"Here's my card. I will be in touch. Thank you for your help. I will see myself out."
The same speech over and over didn't get any easier. But he knew right now this was the easy part. Trying to catch whoever killed Giles and tried to kill Tommy was going to be far more difficult. As he closed the door and got in the car he said to himself, "Where the fucking hell do I start?"
He dialled the chief super.
"I'm going to need a team, this is going to be really ugly and I think we're going to need all the help we can get." The chief super agreed. "Yes, do whatever it takes, we can't have this on our patch."
Ken started the car and began to make progress back towards the station. Time to get a team together and see if he couldn't catch this bastard.
Michelle sent a text to Valerie, "Can I come over?"
"Of course you can come over. But I have to go and identify Giles' body. So I will let you know when I get back. Of course I am always here to help you in your hour of need, as I hope you will be there for me."
As Michelle read the sentence her phone rang.
"I would suggest that we don't send anything by text. However, of course we can speak whenever we want. But I am very aware that the police may be watching our every move."
Michelle said quietly "He isn't fucking dead."
Valerie stopped in her tracks.
"What do you mean he isn't dead?"
"What do you think I fucking mean? Tommy isn't dead, he's in hospital!" She took a sharp intake of breath. "The

DS has told me his injuries are considered life-threatening and there is a good chance he won't survive, but he didn't fucking die."

"If his injuries are life-threatening then he may as well be dead. Stop worrying. Let me go and get this over with, and I will let you know when I get back. Until then keep doing what I tell you. Absorb, process, then go ape shit, we don't know anything about Tommy or his injuries, but if they don't expect him to survive he's hardly in the best place is he? I will call you as soon as I get home." Valerie ended the call.

Michelle didn't know whether to laugh, cry or explode. However the one thing she was sure of was that Valerie was right, whilst they could be the grieving wives together they couldn't let anybody have any idea that they were involved. Michelle decided a bottle of wine was in order.

The DS got back to his desk and began to piece a few things together. The first thing he needed to understand was why the hell Tommy and Giles were together in that remote place that night. He had already gathered all of the mobile phones and communication equipment from the Range Rover. He had forensics examining all of it right now, perhaps they would hold the key. And who the fuck uses a crossbow? It was something he had never come across as a weapon in all his years as a detective. But certainly, whoever it was had definitely known how to use it, though he was pretty sure that both men should have been dead so how on earth Tommy survived nobody really knew, but he would make bloody sure he found out.

It was a very simple process for Valerie to identify her husband. And even more simple for her to shed her tears and grieve when she saw him. Even if inside she was smiling. She would play the game. But ultimately, she was now in control. And for her and Michelle things would change. No longer would they be in the background, no longer would they be manipulated, no longer would they be pushed into a corner.

It was the next day before everything had calmed enough for the two women to meet. Arranging a coffee, they figured that a public place would be as good a place as any to start. Even if it would be in a far more discreet area and they would be upstairs out of the way of the public.

Valerie arrived first. She disappeared up the stairs out of the eyes of the regular guests. Michelle soon joined her.

"They say I can't see Tommy. Why the fuck can't I see him?"

"Because if it's anything like Giles, he probably has a crossbow bolt sticking out of his head."

"So how the fuck didn't he die?"

"Because that's the sort of lucky bastard Tommy is."

"So what do we do now?

"Now we wait. At least one half of the plan has gone exactly how we wanted it to." Giles' affairs would now be getting investigated, they will find out what a corrupt bastard he was. Who knows how high it will go? The only thing we have to be careful of is that DS Nicholson. He is not stupid, and if we let our guard down, I am sure he will see through us."

Michelle smiled, "I'm bloody sure he was trying to see through my tracksuit, that's for sure."

Valerie laughed. "Well, if that's true you make sure you keep doing what you're doing girl, because the one thing we need is him not to look too deeply into us! Especially with the phone calls with Marco."

She then produced two phones from her handbag. "Pay as you go, untraceable. There is fifty quid on each, use these whenever you need to speak about anything that's going on. And as far as anybody else is concerned I am a grieving widow who knows absolutely nothing about what has happened and you are a potentially grieving wife who also knows nothing."

The investigation begins.

"Listen up team," DS Nicholson began. "I want a full background check on the two victims. Bank statements, work information, Christ! I want to know who their tailor was. Go back as far as you need to. I need to understand why somebody wanted these two gentlemen dead and from everything I've learned so far one is a lot easier to understand than the other. Check work records, check employees, start with that club that Tommy Shelton owns, let's see if we can get any background on anybody there. The other half of you, we can hardly do door to door, it was the middle of fucking nowhere, but check out the local villages and check out the golf club Giles Williams is the chairman of. Who knows, somebody might know something."

The team split up and did as they were asked.

Detective Sergeant Nicholson suddenly decided that it may not be very smart, but it was probably very necessary. He dialled the chief superintendent.

"I don't suppose we can have a chat Sir, can we?"

"What on earth do you need to talk to me about?"

"I need to ask you about Giles Williams."

"Do you enjoy rubbing people up the wrong way Detective Sergeant?"

"Not at all Sir, but by your own admission you say that you knew the man and certainly had known him for some time. All I'm trying to do is get some background on who on earth may want to do this terrible thing to him."

"Very well, come to my office in 30 minutes."
Detective Sergeant Nicholson felt uncomfortable questioning his superior officer, as whilst he had nothing to do with what had happened, he needed to dig deeper. Because on the surface Giles Williams was unblemished. Ken had been in the job long enough to know that everybody had a blemish somewhere; you just had to look hard enough to find it. He knocked on the door.

"Come," the voice said abruptly. "Is this official, Detective Sergeant?"

"Not unless you wish it to be, Sir" Ken said. "All I really need to do Sir is just understand what sort of man Giles was."

"Sit down Detective Sergeant and I will tell you all I know of Giles Williams."

The chief superintendent regaled the stories of Giles' wealthy family and that they had always been fine upstanding members of the community. He may have been a little bit of a rogue at times in the past but nothing more than parking tickets and the odd speeding fine. He had never been in trouble with the police, though as a businessman apparently, he was quite ruthless and didn't suffer fools gladly. He had a habit of buying companies and breaking them up, keeping the profitable parts and getting rid of the rubbish, even if that meant to the detriment of some of the community. However, he had also donated massively to the local area, always been willing to help and certainly wasn't shy with his cash helping out charities, schools and many organisations have been grateful in one way shape or form from Giles' cash."

"What about his wife Sir?"

"Valerie? She has been by his side the whole time. They have had their ups and downs I'm sure like most couples have, but she has stood by him and certainly enjoyed his generosity. He was one of the most likeable men I have ever met. Despite his size, he played a mean round of golf, and other than that, I can't really tell you much detective. I cannot imagine anybody that would want to kill Giles Williams."
"Thank you Sir. I appreciate your time."
"I need you to catch this bastard Ken. I can't believe that Giles is mixed up with Tommy Shelton. And even if he is. Nobody deserves to die the way he did."
Detective Sergeant Nicholson asked one more question.
"In your experience, have you ever known anybody who uses a crossbow?"
"Only in the movies"
The detective thanked him once again and left.
Once again Giles seemed untouchable, almost too perfect. Something must have made this happen.

    Rosy was panicking. She hadn't heard from Giles nor had she seen him. And with the club due to open in a few days this was definitely not like him. Just as she picked up the phone and dialled Giles' number again, the intercom buzzed.
"Who is it?" she answered snappily.
"It's the police, open up, we need a word."
Rosy did as she was asked.
"How can I help you officer?" She enquired.
"Can I ask who you are, and have you seen Giles Williams lately?"

"My name is Rosy Wilde, I am the manager here, and no," she replied, "I am very worried about him. He went out a couple of days ago and I haven't seen him since or heard from him which is most unusual."
"You need to sit down Miss Wilde"
She replied, "Just call me Rosy."
"You're going to need to sit down Rosy."
"What has happened?" She demanded.
"I have to inform you that Mr Williams has been killed."
Rosy's face looked completely shocked.
"What?" She shouted. "How, when, where, why?"
"Calm down Rosy," the officer said gently "we don't know any of the answers to that yet, I was hoping you might be able to help me. All I can tell you is that Mr Williams has been murdered brutally, and we need to try and understand why and who may have been responsible."
Rosy's whole body shuddered.
"What do you mean murdered?"
"Exactly as I say Rosy, Mr Williams has been the victim of a brutal murder."
Rosy took a deep breath.
"Do you feel up to talking?" the police officer said.
"Yes, of course, I will do anything I can to help."
As she did so, Gigi appeared around the corner.
"Is everything okay?"
"Everything is fine Gigi, you carry on"

Rosy proceeded to explain to the officer that she had not long worked for Giles, he had employed her as the bar manager, and she had been running the golf club for the last few months. She knew Tommy Shelton, and yes, Giles and he often played golf together. In fact, she thought Tommy and Giles were perhaps business partners. But more than that she didn't know, as she had only been there a short time.

The officer thanked Rosy, and asked if he could come back to perhaps chat to other staff when they needed to.

Rosy waved him off with a cheery "Goodbye!" And went back into the club.

She sat down. Didn't know whether to laugh or cry. The new club. What the fuck would happen?

She went to find Gigi.

"Giles is dead," she said bluntly.

Gigi didn't flinch.

"Someone killed him."

"Shit!" The young girl whispered.

Rosy continued. "Tommy is in hospital. They don't think he is going to survive. The police will be back and will want to speak to you I am sure. So no mouthing off OK?"

Gigi looked at Rosy rather harshly. "I'm not stupid!" I won't say anything."

"I know you won't, I just needed you to know."

Gigi blushed. "I'm sorry," she said quietly. "It was a shock. What will happen with the new club now?"

"I have no bloody idea right now," Rosy sighed. "But it's going to be a bloody mess of a situation."

She took out her mobile. Sending a text to both Geoff and Eugene, she waited for their response.

She didn't have long to wait. They appeared in the bar almost immediately.

"WHAT THE FUCK DO YOU MEAN DEAD?" Geoff was angry. His demeanour always came across as such. But this time he was beside himself.
Eugene quietly said. "Where was he, and how did he die?" Rosy shivered as he spoke. There was always a venom to Eugene's voice. He spoke in low tones, and quietly.
"He was out of town, that's all I know. And the police won't tell me. I was just told it had been a brutal murder"
"And Tommy?"
"Tommy is alive... Just, apparently."
Geoff flinched. "How the fuck is he still alive?" He shrieked. And he punched the wall. "I will fucking find out who did this," he snorted. "And the cunt will pay." And he stormed out of the hall.
Eugene smiled at Rosy.
"Give him time to let off steam. Clearly either the old man upset someone. Or Shelton did," and he slowly walked away.
"Do you want a drink?" Rosy asked.
"Yeah," Eugene said slowly.
Rosy poured a scotch. Eugene thanked her.
"What the hell am I going to do about the other club?" she asked.
"Chill," Eugene spoke softly. "Give it time. It will sort itself."
Rosy looked at him.
"How the fuck can you be so calm?!"
"Not much point in going ape shit yet. The old man is dead, nothing's gonna bring him back. So just take our time. Find out who did this. And then pay them back."
He sipped his drink slowly. Rosy smiled.

"You are so chilled," she said.
"I am for now," he muttered. "I won't be when I find out who the fuck did it!" And he finished his drink and left.

Detective Sergeant Nicholson sat at his desk. The last couple of days had seen the quiet little village and its surroundings rocked by the discovery of the body of Giles Williams, and the attempted murder of Tommy Shelton.
He had been shipped out of London. He knew damn well his senior officer didn't like him, or his methods, and was fairly confident this was part of the reason why he had been put out here. Not to mention the disciplinary that had been swept under the carpet. Not that he cared. He had been looking to get out completely, and had lost all his fight for the force. For now, at least, it was re-awakened.
He had his team out, knocking on doors, asking questions. He felt a little useless, not knowing enough, but with the amount of cocaine, and the uncut diamonds, he was bloody sure Giles wasn't as white as he made out, and it only reinforced Tommy Shelton was a bad apple.

Michelle played the doting wife. She went to the hospital. She sat by Tommy's bedside. She cried. She looked desperate and alone.
Inside she smiled. The doctors had told her, even if he survived, he would almost certainly never walk or even be able to function bodily without help. The crossbow bolt hadn't killed him. But it would leave him permanently paralysed. Perhaps permanently brain damaged.

Michelle couldn't have been happier. Much though she had wanted him dead, the thought of Tommy not being able to do anything about pretty much anything made her feel somehow powerful. She sat upright. Her chest swelled. She whispered in his ear. "It's my fucking turn."

Valerie played her part. She cried at the right time. She had no idea why or how this terrible thing had happened, and couldn't believe her husband was linked to anything illegal. He did so much for charity and the local community. Fine upstanding pillar of the community. And then the prize dig. 'Friends with the Chief Superintendent.' That should make the police feel a little uncomfortable.

Callum heard the news. He smiled. Bout time that fucking wanker Tommy got his just desserts. But Giles? He couldn't understand. What the hell did that silly old sod have to do with it all?
He couldn't care less. He had Sam. The baby. And a great future. His ribs were still painful. He smiled and winced. He wouldn't be going to work again today. As he pondered, the door knocked.
"Who is it?" he asked.
"Detective Sergeant Nicholson."
"Oh for fuck's sake!" Callum muttered. What the hell did he want?
"Hang on, I'm coming," he said slightly breathlessly.
He opened the door, as the DS showed his warrant card.
"Pretty sure I don't need to see that," Callum said with a smile.
"Nevertheless. I take it you have heard about Tommy Shelton and Giles Williams?"

"I have heard," Callum replied. "Tea, coffee?"
"Coffee please, can we have a chat?"
"Official?" Callum asked.
"Off the record for now," the Detective Sergeant said in a low tone.
"Sure," Callum said brightly. "Come through."
"How are you doing after the accident?"
"Not so bad. Ribs are bloody sore, and I'm gutted about my car, but I will live."
DS Nicholson smiled. "More than Giles Williams did, and Tommy Shelton isn't far behind."
"Couldn't happen to a nicer bloke!" Callum said the words angrily.
"Why do you say that?"
Callum froze. He couldn't say anything about his father's death. "I found him a car, the car went wrong, and he spoke to me like a piece of shit," he said. "So I made sure he wouldn't do it again."
"I see. And how did he take that?"
"I didn't particularly give a shit. To me he is nothing more than a small-time crook who had it coming."
"What makes you say that?"
"Oh come on!" Callum said sarcastically. "Everyone knew you could get a bit of gear in Spice. Even the bloody name is a drug!" And he laughed.
The policeman was less amused.
"So you think it could be drugs related?"
"No idea." Callum was suddenly defensive. "That's your job, isn't it?"

"It is indeed." Ken smiled. "But we all need a bit of help now and again. So why would anyone use a crossbow to kill Giles Williams and attempt to kill Tommy Shelton?"
Callum thought back to the old man, and the dog.
"Crossbow?" Callum smiled, "Christ! Who was he, Robin hood?" I have no idea about Giles," he said, "but there is probably a list as long as your arm for Tommy."
The detective finished his coffee.
"Don't breathe a word yet." He said in a soft quiet tone.
"A word about what?" Callum smiled.
"Good man, I'm glad we understand each other." Was the reply. And he left.
Callum smiled. So someone *had* been around deliberately to kill Tommy. But why Giles?

The DS was having just the same thoughts. How on earth was a seemingly 'perfect' individual, with a blemish free record, mixed up with a small time, or maybe not so small time, drug dealer?
After all, the amount of cocaine recovered at the scene wasn't enough to make anyone rich, but, after the forensics, it was almost pure. Totally unheard of in the club scene. So this was something else? Something exclusive? Uncut diamonds too. Definitely not your average merchandise. Whatever this was. It was somehow connected to the package that had been found with the bodies.

Tommy lay motionless. The drugs and painkillers numbing the outside world. His mind was restless, however. Despite the crossbow bolt entering his skull it had not penetrated fully. So whilst his brain had been damaged, and there was every chance he would never walk or even be able to function normally, his mind was very much alive.

Michelle kissed him on the cheek and left. The police presence outside the door remained. She smiled. Tommy would be hating every minute.

The Warren.

Giles' secret club, The Warren, remained firmly closed. Rosy had informed all of the guests of the tragic events, and until such times as everything had settled, the club would not be opening.
She continued to run the golf club, and answered all the police questions. Geoff and Eugene had been interviewed. And despite the misgivings from one of the team about the pair of them, especially Geoff who certainly had a cocaine habit, there seemed nothing untoward.
Detective Sergeant Nicholson and his team had, after almost a week, nothing. Tommy Shelton was a drug dealer. But no one had any ideas of the scale of his operations. As for Giles Williams. He seemed untouchable. No one had a bad word about him. Christ! Even the chief super was friends with him…
The clues surely lay with Tommy.
Ken did not believe anyone was perfect. Much less Giles Williams. There had to be something.
He decided to go back and see Valerie.
She greeted him with a cheerful hello. Too cheerful for a woman whose husband had just been murdered?
"I wonder, did your husband ever mention anything about diamonds?"
"No, never." For once telling the truth was easy. She knew nothing about the diamonds.
"What about any business associates Giles may have upset?"

"Oh, there have been plenty of those over the years. But I don't think anyone would want to kill Giles over it," she laughed.

"You seem remarkably cheerful for a woman whose husband has just been murdered Mrs Williams." The DS was not known for his subtlety.

"And how would you know what I am feeling?" Valerie snapped. "You may see my outward persona that way, and ask anyone, they will all tell you I am a cold-hearted cow." She drew breath.

"Am I going to miss him? Of course I am. Am I stricken with grief that he is dead? No, detective. I am not. Giles and my marriage was a sham. A good look to save face at the golf club. Or whatever function he needed me to be at. Did I want him dead? Good God! No! Do I want him back? No not really."

He sat expressionless.

"Did you have anything to do with your husband's death, Mrs Williams?"

"No, I didn't, nor did I see it coming. However, the deeper he got with Tommy Shelton the more I feared something bad might happen."

"Why do you say that?"

"Because Michelle and I are close detective. We talk. We have coffee. We spa. Tommy had a drug problem. It's no secret. And Michelle feared it was getting out of hand."

"I see. Anything else I need to know about your husband?"

"I don't think so," she said succinctly.

"Mind if I look around?"

"Don't you need a warrant to search my house?"

"I said look around."
"Be my guest, I will be watching you."
"I'm sure," came the reply. "Did Giles have an office?"
Over there. Valerie pointed. "His study, as he called it," and she laughed. "More like his porn den."
Ken opened the door and stepped inside. He left the door open.
Valerie kept a close eye.
He sifted through the papers on the desk. Nothing but invoices for building materials. Nothing out of the ordinary.
He sat in the chair behind the desk. There were three drawers either side of the desk. He pulled at the top right. It opened easily. Thumbing through the contents more invoices. Many of them mentioning The Warren by name.
The next drawer had general crap in it. Pens. A small hip flask. He opened it. Scotch. Nice. Smells decent, he thought. The third drawer won't open. Locked. He tried the drawers on the left. Same story. Top two had general bits and pieces. Bottom one locked.
"Don't suppose you have a key for these?"
"You suppose right, I don't. And if you want to break them open, you will need that warrant."
Ken smiled. This whole bloody village was sewn up tighter than a drum. Why the hell had this been allowed to happen?
"I will be back," he said softly. And left.
Valerie called Michelle. "The detective will be paying you a visit."
"How do you know?"

"Because he has just left here, and he has more questions now than before he came. I told him I'm not sad about Giles' death. Mistake perhaps. But it's true. You play it how you want. But he knows my marriage is… er was, a show," and she hung up and burst into tears. Angry spiteful tears.
"You fucking hit me you bastard. You got all you deserved." She banged her fist down hard.
Valerie was right. The policeman pulled up in the drive. Michelle saw him coming. She opened the door, it took him a little by surprise.
"Good afternoon," she said in a low rather sad tone. "Can I come in?"
"Sure. Coffee, a beer, something stronger?"

"Just a coffee is great, thanks."

"Come through."

He couldn't help noticing she wasn't wearing much. Ever since he had first met her he had thought she was attractive. Pull yourself together man, the voice in his head told him. This is why you had to leave London.

"Take a seat." Michelle offered.

He sat on the stool at the breakfast bar.
"Nice house, did drug money pay for it?"
"I have no idea," Michelle replied. "You're the detective you tell me."
"I understand you and Valerie Williams are very close."

"We enjoy each other's company. Is that a crime now?"
"Why is everyone in this bloody village so defensive? And why on earth do you think your husband ended up with a crossbow bolt in his head?"
"Probably because they couldn't find his heart." Michelle laughed.
"So you think it's funny too do you? Valerie Williams laughed and was in a good mood despite the fact her husband is dead."
"I wouldn't be too sorry if Tommy was dead too."
"And why is that Mrs Shelton?"
"Because he had become a monster, if you want the truth, I have no idea where the money came from. I know that the club was doing very well but I also know that my husband had, over the years, become a completely different individual to the person I met and fell in love with."
"Valerie Williams tells me Tommy had a cocaine habit?"
"He definitely had a cocaine habit. And he was getting worse. He also had a propensity for the girls at the club but I suppose she didn't tell you that. My marriage was a joke. Tommy had got to the point where he would even hit me on occasions."
"Why did you never report it to the police?"
"Because officer, if the wrath of Tommy wasn't bad enough, drink or drug fuelled, Can you imagine how he would have reacted to the police? I think if I had done that it would probably be me that was dead."
"Did you attempt to kill your husband or were you involved, Mrs Shelton?"

"No, I did not attempt to kill my husband nor was I involved. If I had been he would be dead now."
The DS looked up, a little surprised at the reply.
"Do you know anything about diamonds?"
"No, I don't know anything about diamonds."
"Do you mind if I have a look around?"
Michelle smiled "I was going to say do you need a warrant for that but I would assume you've already had that speech with Valerie, so, if this is official then you need a warrant."
"It's off the record for now."
"Then be my guest, if you want to start with Tommy's den. It's over there, go through the living room and to the door on the left."
"I think that's the perfect place to start, don't you?"
"Don't ask me what went on in there, I have absolutely no desire to know. However, I will be watching you."
"Funny, I had exactly the same speech not too long ago."
"And did you find anything?"
"I found two locked drawers in a desk, and I will be going back with a warrant."
Once again there was a desk, only this time there were only three drawers, none of them locked, all of them containing bottles of rum. Some, it seemed might have been exclusive, but in reality the policeman knew nothing about rum, but the bottles looked expensive. He couldn't find too much of interest.
After a brief poke around, he bid Michelle farewell and gave her his card.
"If you need anything, he said, give me a call."

"I am sure I can give you a call, but I'm not entirely sure it will be anything that you could give me even though I might need it," she laughed.

Ken didn't quite know what to do or say. He felt his cheeks go red.

"And just for the record, no, I don't have anything on under here, perhaps next time you shouldn't make it quite so obvious."

He said goodbye and left. All the way back to the station all he could think about was how could he have been so stupid.

All Michelle could think about was he was quite attractive, and she knew that he found her attractive. Perhaps she could use this to her advantage, especially with the new found strength that she had been given. Despite the fact that Tommy hadn't died, Michelle felt she could take on the world.

She telephoned Valerie. "I think the copper likes my ass," she laughed.

"Then you make sure you use that ass to your advantage. In fact to our advantage."

"Did he find anything?" Michelle asked.

"He found two drawers that were locked. He is coming back with a warrant. The truth is Michelle I have no idea what they're going to find. At the moment everything is hanging on Tommy and drugs, and from what I understand, there was a big quantity of cocaine found at the scene, and they are pinning all of that on Tommy. They definitely know he was dealing, and they certainly know he was taking, but I keep being asked about diamonds?"

"I have been asked about diamonds too, but I have no idea about diamonds."

"Neither do I, but they must be connected somehow."

Crossbow Charlie.

For the first time Eugene, Geoff and Harvey met at the golf club. United in their grief for their respective employers but also each one of them eager to find out exactly what had happened. None of them could believe that there was complete silence, and nobody knew who had done this.
All they knew was this was a professional hit. Ultimately, they believed that Tommy was supposed to be dead as well, and it was more by that useless piece of shit's good luck that he was still alive.
Albeit he would probably never be the man he was.
"Who the fuck uses a crossbow?" Harvey said.
"I have been asking myself the same thing over and over, why would you use a crossbow? Why not use a gun it's cleaner quicker and would probably have killed Tommy Shelton." Eugene replied.
Geoff chimed in with his own thoughts. "Silence," was the only word he said.
The other two looked at him, puzzled.
"What the fuck are you talking about?" Harvey said.
"Silence," he said again
"We heard you the first time, dickhead, what are you talking about?"
"He used a crossbow because he didn't want to make any sound."
"It was in the middle of fucking nowhere, who gives a shit about what sound you were going to make?"

"I don't know the fucking answer to that do I. All I know is there is no logical reason otherwise." Neither Eugene nor Harvey could come up with an argument to that, however, the point stood, if you were in the middle of nowhere in the middle of the night, why on earth would you want to be quiet?

"The police have a warrant, they are coming to search the club top to bottom." Harvey said. "So I guess I will be out of a job fairly soon. One thing Tommy did was never be particularly tidy. I'm sure they will find shit everywhere and shut the place down."

"Bad luck man," Eugene said. "It would appear that Giles is as squeaky clean as his image and so far nobody has found anything other than the fact that he got mixed up with the wrong man. Your boss."

And he laughed.

"Not especially a laughing matter," Harvey said. "I still have a kid to support."

"And I need to find out what bastard did this. If there is someone on our patch and yes, I do mean our patch, that wanted rid of Tommy and Giles badly enough, they could be out for us next."

Both Eugene and Geoff nodded at the prospect.

"So how do we find them? The police are already looking."

"The police don't know the Underworld like we do. But we do have to be very careful."

"That new DS is not stupid, I am very wary of him."

"Where the fuck has he come from?"

"London apparently, has been brought in to clean up the drug problems in the local rural areas."

"Crossbow fucking Charlie did that for him all by himself," Geoff laughed, and all three men nodded in agreement.

Rosy brought over three more drinks whilst Gigi fluttered her eyelashes and looked at Geoff. He went red with embarrassment.

"I think she likes you," Harvey smiled.

"I think you could be right," Geoff answered, "and maybe when the time is right, I will have a piece of that young filly"

"You sound more and more like bloody Giles every day." Eugene said. "So, what's the plan?"

"The plan is to fuck her over the desk once this place has closed."

"No, you prick," Eugene rolled his eyes, "for crossbow Charlie."

"Oh!" Geoff laughed. "Well you can't have much of a plan for a ghost, can you? How the fuck do we plan something we know nothing about?"

Harvey chimed in, "We know he used a crossbow."

"But we don't know why do we?"

Harvey looked toward the floor. Then looked up. "Well, I don't hear any better suggestions!" He said angrily.

"Calm down boys," Geoff said in a low voice. "We don't know anything. But we do have contacts. We do have our ears to the ground. So, for now, let's just keep it that way. Low key. Do some digging. And keep that fucking copper at arm's length. Agreed?"

"Agreed."

Marco emptied his glass. He sat looking around his restaurant. Stephanie was in the back, doing the last of the clearing away. He picked up his phone. Sent Anesh a message. "All seems calm my brother."

Anesh replied almost instantly. "Give it time," was the simple message.
Marco smiled. He was always more impatient than Anesh. He wanted it all. Now! And he had a sudden realisation he wanted Valerie. No real idea why. But he liked her. Never mind the sex. She excited him. Her mind. Her strength. Her vision. And, if he was honest, the balls to want her husband dead. Marco had never had a serious relationship. He had always enjoyed the ladies. And probably always would. But, as he sat alone, he realised that she was the first woman he actually could see sitting here with him. He couldn't guarantee he would be totally faithful to her, but he at least liked the idea of having her around. He sent a message back to Anesh.
"When everything settles, I want Valerie."
His phone rang.
"What the fuck?" Were the first words that greeted Marco.
"I want Valerie," he said again. "I am ready to have a person in my life."
Anesh laughed. "And what do you propose to do with your cock? Just devote it to one woman too?"
And he laughed again.
"Well," Marco began.
Anesh stopped him.
"You see, there is no way you could be faithful to a woman."

"Perhaps not my brother. But, if she knew that, and could accept that I would try, then there may be a chance?"
"Shit! Marco, it sounds like you actually mean it."
"I do my brother," Marco spoke softly in his deep bass voice, "I do."

Bollocks! Valerie said under her breath. She looked at her phone. The doorbell camera showed that bloody DS Nicholson.
"How can I help you?" She smiled sweetly as she opened the door.
"You know that warrant?" He paused for effect and rummaged in his pocket. "Surprise!" He smiled holding up a piece of paper. "So let's see what's in those drawers shall we?"
And he marched inside.
Valerie was decidedly unimpressed by this. "Who the hell do you think you are?"
"I'm the man tasked with finding your husband's killer Mrs Williams. Now if you don't mind, I'd like to do my job." And he headed for the study.
Reaching the desk. He double checked. The bottom drawers were indeed locked.
The truth was, Valerie had no idea what was in those drawers. But her gut told her, if Giles kept them locked, it was either illegal, immoral, or both. She gulped.
"Coffee?" she asked as nonchalantly as she could.
"Please," he replied. As he did so the small bunch of keys he had had for years worked their magic. No idea how sometimes, but the locks proved far too easy to pick on the desk. Opening the left-hand drawer revealed two

small diaries. He took them out and opened the black one. Lists and lists of names. Next to them, either amounts or objects, bottles of whisky, champagne. As he scanned through, he found 'Oscar the chief super = 20 year malt (at the very least the lucky devil!)'.
He quickly slammed the book shut. His mind already didn't like how close his superior officer was to Giles. This just made the whole thing a hell of a lot worse.
He opened the right-hand drawer. A laptop and a charger. And that was it.
Valerie arrived, "Here you go," she said, very matter of factly. "What have you found?"
"Oh, nothing too interesting. A diary and a laptop."
Valerie felt her shoulders fall.
She only hoped Ken didn't spot it.
"Oh!" Was all that would come out of her mouth.
"So I shall be taking them to forensics."
"Of course."
"Did you have anything to do with your husband's death?"
"I have already told you I didn't."
"You have Mrs Williams. But your body language is telling me you are hiding something. And if I open that laptop and find you are lying, I will throw the bloody book at you for wasting my time."
Valerie looked at him. Angry. She had let her guard down.
"Is that a threat?" She spat the question.
"No," he paused, "it's a promise," and he smiled. He had her rattled. He quite liked that.
"Giles liked young girls." She blurted. "I don't know how young he never told me."

"I see. And you never thought to bring this to the police?"
"BRING WHAT?!" She exploded. "That I caught him fucking his 20-year-old secretary? Yeah I really wanted to announce that." And she turned on the tears.
"20 is not an offence," he replied blankly.
"No shit Sherlock!" Valerie's hackles were up now. "But I know he always liked the idea of teenagers. I heard him talking more than once at parties about 'that fine young filly' and I just never quite trusted him. I never had any proof nor did I look for it. But I knew it could happen. I don't think it ever did. But it could have."
"Thank you Mrs Williams, I will give you a receipt for the items I have taken."
"You can keep the fucking things for all I care. See yourself out," and she left the room.
The sergeant did as she had asked. She watched him look back at the house and shake his head. The laptop under his arm. He got into the car and left.
Valerie was fuming. This could ruin everything. She had no idea what Giles was hiding on that bloody laptop.
  The detective got back to the station and went straight to his office. Put the laptop down in front of him. He was useless with technology. Forensics would have to crack that. But he could read. The black diary was clearly a list of payoffs, gifts, and keeping people quiet. The chief fucking super! Christ! What was he going to do with that?
The red diary is less easy to fathom. In bold black letters "The Warren" on the front. Inside lists of

materials. So clearly a building. But where? No mention. Fine wines. The best booze. But nothing else.

At the back of the diary a list of people. Minor celebs. Local mostly. And there, in black and white, 'OSCAR OLD CHAP'.

Ken was speechless. Whatever The Warren was. He needed to find out. And find out just how deep his chief superintendent and Giles Williams were with each other. For now he couldn't share this information with the team. Not yet. He needed to be sure.

He dialled the Forensics lab. "Great," he said breezily. "I will bring it right down," and he got up to leave.

As he shut the door the chief superintendent was coming towards him. "Any developments?" He said.

"Nothing concrete Sir," Ken lied.

"Well keep me informed there's a good chap."

"Oh, I will Sir. I bloody well will," he muttered, out of earshot to his boss. As he went down the stairs his mind just kept saying... he doesn't have a clue, I can't fucking believe he has no idea.

Annie.

He placed the laptop on the counter, and was greeted by a petite, attractive dark-haired woman.
"Where is Jack?"
"Oh, he has had to take some urgent family leave," she replied. "Hi I'm Annie."
"Well, you are definitely easier on the eye than Jack!" He laughed. "Can I leave this with you? I could do with any results on the quick really."
"Important is it?" She smiled.
"As important as murder and attempted murder can be I suppose," he said a little sarcastically.
"Shit!" Annie gasped. "Tomorrow morning OK?"
"Blimey! You are confident."
"Always!" She looked at the DS and winked.
"See you tomorrow," he waved, and walked away feeling chirpy. She was hot, and he definitely didn't mind seeing her instead of Jack!
Little did Ken know that Annie was a computer geek. Tech was her thing. She loved forensics, but the computer side of things would always be her first port of call. She loved nothing more than defeating passwords, knocking down any barriers that were in her way, and especially loved accessing deleted files. She smiled a wicked smile as she opened the laptop and turned it on.
    The next morning it dawned bright and clear. Completely the opposite of Ken's mood.

His mind was even more confused at the current case. He only hoped that perhaps the laptop held the key. He didn't have to wait too long as he swung into the yard at HQ and made his way to his office.

There were not too many people around, but I suppose at 6:00 am there wouldn't be.

Annie was already at his desk.

"You are a sight for sore eyes," he smiled "Especially at this time of the morning, what do you have to tell me?"

"Oh, I have an awful lot to tell you!" She said excitedly. "Why don't you go and get a coffee and we can have a chat?"

Ken didn't need asking twice, he would definitely need a coffee before his day started. He came back with two steaming mugs of coffee.

"Okay Annie, so what do you have for me?"

"I have a very elaborate computer system for you."

The sergeant looked to the skies. He was the world's worst when it came to tech.

"Is this going to be all computer geek speak?"

"No, I will keep it simple for you old ones," she laughed.

"Cheeky cow!" He said tongue-in cheek.

She opened the laptop, and started to explain. "The password was actually very simple. It didn't take much. It was just his wife's name. I had to juggle it around a little bit. There was a combination of letters and numbers, but it was nothing too difficult. The difficulty comes once you get inside," and she grinned. Every file that's in here is encrypted in some way. I don't know who did it but if it was Giles he was much smarter than everybody gave him credit for. Anyway, it took me most of the night but I've managed to resolve it."

"Most of the night?"

"Yes," she stopped and went red in the face. "Computers are my thing, and once you told me what the case was, I couldn't stop myself."

"So? What did you find?"

"Basically, I found Giles's pornography. He likes young girls. Very young girls! Nothing too bad we're not talking eight nine ten year olds here, but we are talking fifteen or sixteen. And nothing too bad sexually. Vanilla you might say."

Ken saw what she meant. But, in the eyes of the law, that could make Giles a paedophile.

"To be honest I know in the overall scheme of things it's all bad but I'm not talking here about some sex pest pervert predator. I think he was just a sad old bastard who liked looking at young girls."

"How did you find all this?"

"He accessed most of it through the dark web."

Ken had heard of it but knew very little about it.

"All of the sites are encrypted so there's no way to trace them, well you could, but you'd spend days. Anyway, he has folders and folders of pictures and videos of young girls. Clearly that's what got him off."

"His wife told me he liked young girls, but she had no idea how young."

"I haven't opened every folder yet as there are still some which are even too encrypted for my amazing brain," she grinned and laughed.

"So when do you think you will get those un-encrypted with your amazing brain?"

"I should have the answers by the end of the day." And she jumped off the desk and made her way back to the lab.

Ken sent out an email. It was barely 6:30 am. He sent an email to all of his team. "Briefing at 7:30, Giles Williams is not so white after all."

He sank his coffee and made his way to get another. With the news he had just had, depending on who else knew in Giles circle of friends and what Giles may have done, somebody could very easily have wanted him dead. Including his own wife. He kept coming back to Valerie. She was too cool, too calm. She was involved, he was convinced.

7:30 duly came around and all of the small team were in one office.

"I have some breaking developments, but I don't want them to go outside of this team just yet. I fear it may go deeper than we imagine and until I have all the facts, I'm not prepared to go public with anything."

He relayed the story of what Annie, a sexy techy girl (he couldn't believe he had just said that in his own mind), had found out. Giles could be, in the eyes of the law, a paedophile. Though he had to conclude there had never been an allegation made against him by anyone and his record was absolutely pristine. However, videos of (potentially) underage girls giving blow jobs to older men definitely made him very twisted indeed. Who knows what else he was capable of?

The team took the information on board.

"I now need you to delve very carefully into anything which may have given anyone a suspicion. If this village can keep its mouth shut about everything else, I'm sure it can keep its mouth shut about a pillar of the community that plays golf with the chief super, who's actually a paedophile."

He decided he may have to go and speak to Valerie again but first, he would see just how much Michelle knew about Giles and his liking for young girls. He dialled her phone number.

Michelle answered swiftly and took him slightly by surprise. Her voice sounded ever so slightly low as I suppose it would if your husband had almost been killed by a crossbow. His mind switched. Why a fucking crossbow? He could not understand.

"I wonder if I could come over?" He said sharply, flicking his mind back into his duties.

"Of course," she replied, "do you have any developments?"

"You could say that," he said abruptly "I just need your help with something."

"Okay. I'm not going anywhere you're welcome anytime."

As the DS got in his car, he paused for thought. There was something about this woman he liked. But he couldn't go through what had happened in London again.

Besides, for now the case was more important. It would seem he had opened a can of worms that certainly needed delving into. And oddly right now, whilst Tommy Shelton was undoubtedly guilty of drugs and other offences, Giles Williams was just as much of a suspect. Even if he was dead.

Giles liked young girls.

He rang the bell at Michelle's house. The door flew open very quickly and she beckoned him in.
"Do you want something to drink?"
"No thanks, it's just a quick chat. I just really need to know how well you knew Giles Williams."
"I knew him as the loud: brash, in your face, people loving, warm-hearted, overweight, golf playing guy that everybody thought he was."
Did you know him as a paedophile?"
Michelle stood, shell shocked.
"Valerie had told me he liked young girls, especially that new one at the club, Gina or whatever her name was, but no I had no idea he had any interest in children. That's disgusting. In fact the truth is Giles loved children."
"Even though they didn't have any of their own?"
"Valerie never wanted children. She isn't the maternal type, Giles was always gutted about it. I knew that, but he enjoyed being around the kids and I never saw anything untoward and that didn't matter whether it was a boy, a girl or anything. I can only say what I saw, and what I saw was Giles enjoying the kids being kids. Every time his attention was anything more than that it was towards eighteen, nineteen, twenty-year-old barmaids that sort of thing. There was never anything inappropriate."
"So you have no idea how dozens of images of young girls happen to be on a laptop we found in Giles desk drawer?"

"I have no idea at all. I'm not going to tell you again, I never thought anything untoward. Are you sure all the girls there are underage?"

"We are still continuing with our enquiries, but I think it would appear that some of them at least are, yes."

"Then I'm afraid I can't help you," Michelle said bluntly.

"And how are you doing in yourself? Do you have any more ideas on who may have done this to your husband?"

"We have had this discussion once before. I could give you a list as long as your arm about people that hate Tommy, but whether anybody would actually have the balls to do this to him, I couldn't think of one."

"Fair enough Mrs Shelton, I believe that's all for now. I appreciate your help with this matter. I would prefer you didn't discuss it with anybody at present, as we are still making enquiries."

"So what you mean is, don't tell Valerie."

Ken smiled. "No, you don't have to do that, I can do that all by myself. But let's just leave it there shall we?"

Michelle warmed to his smile. She could see deep down he wanted justice and was only doing his job. She enjoyed his warm face, his dark eyes and the way he always admired her whenever he turned up.

Pathetic perhaps and maybe even a hangover from the websites, always wanting to know she was the best. It became rather childish but was something she couldn't really prevent.

"I will see myself out," and he stood up and left.

Making his way immediately to Valerie Williams house. He waited at the gates but there was no answer. "Bollocks!" He exclaimed, and was just about to pull away when he saw the Mercedes in his rear-view mirror. He got out of the car.

Valerie wound down her window.

"To what do I owe this pleasure?" she said agonisingly.

"You and I need to have a chat, Mrs Williams. It's about your husband's laptop."

Her heart sank.

"Well, if you get that bloody thing out the way I will open the gates!" She snapped, clicking the remote as she did so.

He duly did as he was told and reversed his car out of the way. Following Valerie into the drive. He parked on the drive as the gates closed behind them. Once again it was the same line of questions and indeed the same line of answers that Ken got back.

"Yes, Giles like younger girls sometimes even into their teens but generally it was the early 20's that made him horny and got him off and gave him what he needed."

Valerie had no idea at all that children were ever involved and the only thing she had ever seen was Giles genuinely enjoying their company and often passing on to her that he wished he had some of his own. When he left, he was pretty much certain that neither of them were lying. So even if Giles had accessed underage porn, it was clear that neither of the women knew anything about it, so the chances are Tommy Shelton didn't either. Also, whilst Giles had almost certainly broken the law it didn't seem much of a reason to get him killed.

Was it just the wrong place at the wrong time?

Should he not have been with Tommy?

Right now, Ken couldn't come to another logical conclusion however he would keep his investigation open and keep his mind open until he had more evidence. As he got back in the car his phone rang.

An excited voice on the end said, "Hello, it's Annie!"

Charlie Summers death.

"Annie," he beamed, "to what do I owe this pleasure?"
"My crazy little brain has been working very hard, and I have accessed pretty much every single file that is encrypted or hidden on this laptop."
"And don't tell me, let me guess. You have something very interesting to show me!"
"I have something very interesting to show you. It isn't pleasant but it's interesting."
"I am on my way back to HQ now. I will see you shortly and you can show me everything you need to."
He grinned and hung the phone up. Deciding to make the journey back to the station a little more exciting and also to get there much quicker, blues and twos were the order of the day.
He made it back to the station in less than twenty minutes.
Making his way straight to his office, he marched through the station as if he owned it. One or two people tried to catch him. He simply put his hand up and said, "later."
When he got back to his desk he buzzed down to the lab. Annie answered the phone quickly.
"You best come up young lady."
She ignored the sexist remark. She had done a bit of delving into Ken Nicholson, and it would seem he was a bit

of a maverick and a bit of a rogue. Most of his superior officers didn't like him much but they certainly liked the results he got. Even if sometimes his methods were not always by the book.

"I am on my way! Make sure the office door is locked!"

"Now that's not something I hear every day, "but don't worry, I will make sure we are not disturbed. This had all better be worth it though."

"Believe me Sir, I am pretty sure it's worth it."

A few minutes later she knocked on the door complete with laptop and charger. She had a beaming smile on her face, almost conveying to the officer how proud she was of what she had found. She set the laptop down on the table.

"I will go and grab a couple of coffees," he said.

"White two sugars please."

"Coming right up!" He disappeared out of the office and into the corridor. The coffee machine dished out shit coffee but it was better than nothing today, and he certainly needed some. When he returned Annie was sitting with the laptop facing her and another chair close together.

He smiled, "Get a grip on yourself." He told himself, she's probably only in her twenties. As he said the words, he suddenly had visions of Giles. Perhaps he had underestimated this man and there really wasn't anything sinister. Perhaps it wasn't child porn, it was just the fact that they were young.

Annie patted the chair next to her.

"Come sit, I still haven't opened every file there are dozens of them. But they are all titled."

He looked down at the screen as he sat down and he could see the excitement on Annie's face.
"How long have you've been working on this?"
"Oh, pretty much all night again."
He looked at her.
"Are you mad?"
"No, Sir I'm not mad, I just love doing this, and when the mood takes me I won't stop until I have all the answers. Everybody thinks they can delete things and they will disappear. But nothing really deletes unless you know how to. Though I have to admit they were very well hidden. For his age Giles was a computer genius."
"He wasn't that much of a genius. You found it all."
"Believe me Sir, if he had lent this laptop to anybody, nobody would have found it. He was a very clever man and certainly wanted to keep his secrets secret."
She clicked on the first file. There were several titled 'W' practice, and then a number.
The video opened. There was Giles in his office. Almost immediately the door opened and Rosy walked in.
"I know her," said Ken. "She's the bar manager at the golf club."
Annie laughed. Ken looked at her.
"What's so funny?" he asked inquisitively.
"Wait till you see what she does with his club!" she laughed.
"Oh my God!" Ken said depressingly. "Do I really have to sit through that?"
Annie clicked on the forward button. You could clearly see Rosy open Giles' fly, take out his cock and slowly proceed to give him a blowjob.

"Who in their right mind would want to go down on Giles Williams?" Ken said out loud. As he said it the door opened, and Gigi walked in. Looking shocked she said, "Oh my goodness I will leave."
At which point, through the crystal-clear audio, Rosy turns around and says,
"No it's your turn to practice. You must remember our clients will only want the best."
She beckons the younger woman over, who proceeds to get on her knees and take Giles' cock in her mouth. You then see, and hear, Rosy instructing her on exactly what to do with it in order to bring the old man to orgasm. In fairness she does everything she's told expertly, and it isn't long before Giles relieves himself.
The DS watches and isn't quite sure whether to be disgusted or admire the two women for their clear expertise.
At the end of the clip, which isn't very long, Rosy stands up and says to Giles, "I'm sure she will be perfect."
Giles winks and says, "I am sure you will, my dear," as Gigi stands up, wipes her mouth and leaves.
Ken sits back in his chair, takes a sip of the coffee and suddenly realises he has a hard on.
The hard on which Annie clearly notices.
"Enjoy that, did we Sir?" She looked down and laughs.
"It's been a while I have to confess," he laughs. His face turned bright red.
"What on earth do you think they were talking about? She will be perfect, and his clients will only want the best?"

"I've got no idea. After all, you are the DS remember."
Ken smiled, this girl was bright, very bright indeed, she would go far, and certainly go a long way to helping his investigation.

"So tell me what else you've got for me."

"There is a folder titled Charlie."

Who the bloody hell was Charlie? Ken couldn't quite place the relevance. He clicked on the icon the screen sprang into life. The film was in Giles' office and quite clearly every single person that had been filmed had no idea they were. Giles sat behind his desk, a huge cigar in his hand and a glass of something, clearly a spirit of some sort, amber coloured and in immaculate crystal glass. Opposite him sat Tommy Shelton, with an equally fat cigar and also a glass of spirit though definitely not the same as Giles, a completely different colour.

The audio was as crystal clear as ever. In fact, Ken couldn't quite believe that the sound quality was so good. Giles began by saying to Tommy, "I told you I wanted nothing to do with it, just you make sure that nothing can come back to me."

Tommy bellowed, "What about me?"

And Giles replying, "You took it upon yourself to have the man disposed of."

Tommy replied "He was fucking my wife."

Giles laughed. "And you weren't fucking anything that moves."

Tommy stood up. The footage crystal clear. He raised his fist.

"Who the fuck are you talking to."

"I'm talking to the man that could have jeopardised our operation. Who gives a fuck if your wife was screwing the local mechanic, or the fucking band of the grenadier guards? You could have kept quiet, you could have let it go, you could have told her that you knew and made her behave."

"What, you mean like you make Valerie behave?"

"That's completely different and you know it. Valerie and I have an arrangement. As long as neither of us announced it then we were quite happy to exist as we are."

Tommy exploded. "I don't know who you think you are. First of all you're not gonna tell me what I can and can't do with my wife, and second of all I got rid of the fucking problem. Charlie Summer is no longer in my way, and there is nobody who can find any fucking evidence to say we did it."

Giles stopped him quickly. "I didn't do anything dear boy, you took all of those actions on by yourself."

"Well old man, you just make sure that the fucking chief superintendent doesn't look too hard hey, go and play an extra round of golf with him and keep him sweet."

"Get out of my office until you have something sensible to say." Giles boomed.

Tommy downed the last of his spirit. He smashed the glass on the desk and said to Giles, "You don't fucking own me old man, just remember that we are partners, our merchandise and our clubs need each other so get fucking used to it."

He walked out of the office as soon as he had left the footage ended.

Ken sat in complete silence. He looked at Annie.
"What the fuck do I do with this?"
She smiled serenely at him.
"I have no idea Sir."
The video provided conclusive proof that Tommy Shelton had Charlie Summer killed. The question was, who knew it other than Giles and Tommy himself.
If either of the women did, that was sure as hell a motive for murder. Never mind the fact that it would appear that Tommy's wife had been sleeping with Charlie Summer. Just for a brief moment in his head, Ken smiled, lucky bastard he thought to himself.
"Is there anything else that is significant?" he looked at Annie.
"To be honest Sir, other than some more practice blow jobs not a lot. There are a few more meetings though no more mention of Charlie Summer."
"You didn't find anything mentioning a place called The Warren?"
"I didn't. Though I guess it's reasonable to assume all the videos with 'W' could relate to it? I have been through almost every file now and as I say, I can find drug references and it's pretty clear that Giles and Tommy were the brains behind all of it. I would guess if I was a detective that Tommy was the main man behind the drugs. I don't know what contacts he would have had. And my guess is that his club Spice, ironically named, after one of the most awful drugs there is out there, was the outlet for the drugs and provided the cover. My other guess is that Giles and Tommy got along because

Tommy's club provided all the young girls Giles needed. But the truth is that's all supposition and guesswork Sir." Ken looked at Annie. "You would make a bloody good detective. How do you fancy a drink tonight after work."
Annie blushed. "I'm not used to being asked out, Sir."
"Well you are now, so if you fancy that drink, maybe we can meet in the Red Lion, let's say seven pm shall we?"
Annie blushed again, "Yes Sir."
"My name is Ken. Maybe Sir in here, but I do not expect you to call me sir when we get to the pub. First round is definitely on me. You are a clever girl, keep looking, go over it again. I want to know that we haven't missed anything."
Annie stepped out of the office feeling very good. Ken watched her go. He was not entirely sure taking her to the pub was a wise move, but right now he needed some way of saying thank you.
Despite the fact it was her job, it would seem that she had gone above and beyond.
What he now needed to do was figure out just what all of this implied. He looked at the clock. It was close to five pm and he decided to simply send an email to the team. After all, nobody really got on with him, they had been thrown together as the local police station would not have been able to cope. He also needed to work out what on earth he was going to tell the chief superintendent. One way or another Oscar's beloved golfing buddy had been in it up to his neck, before he pretty much lost his neck.
Wearily, and with a heavy head he stood up and collected his coat. Although he had enjoyed the action of London

he had never ever imagined a sleepy little place like this would provide even more of it, and the truth was he wasn't entirely sure he liked it. He had ulterior motives for the invitation to the Red Lion. But they were no more difficult to work out than he lived in one of the rooms above it.

He drove slowly home, his mind working overtime. He parked the car, went inside and decided a hot bath was the order of today. As he walked through the bar he looked up.

"Evening Ray," he smiled.

"Evening Detective Sergeant," Ray the landlord returned. The rest of the bar went slightly quiet. Ken didn't mind that, it was always good to make sure that everybody knew he was a copper. Much less chance of them stepping out of line.

"Are you still doing food?"

"Yes, usual tonight, till nine o'clock."

"That's good, I have a guest coming at seven pm. I will be down in an hour or so." And he trudged up the stairs.

Annie had whizzed home in her little car. Her stomach full of butterflies. Being the geek she was, she hadn't actually been out with too many men. And certainly, never a detective sergeant!

She guessed his age was mid 40s. That was okay, she was pretty sure he thought she was younger than she was. She was 32, but she had looked after herself. With white China skin and dark hair and dark eyes, she was a very pretty girl but quite shy and introvert.

Her love for all things investigative had definitely held her back at times with her social side.

She dressed plain and simple. Jeans, boots, and a blouse. The taxi arrived at 6:30 just as she booked it. She got into the back and made her way to the Red lion.
Ken was already at the bar, halfway through a pint when he saw her come in. She smiled a broad white straight teeth smile. She was indeed very attractive, he thought.
"What can I get my star techy geek?" he laughed.
"Just for that cheeky remark, I will have a large sauvignon please."
"A large sauvignon Ray, put it on my tab would you?"
He looked at Annie. "Now, this is a social evening really, for me to get to know you and to appreciate your efforts with that bloody laptop."
"I was just doing my job Sir."
"If you call me sir once more, I will send you home now."
"Sorry Ken," she said meekly, "but it's true I was just doing my job."
"I know you were, but you are doing exceedingly well. Anybody who has a passion for something I respect, and anybody who's good at their job I also respect, so you tick both of those boxes. Now I said this is a social evening, so let's have a drink, something to eat and chat about, I don't know the weather, anything but bloody work."
Inevitably there were questions thrown in over the meal. Ken bluntly asked Annie, "Do you think after what you have heard on that video that's motive enough for murder?"
"I think a bag of chips can be enough for murder Sir, sorry Ken, it just depends what drives you. But if you are asking me that if I found out my husband had killed my

lover then most definitely it would be grounds for murder."

Ken smiled, he agreed entirely, proving however, that Michelle knew her husband had murdered her lover would be far more difficult.

The evening flew by. Though she was around twelve years his junior, it seemed they had a lot in common and got on really well.

"Last orders!" Ray shouted as he rang the bell.

Ken looked at Annie. She was slightly tipsy now.

Three large glasses of white wine had definitely gone to her head. However, she also had not felt so relaxed for a long time. Her last boyfriend had not been particularly good to her. Though she had liked him, he was just a bit ordinary. Plain. Nice enough. But perhaps too nice. She needed a little bit of rough she thought. Something or someone with an edge. What that edge was, she had no idea.

Ken looked at her. A glint in his eye.

"Fancy a nightcap?"

"Yes!" She squealed.

Ken got up and walked to the door leading to the upstairs. He smiled as he looked back. Beckoning Annie, he smiled at Ray.

"Goodnight Ray," he said.

"Looks like it," laughed the landlord.

They climbed the wide staircase together and reached his door.

As soon as he opened the door, she literally forced herself onto him. The 'movie moment' kiss. Hard. Against

the wall. She fumbles with the buttons on his shirt as he pulls her blouse out of her jeans.
His hands eventually can't wait. He rips at her blouse. the buttons fly everywhere. She gasps... her breasts exposed. The bra is lacy, sexy. He bites her neck, and his hand undoes her bra strap. She squeals, as his mouth encircles her nipple. Biting, gently at first. He feels it stiffen and his left hand massages her other breast. He pushes her back. Gasping, she falls onto the bed.
Ken took off his shirt and unzipped his trousers. As his cock was released, she sat up.
The tip close to her mouth. He looked down as she looked up. Their eyes met and she lowered her head and softly took his rock-hard cock between her lips. He shuddered slightly and held her head gently. As she went deeper, he raised his head and moaned softly. Deeper still she took him. The tip hit her throat. She didn't gag. Cupping his balls, she took his whole length.
Ken shuddered again. Softly he muttered, "amazing."
She pulled him out of her mouth. His hard cock covered in saliva. She wanked him slowly. He smiled and pushed her back. She laughed as she fell, and he knelt between her legs.
"Get naked," he commanded as he opened her button on her jeans. She lifted her arse up. As he pulled at her jeans, they were tight enough to drag her thong with them. Suddenly she felt embarrassed. Covering her smooth pussy with her hand.
Ken stood up. His cock still wet. He removed his trousers. Slight beer belly, but she didn't care, her eyes were greedily on his cock.

She reached out and he pushed her back.
"No, I'm gonna eat you to orgasm," and he pushed her back. She lay down and parted her legs. Her pussy lips glistened. Wet. Expectant. He knelt, admiring her wet clit. Softly kissing her thighs. Licking. biting. Hot breath closer now. The tip of his tongue expertly ran along her lips. Brushing her clit so softly and unexpectedly she moaned.
"Oh fuck, yes!"
Grabbing his hair. Her mind no longer able to hold back. "Eat me!" she demanded. And pulled at his hair, pushing his head onto her pussy. "Bite me, lick me, fuck me!" She shouted.
Ken let his tongue press hard against her clitoris. Her body shook. She squirted hard. It caught him by surprise.
"Fuck!" She screamed.
Ken smiled. "And I thought it had been a while for me." He said to himself.
Knowing he was now in total control he stood up. Walked around the side of the bed.
Annie looked disappointed. Her breath was short.
He knelt on the bed. His cock next to her mouth. "Suck it," he said. She did as she was told. As he slipped into her mouth, he pushed two fingers inside her. She squirted again, and his cock was taken into her throat. He pushed it, hard. She gagged. And a third finger entered her.
Annie exploded. Her pussy drenched his fingers as they fucked her. She choked on his cock. Her head spun. She lost herself totally in the orgasm. It was simply massive

and something she had never experienced. Her body shook. She spat out his cock, and momentarily lost herself completely.

Her breath came in short gasps. Ken didn't quite know what to do for a moment. The juices covering his fingers, her legs, and the bed. He smiled as she came back down. "WOW!" She said smiling. "So, are you going to fuck me or not?"

Ken grinned. His cock rock hard. He hadn't been like this for a long time. Annie's young body turned him on. Her perfect skin, white, smooth. He touched her sensually. His mind racing. Wanting this to last. He loved being in control. But he knew he wanted to come also.

"Stand up," he said. Soft, yet a firm command. Annie did as he asked. He admired her body. Kissed her mouth. His tongue teased across her lips.

He sat on the bed. Annie touched his cock. It twitched. She knelt.

"No," he said. "I'm not going to fuck you."

Annie looked gobsmacked. Before she could say anything, he answered, "You are going to fuck me," and lay back. He moved up the bed. His hard cock magnificent. Proud. Tall. She smiled.

"Yes Sir," she said, and lowered her pussy onto him.

Her tight pussy gripped him as she slowly began to ride him. Her head fell back, she fucked him gently. He pawed at her breasts. Pulling her closer. She let him play with her nipples. She began to fuck him faster. As she leant forward, she could feel her clit being caressed by his body. Manoeuvring herself so she could make sure she

got maximum exposure on her clit, her mind began to spin again. Ken could just reach her arse.
She fucked him harder. Slamming down on his cock. Her breath short again. Annie looked at him.
"You are a bad man Sir. "And I'm going to come all over your cock."
"Fuck me," he said breathlessly.
She rode him harder. "Oh fuck!" She said. "Oh fuck!" "Oh fuck!" Faster! Her head spun.
He held her hips. Pressing against her clit.
"I'm going to come!" She shouted. As she did so, she fell forward.
He slid his finger up her arse. She screamed. And bit his shoulder. Hard. Her pussy squirted again. And his cock exploded its semen inside her. He could feel the tip of his cock as his finger fucked her arse. "Fuck!" he shouted.
His breath faster. His forehead glistening with sweat. He slipped his finger out. And wrapped his hands around her as she shuddered.
"You OK?"
"I'm OK." Her eyes closed. "I'm fucked," she laughed. And cuddled into his chest.
Shit! He thought to himself. This could get very messy.

The Chief Super.

Ken left early with a simple note, "See you at work." He looked back at the younger woman lying in his bed. "I really shouldn't have done that," he muttered to himself, but it was bloody good. He smiled. However, he now had a team to brief, potentially a chief superintendent to interview, and a whole different crime facing him.

As he drove to work, he pondered on his next move, and decided that he would tell the team that it was time to bring all of the people involved into the station. That included Rosy, Gigi, probably Geoff and Eugene, Harvey and question them all much harder and under duress. And of course, the wives of the two victims. One of them especially. After all, one of them had such a reason for murder (if she knew what he knew), of course she would be the prime suspect.

He reached his desk just after six am, usual routine, coffee first, strong and sweet enough to kick start the day.

He went over to the board which had everyone's ideas on it: thoughts, links, ideas. Although it was very old fashioned, it was still a method that he thought worked and he would continue to employ it. After his second coffee all the team were together. He told them exactly what he wanted; who he wanted brought in, how, and more importantly, the line of questioning as he now had categoric proof that Charlie Summer's death had not been accidental.

There were now cases within cases never mind the fact that Giles Williams could have been a paedophile, and that most certainly there was something else going on in the background.

The Warren kept eating at him. He had no idea what it was and perhaps it was time to talk to his chief superintendent and see if he had any ideas.

He decided he would not speak to either of the wives yet, he would much rather find out what everybody else knew before he tried that. He also needed to go and speak to young Callum Summer, though again he would keep his powder dry. This was not a time, right now at least, for rocking any more boats. Gather the evidence in the traditional way. He smiled to himself. 'In the traditional way', something he had never been particularly good at, always wanting to find his own way, his own path. However, on this occasion it needed to be a rock-solid case and he would make sure he did everything by the book, in particular when it involved a chief superintendent.

As he got up from his desk and left the office he saw Annie.

"Good morning," he smiled. "I trust you had a good night sleep?"

"I did thank you very much."

"See you later," he waved and was gone. He had decided he would go and see Callum Summer, just a friendly chat, nothing more.

Callum was at work in the garage. His ribs still aching but at least he could get back to work.
His father had given him a sense of worth and he had no intention of changing that.
"Callum Summer?" The DS shouted from the workshop.
Callum shouted, "Up here!"
He made his way up the wooden staircase, to find Callum sitting very efficiently behind the desk finishing a phone call.
Nothing very dramatic in any of it. He looked at the young man. Big built, strong, you already knew that his mind was strong too.
"How are those ribs feeling now?"
"Oh not so bad, still a twinge now and again but not so bad,"
"That's good to hear."
"So, to what do I owe this pleasure? Do you want a coffee by the way?"
"No I'm fine, it's just a quick visit. As you know I'm new to the area and just learning about things really, and I came across some old case notes the other day. As it cropped up I thought I'd come and ask the man who should know."
"And what are those case notes?" The voice changed, it faltered slightly.
"I didn't realise you had lost your father Callum. What happened?"
"My dad died in a car crash."
"I'm sorry to hear that, was the crash his fault?"
"No!" Callum said sharply. "It wasn't his fault, okay!"
"So it was someone else's fault?"

He saw Callum's fist clench. "I am convinced it was somebody else's fault, but there was never any evidence, so I suppose as time passes you believe it yourself."
"Well, like I say, I didn't wish to dig anything up and I apologise for bringing it up, just made me curious when I found the case notes. What do you mean you couldn't find any evidence."
"I tried to make the accident happen myself, my dad was getting on a little bit, mid-fifties, bit slower, beer belly, but he could still fucking drive man. There is no way the accident happened the way the police say it did."
"I'm sorry I brought it up."
"Don't be," Callum said quietly. "But I'm telling you, my dad didn't just crash and die. If I didn't know better, I would reckon someone ran him off the road. But, no CCTV, no skid marks, no nothing!" And he broke into tears. "Just my dad. Burned to death in his own car."
"Shit! Son, I'm sorry. I didn't read all the notes, just a brief glance. You OK?"
Callum looked up. "It still hurts officer" he paused. "It still fucking hurts."
"I can only imagine," Ken said quietly. "I will see myself out."
His team did as they had been asked. They brought in everyone.

Rosy: A wise old bird. Kept her mouth shut about pretty much anything. Said Giles had told her he would reward her well after his blowjob. Rosy wasn't getting any younger and she definitely still liked a bit of sex.

So what if it was Giles? She had no idea about Giles and young girls.
Though she had always noticed he enjoyed Gigi serving him. Just assumed it was coz she was a pretty little thing.
Of course she was teaching Gigi. The poor girl was a bit naive. And Rosy was just guiding her sexually. She just happened to walk in when Rosy was with Giles.
"Clients? You must have mis-heard officer, Clive is Gigi's boyfriend. The only clients we keep happy are behind the bar at the golf club." She was definitely a wise old owl who knew her way around the system, and definitely knew what to say or not to say.

Gigi: "Of course I was shocked when I walked in on them. Rosy told me to stay as we had been chatting about my boyfriend Clive, and he had already told me I didn't do it right. So I watched."
 And Rosy then said, "Now you try."
"Of course I didn't want to. But I want to make my boyfriend happy. So I did it." Then tears and "Please don't tell my boyfriend."
"No, Giles had never done anything inappropriate. She was sure. She didn't know what the video meant by 'clients', unless Giles had thought she would be giving blow jobs to other men in the golf club."

Harvey: "I know nothing about Giles Williams except him and my boss (Tommy Shelton) play golf together. Other than that, and the fact he seems to be 'Mr Big' in the local community, I couldn't tell you anything."

Geoff: "Who doesn't like younger women? That's not a crime. Sure, Giles had enjoyed the odd hooker, always early 20's, and yes, he had indeed made sure Giles was not disturbed on odd occasions. Nothing illegal in that. Giles loved kids and was exemplary in his behaviour around them. Though always got a twinkle in his eye if there was a new barmaid around and she was young and pretty."

Eugene: "Who doesn't like younger women?"
To be honest, it was as if Geoff and Eugene had eaten exactly the same speech. Almost word for word they dealt out the same old crap. Giles was a pillar of the community. Of course he had the odd indiscretion. Of course he turned a blind eye. Of course, the new barmaid had caught Giles' eye.
But Giles loved kids. No way on earth could he be interested in children. He plays golf with the chief superintendent don't you know.

After a long day of questioning all of the people on the periphery of the case, the team was exhausted. It seemed once again, that the whole thing was locked up tighter than a drum. And each one of the members involved with either Giles or Tommy, had their act perfectly polished. No one prepared to crack. Everyone singing from the same hymn sheet.
  Once they had released everyone, Ken gathered the team together. None of them were particularly local. Certainly, none of them knew Ken. He thanked them all for their efforts today.

One voice said "What's the point Sir? We haven't done anything or learned anything."
Ken looked at his colleague.
"Terry, what we have learned is that in one way shape or form all of these people are involved. All of them tell the same story, almost too perfectly. We may not be able to prove anything just yet but I can assure you every single one of them out there is guilty in one way or another. And I will find a way to prove it. Now go home, get some rest, as you never know what might happen with the dawning of a new day."

The team disbanded and made their way home.

Ken decided it was time to speak to the chief superintendent. He hoped he would catch him. As luck would have it Oscar hadn't left for the day. Ken tapped quietly on his door.
"Come," said the voice in the office.
How very antiquated Ken said to himself. He stepped inside the office. Having only been in there a couple of times, he still admired the plush chairs, and the elegant pictures on the wall.
"Sir," he said. "Do you have a moment?"
"I have a few moments, yes," Oscar said quietly. "Do you have any developments?"
"I have several developments, some of which I might need your help with."
The chief superintendent smiled to himself and thought, "You see I'm not useless, despite what people think I'm still a good copper."
"There's no subtle way to say this Sir," Ken blurted out. "We believe that Giles Williams could have been a

paedophile. However, it would also seem that he was an extremely clever man with computers and at present we are struggling for concrete evidence, but I can tell you he liked the young girls."

"Oh! Come now Detective Sergeant! Don't we all like to look at a young girl now and again?"

"Oh! He did a lot more than look Sir, though I will admit the only thing we found on his computer were pictures. So yes, he definitely liked to look. It would appear that some of the girls in some of the images may be younger than 16. However, as they come from the dark web and are almost untraceable it's becoming very difficult to prove."

Ken paused. "However, Sir, I have a much bigger problem which only came to light yesterday thanks to the help of the excellent Annie in Forensics."

"Yes she's a bright young thing."

Ken smiled, "She certainly is extremely helpful and, also, as it turns out something of a computer Whiz kid. She managed to crack Giles' laptop, which I might add was hidden in a locked drawer."

"Would you like a drink Ken?"

"Thank you. Yes Sir, I think I would."

The chief super poured two small glasses of whisky. "And what else did this laptop reveal?"

"I had only just joined this place when I heard about a car accident, a horrific accident actually, in which a man was trapped in his vehicle and burned to death."

"Yes terrible business, Charlie Summer, everybody liked him. Bit of a loner but a very nice man. He even looked after my wife's car on occasions."

Ken smiled at the comment. His face then fell. "There's no easy way to say this either Sir, but I can prove beyond any reasonable doubt Charlie Summer was murdered. And I can prove that Giles Williams knew about it."

The chief superintendent sank back in the chair. "But there was a full investigation. "Nobody could find any trace of foul play."

"That may be the case Sir, but I assure you I have all the evidence I need. The problem is, at the moment, one of the suspects is lying in hospital with a crossbow bolt hole in his head and the other one is dead. Whilst I fully realise I'm still investigating the murder of Giles Williams and the attempted murder of Tommy Shelton, I believe they may be linked to the death of Charlie Summer. With your permission I want to reopen the case."

"Yes of course, do whatever you need."

"Thank you Sir," said Ken as he downed the last of the Scotch. "I will pursue other lines of enquiry as well as of course looking for justice for them all. However, Sir," he paused, "It may well be that Tommy and Giles have had justice of some kind already served to them."

He smiled internally, careful not to let the chief super know his real thoughts. And the truth was Ken didn't really give a toss who had killed Giles Williams and tried to kill Tommy Shelton, from everything he was finding out about them they had it coming. But he was still a DS and a bloody good one. One way or another, he would find out who did it. He placed the glass on the desk, stood up and made his way to the door. He looked back. "Thank you, Sir," he said quietly. "Just one more thing."

Oscar sighed. He was already in shock over the news of Giles, though his mind now kept repeating the words he had heard many times from his golfing friend "bloody fine filly that."

"Of course."

Ken looked directly at his superior officer. "Do you know anything about a place called The Warren?"

Oscar froze. "I heard Giles mention it a few times. He said he was going to go back to the old days of dancing girls, cabaret and all that sort of rubbish."

"Thank you Sir." Ken put hand on the door handle.

"Why do you ask?"

"No reason Sir, I found a notebook with building materials and I couldn't work out what it meant. You have just cleared it up for me."

"Jolly good show." The superintendent replied.

Take me to bed Detective!

Ken closed the door with a smile on his face as he did so. He made his way down the stairs and out to the main entrance. As he did so he almost literally bumped into Annie coming up the stairs.
She smiled at him, "Hello Sir," she said brightly.
Ken smiled, he was a little worried, was she here by accident or by design?
"Do you fancy a drink?" She said shyly.
"I would much rather have a drink indoors and chill out," he said.
"Great!" she beamed "Why don't you come back to my place? We'll get a takeaway."
"That sounds like a great idea," he said, not entirely sure in his own mind it was a great idea at all, but right now any escape from this case would be welcome. "I will follow you." He grinned as Annie skipped out of the station.
Within a short space of time, they had arrived at a small block of flats, only three stories high, plain, simple, nothing fancy a bit like Annie really. She used a fob and opened the main door.
"I live on the top Sir, but it's not too far as you can see," she bounded up the stairs. Ken followed her.
"So, do we talk shop now? Or do we just relax and leave work at work?"
"We can if you wish Sir."

"Stop calling me sir! How many times am I going to tell you to stop!"

"Sorry Ken." She opened the front door and stepped inside pointing to the first door on the right. "Why didn't you go in there and make yourself comfortable. I will be back in a few minutes."

Ken did as he had been instructed. He opened the door to a small living room with a large window, two main chairs facing the fireplace, a TV in the corner and a sofa on the other wall. Considering what he already knew of Annie he didn't think it was too forward to take his shoes off. He placed them neatly by the side of the sofa. He sat down in one of the armchairs and let out a sigh of relief.

As he did so Annie appeared with two glasses of wine. "I haven't found anything else in that laptop Sir. Giles clearly thought that nobody would ever find it and certainly go through it, so he kept some meticulous records in some respects but only of specific things that he wanted to keep. It wasn't like a diary or a journal. My guess is he was frightened of Tommy. But I'm not quite sure why, so he kept the video just in case and thought it was enough to distance himself from any wrong doing."

Ken sipped his wine. "Are you sure you don't want to be a detective?"

"I would love to be a detective, but I failed the exams so forensics was my next best thing. Believe me I love it. Now what do you want to eat?"

Ken looked at her. "I'd like to eat you," he smiled.

Annie blushed. "I'd like to let you," she grinned. "Why don't you go and take a shower and meet me in the bedroom. The bathroom is opposite. I will see you in a few minutes." She got up, took the glasses and made her way down the small corridor to the bedroom at the end. Ken smiled and unbuttoned his shirt and again did as he was instructed.

Ken came out of the bathroom and padded along the corridor he knocked at the bedroom door.

"Come in."

He opened the door into almost total darkness. Curtains drawn, no lights on. As he stepped inside Annie pushed him.

The move was unexpected. Ken didn't quite cry out, but he did stumble forward, putting his hands out to stop himself he fell onto the bed. He heard Annie quickly run around.

"Now I've got you," she laughed, and Ken smiled. This meek and mild woman at work was something of a bedroom monster but for now it was all the release that he needed.

Annie sat and straddled him.

He could hear a strange rattling sound. He put his hands up to touch her, feeling her naked skin he began to play with her breasts pulling and turning and teasing her nipples. She moaned softly, "I love that," she said quietly. As she did so he felt the metal wrap around his wrists. Annie Washford whispered quietly, "You are under arrest. Put your hands up and don't say a word."

He lifted his hands above his head only then did he notice the metal bed frame.

He grinned again as Annie clicked the handcuffs around the frame of the bed, his arms now above his head. He was unable to move. Annie kissed him on the mouth then kissed him lower going across his chest and down his stomach. His already erect cock pressing at her, she took his cock deep into her mouth.

Ken smiled. "You are a little minx, aren't you?"

"No talking!"

Ken closed his eyes again, "Whatever you say."

She took him deep into her throat, no gag reflex this time. After she had done so and having created a huge amount of saliva, she spat on her hand before taking his cock back into her mouth.

As she went deep, Ken moaned softly and Annie put one of her fingers up his arse. It wasn't something he had experienced very often but as his cock hit the back of her throat it was perfect. He moaned loudly, not quite sure which sensation to enjoy first. For the rest of the evening he allowed Annie to do whatever she wanted to him. Laying back, enjoying the pleasure and allowing his mind to escape. She even had a whip. At one point she undid the handcuffs and told him to bend onto all fours. However, this was one step too far.

He felt the strap on dildo. "No," he said quietly "I don't mind your finger up my arse, but you are not going to fuck me there."

Annie laughed. "I will, one day."

Then suddenly and without warning, all of the toys disappeared. All the extras.

Ken, still hard, was puzzled.

She stood up, kissed him sensually, and said, "Now make love to me," and she laid back on the bed.

Ken kissed her softly as she spread her legs and allowed him to slide inside her. His rhythm building slowly, she held him tight, and he imagined that this was the first time she had felt like this. Certainly, her body language told him she was enjoying being sensual and close. He made love to her not hard and fast but slow, sensual.

She wrapped her legs around him and whispered in his ear, "I'm going to come, make me come Ken," he didn't change his rhythm, perhaps just getting a little faster. Very soon Annie bit his shoulder as the orgasm swept over her, and she cried huge sobbing tears.

Ken looked down at her. "Are you sure you are okay?"

"I am perfect, but you have not come."

He looked at her, pushed the hair from her forehead and said, "Tonight was all about you."

"Thank you, I don't think it's ever just been about me."

Ken sat on the side of the bed. "Well tonight was definitely all about you."

Annie squealed with delight. "I love that thought, so what do you want to eat?"

Ken grinned. "I didn't even get to eat you!"

As he laughed, Annie dragged him backwards and forced him to lay flat on the bed. Ken didn't stop her.

"Put your hands up," she laughed "You are under arrest." As he put his hands up he felt Annie climb off the bed, then back onto it. She was straddling his face.

"You wanted to eat me. Now eat me to orgasm!" And she gently lowered herself onto his tongue.

Ken did exactly as he was told. Her body writhing and teasing as he flicked his tongue over her clit and bit her pussy lips gently. It didn't take her too long before she gushed. She hung on to the bed frame and came in his mouth. Her body shaking with the intensity of the orgasm.

Once she had breathed deeply and allowed herself to come down, she laughed.

"You will now need another shower, and we will sleep in the other bedroom, this one's a bit damp!"

Ken smiled, "I'm going to shower," he said. He hadn't noticed the other door when he had made his way to the bedroom, but as he came out there on the left was another door. He looked back at Annie.

"You are just full of surprises aren't you?"

"I can be. This was my Grandmother's place. She left it to me in her will, so I now have a den of iniquity," she laughed, "and also a boudoir."

When Ken came back and made his way to the other room, there were no handcuffs. It was decorated beautifully. Minimalist white with pale blue. He got into bed, put his arms around Annie. Kissed her and was asleep within minutes.

Annie smiled. She actually had never had a man in this bed! She'd had more than her fair share of men in her den of iniquity, but no one had ever spent the night. She kissed him on the forehead and closed her eyes.

When he woke the next morning Annie was already gone. She had left a note and the key. Lock the door behind you. A kiss and a smiley face.

There was a sudden panic. Ken wasn't sure that this relationship was what he wanted. For a start she was more than ten years his junior though he had to admit they got on but it all seemed a little bit rushed, a little bit too fast. Having said that the sex was fantastic, and she was a clever girl who potentially had unlocked a key to this case. What he was worried about most was London. About getting involved. About being too emotionally close to somebody. The job didn't allow that. Even though he tried very hard to keep to nine to five, he knew deep down he could never do it.

He got into work and decided to gather the team up. The investigation had definitely changed. And especially now he had the approval of the chief superintendent he was going to make damn sure that he stirred everything up.

He told the team very clearly, "I want every movement and piece of money that Michelle Shelton and Valerie Williams have moved around in the last year. I want to know if they were involved in the murder of Giles Williams and the attempted murder of Tommy Shelton." He then began to relay to the team the evidence he had found regarding the death of Charlie Summer. It was categoric that Tommy Shelton had been involved in having him killed even if he hadn't done it directly. This put a whole new complexion on the potential reason for Tommy being shot with the crossbow. He relayed the story to the team that Michelle Shelton had been sleeping with Charlie Summer.

Tommy Shelton knew this and took exception to his wife screwing around. Clearly, he decided that if he eliminated Charlie Summer, he eliminated the problem, and his wife would no longer be screwing around. Unfortunately, what he didn't know was that his business partner liked to keep records, hidden records that he didn't think anybody would find, but the little genius in forensics did,

Annie, there was a whistle from the back of the room. "Calm down Terry," Ken said and laughed. "We all know she's a pretty little thing but she's also very smart, and she managed to unlock everything that was in that computer. Hence, we know about Giles and his young women and we also know, though I still can't work out why Giles recorded himself telling Tommy that he knew he had killed Charlie. I cannot understand it, however, know it I do, and I want to find out if Michelle Shelton was involved. So, two of you go and bring her in for questioning, two more of you go through bank details of both Valerie and Michelle and don't let any of the banks give you any crap, this is a murder case I am not going to put up with any of their bullshit."

"What about you Sir? Where are you going?"

"I am going to see Valerie. I'm sure she will be really pleased to see me again. I'm going to find out just exactly what she thinks her friend has been up to." He paused.

"Let's get to it people"

Before going to visit Valerie he decided it would be a good move to drop in on Annie. He still wasn't sure that what he was doing was the right thing but for now it felt good and he certainly didn't want to upset her.

She saw him and smiled.

They knew they had to be discreet, the force didn't particularly like anybody being together, it made relationships at work very difficult.

She whispered, "I left you sleeping, you looked so peaceful, and besides I had a lot to do here."

"That's absolutely fine, here is your key."

"You can keep it if you want to," Annie smiled and looked deep into his eyes. "But I guess that would be going a bit fast."
"Maybe just a little. It… it's not a no, it's just a not yet."
"That's fine. I kind of expected that."
"I will see you later." And he strode purposefully back up the stairs and out of the station.

The gates were closed at Valerie's house. He rang the bell but to no avail.
"Bollocks!" He need not have worried, as just as he was about to vent his frustrations his mobile rang.
"Yes, Terry,"
"We've come to pick up Michelle guv and Valerie is here too."
"That's absolutely fine. Bring them both in, I will see you back at the station," and he laughed to himself. "These two are as thick as thieves." he said to himself. He began making his way leisurely back to the station.
When he got there he decided he would interview Michelle.
"Terry, you take Valerie. I want to know everything. I want this to be a full-on interrogation, and I want her to be worried. Somebody knows something and somebody will fucking tell me."
"Yes guv. No problem."
Ken opened the door to interview room number two, powerfully swinging it hard. He sat down in front of Michelle. He had decided to bring Detective Constable Jane Fraser into the interview. Jane had been on the

Force a long time, but she had never really wanted promotion and was just seeing out her days until her pension. She didn't particularly like Ken nor did she dislike him; she certainly didn't like some of the methods he employed but she had known from colleagues in London that he got good results. She made sure she recorded the interview. Once the formalities were out of the way Ken decided just to get straight to it.

"I understand you were having an affair with Charlie Summer?"

"And what business is it of yours if I was?"

"I'll tell you why it's my business shall I? Let's put two and two together and stop fucking about. You were having an affair with a man who died in a car crash."

"No shit Sherlock!" "Wow! Do they give out medals for this amount of intelligence?"

"Your husband knew you were having the affair?"

"Yes I suppose he did," she said sarcastically.

"And now your husband is clinging on to life. So you see Michelle, the common denominator here is two men, both in some way and how deeply I don't know yet, in the case of Charlie Summer, but I will find out, who were both involved with you and now one is dead, and one is almost dead. That leads me to question if that's just a coincidence. And I don't believe in coincidences do you?"

"I believe in coincidence all the time, officer, don't you? I mean just imagine how else it could be that both my lover and my husband were killed."

Ken paused for a moment. "Where were you on the night Giles Williams and your husband were attacked?"

"I was at the spa with Valerie and then at home in my bed. You can check if you like, though you may find it difficult to check my bed."
"Oh, don't worry I will be checking with Valerie. She is being interviewed right now."
"Good! And she will back up what I just told you."
"How did your husband seem on the days before his death?"
"Agitated, angry, although he was always angry."
"I would think if my wife was screwing another man, I'd probably be angry too."
"Well perhaps if he looked after his wife a bit better, she wouldn't have been fucking somebody else would she? Touché officer."
Ken had had enough, his blood was beginning to boil and he had certainly had enough of Michelle and her arrogance.
"How did Charlie Summer die?"
"You know full well how he died. I'm sure you've read the reports if you've discovered he was my lover."
"Ah, you see Michelle, Charlie Summer wasn't in the reports as your lover."
"So how the hell do you know that I was sleeping with Charlie?"
"Because new evidence has come to light," Ken said, sitting back in the chair. He folded his arms. "New evidence which indicates that Charlie's death was not an accident."
"I knew it!" she breathed.
"Knew what exactly Michelle?"
Michelle froze. "Bollocks!" she thought.

"I knew it wasn't an accident. I knew that Charlie was too good a driver to have crashed. So did his son Callum."
"I will be speaking to Callum too. I have one more question for you for now Michelle, did you suspect your husband had killed Charlie Summer?"
"Yes, officer if you want the absolute truth yes, I did. I was pretty sure that he had found out about me and Charlie. I didn't care, I was planning on leaving anyway I just needed to put some things in place. Unfortunately, I never got the chance to do that because Charlie's life was taken before I could. I had no proof that Tommy was involved. Let's just call it women's intuition, shall we?"
"Did Giles Williams know that Tommy had killed Charlie?"
"I have no idea, why don't you ask him, oh, you can't he's dead!" She said sarcastically again.
Ken stood up and smacked his palm on the table.
"Don't fuck with me Michelle! If you are behind this, I will find out, I will prove it, and you will pay."
Michelle stood up and was in his face. "So big man," she said sarcastically. "You think you have something on me do you, prove it. I was at the spa with Valerie. I went home to bed alone. I had no idea where Tommy was to be honest, he was probably fucking one of the barmaids or one of the stupid tarts at his club, that would have been the norm. And if I mentioned anything when he got home, I would normally get a slap so that would have been normal too. Was he pissed off when he found out about me and Charlie? Of course he was pissed off. He thinks I was his property. That he owned me. Well he doesn't fucking own me anymore does he Detective Sergeant!" And she laughed. "So I'm sorry, I can't help you with

who, how, or why my husband and Giles were where they were that night. I have even less idea who may have killed Giles and tried to kill Tommy but I can tell you it wasn't me and it had nothing to do with me. Am I sorry that it happened? Not a chance. I'm only sorry that he survived."

"I have that on record," he said.

"I don't give you a fuck if you have it on a stone tablet! Did I care about my husband, no, was I going to leave my husband for Charlie Summer? Yes! Did my husband find out? I think so, and I'm certain that's why Charlie died. And you have just confirmed that. So basically, my husband is a killer."

"I didn't say that Michelle," he backtracked, "I said he may have had something to do with his death."

"So he paid somebody to kill him," she said very matter of fact.

"That's a possibility, yes. I don't have any further questions at this time Michelle but I must tell you that right now you are the strongest suspect I have."

Michelle fluttered her eyelids, "You mean poor little weak, innocent, feeble me," and she sat and raised her arms squeezing her biceps. She laughed again. "Can I go now?"

"You can go now."

"Jane, would you be kind enough to escort this lady out of here."

"Certainly Sir." "This way ma'am."

Before long Michelle was back in Valerie's car. The pair of them were extremely confident.

"They can prove nothing." Valerie said.

"They are asking for bank statements." Michelle answered.
"Let them have bank statements they won't find any payments, they won't find anything."
Valerie was super confident.
For once Michelle did not hide behind her but stood firm, shoulder to shoulder with her friend. "No, you are right, they won't find a fucking thing, but I want to know how they know."
"Giles and that fucking laptop that's how. I didn't even know he owned it, much less that it was locked away but apparently, he kept some records on there. Forensics must have opened it."
"So, what do we do now?"
"We do nothing, we let the police do their thing and unless they can come up with some proof which they won't be able to, we are in the clear." Valerie smiled.
"Shall we go and get a drink?"
"Yes, let's do just that." Michelle answered.

"Do you fancy a coffee, Jane?" Ken asked. "I could do with a chat and your opinion."
"Certainly Sir," and they made their way to the canteen. Ken came back with two coffees and two pastries.
"So, you're an experienced officer," Ken said bluntly, "What do you think?"
"I think she's involved. I don't know how and I'm pretty certain she didn't fire that crossbow, but I think she's involved somehow."
"I think you are right," but how the fuck I prove it I don't know. Valerie and Michelle have their stories sewn

up tighter than a drum, and of the two people who could argue with her, one is dead, one might as well be dead, and everybody else who has touched in this case, whether that be the heavies that belong to Giles or Tommy or even Charlie Summer's son, all keep their mouths shut firmly, and telling us only what we want to hear. Without any more evidence I don't see a way we can get to the bottom of this right now. I'm sure it will come but it's going to take a lot more investigation."
As he finished his sentence Terry appeared.
"Nothing Sir, we got absolutely nothing. We have been through all the bank records, nothing, no strange payments, no money in, no money's out certainly nothing that would raise alarm bells, nothing that would tell me if they're involved. If they are, I don't know how."
"Get the team together. In my office, shall we say 3:00 pm?" He looked at his watch.
"That gives me half an hour to have another one of those bloody pastries," and he laughed.
"Very good Sir."
At 3pm Ken made his way back upstairs. He got the team together. He got everybody's input. Then very quietly he whispered "Right now team we have nothing, all we know is that Tommy had Charlie Summer killed. We don't know who did it. The only thing we know is how he died. We know that Giles Williams knew about it but was trying to keep himself distant as though it was nothing to do with him. Something which apparently Giles is very good at."
At which point Terry piped up "Well he is now Sir," the team laughed.

"This is very true Terrence," Ken said with a smile on his face. "So the bottom line is, we have a paedophile and a drug dealer, one is dead, one is almost dead and we have Charlie Summer who we know was murdered. And the only man right now who can tell us about that is the man who's nearly dead. Anybody else is either silent, staying silent, has never spoken, or is too clever, so right now we are banging our heads against a very carefully constructed wall. And the truth is I don't know about you, team, but for me, I don't really care. Of course, I'd like to see justice, but if a paedophile and a drug dealer end up off the streets and potentially off of this planet, I don't see how that is a bad thing. I probably shouldn't say that, certainly don't let the chief super hear me say that."

Ken calls in some help.

Jane chipped in, "But surely Sir, we do have to find the killer?"
"We have to, you're quite right Jane. But there are degrees of looking, aren't there? Anyway, I think it's time for a drink don't you all?"
The team nodded in agreement.
"First round is on me!"
He sent Annie a text. "We are going to the pub over the road, it would be great if you could join us."
Annie sent back a smiling face.
"We need to be discreet for now, but I'd really like your company."
A smiling face and a kiss emoji came back.
Ken smiled to himself.

He stopped for a moment just to look around and take in all of the events. The small sleepy village had absolutely no idea what was going on. Why would they? The town he was sitting in generally thought it seemed that Tommy was a bit of a wrong 'un and Giles was the perfect human being. He looked at his team and smiled. It was the first time they had really got together. They didn't do a bad job. Jane certainly didn't like the way he did his job sometimes, but overall, he couldn't have asked for more. He stood up to go to the bar. "Another round everybody?"

The team chorused as one. "Yes guv!" Just as Annie walked in. The rest of the evening went just the same way. The team of detectives letting their hair down and generally having a relaxing time. One or two perhaps had one too many, and at the end of the evening Ken told them all no rush tomorrow.

"Shall we get a cab?" he said to Annie.

"I think that's probably safest, don't you? Hardly fitting for the police to have had one too many drinks and drive home."

"With a smile, he put his arm around Annie, and they left the pub.

Over breakfast the next morning Ken decided to ask Annie a question. She was a bright girl after all. "Why on earth would the killer use a crossbow?"

"Good morning to you too, Detective Sergeant!" Annie laughed. "What a way to say good morning."

Ken laughed too. "Sorry, do you want coffee?"

"Yes please," she said. "As for the crossbow thing, silence."

"Silence?"

"Well, I don't know the total details of the case, but I don't know anybody that would use a crossbow instead of a gun unless it was to do with noise."

"Both men were shot in the middle of nowhere. No houses around, no people around for miles. It was gone midnight, probably closer to 1am. There wasn't another soul around and the only things that would have heard anything would have been the rabbits and the deer in the trees. So how on earth can it be to do with silence?" Ken looked puzzled.

"Oh, that's easy then. Your killer is deaf." She said it so matter of factly, Ken was gobsmacked.

"How the hell do you come to that conclusion? Surely if he is deaf any form of noise wouldn't make any difference."

"I totally agree, but that's not the point. You told me this was a professional hit right, the man knew what he was doing, no mistakes, nothing left to chance."

"I did tell you all of those things."

"Then I'm telling you he is deaf. He probably has a collection of knives, a collection of crossbows, and if I was guessing a cheese wire or some sort of garrotte, but he doesn't use anything that makes any noise. He lives in a world of silence, and he likes his world of silence."

"How the hell did you manage to work that out?"

"I saw it on a programme once I think, and even if I didn't it's just how my tiny brain works. Logic says he has no noise around him so why would he want to make noise? It's irrelevant to him."

"And just how many deaf professional killers have you met?" Ken laughed.

Annie looked at him patronisingly. "You are the bloody detective, remember!" She smiled "I'm going for a shower. You best leave and get in before me. I will see you at work."

"OK, Annie, I will see you later. Oh, and Annie thank you."

"What for, the amazing sex or my amazing intellect?"

Ken didn't hesitate with the reply. "Both, but more your amazing intellect," and he laughed as she threw her toast at him as he raced out of the door.

"Bastard!" she yelled, laughing.

As he made his way into work he dialled an old colleague from London. "Pete you old devil," he said brightly.

"Bloody hell, Ken Nicholson, now there is a blast from the past!" The voice said down the phone. "To what do I owe this honour?"

"Well, my old mate I would love to say it's a social call but it's not."

"How is life out in the sticks with all those carrot crunchers?" Pete laughed.

"Believe it or not mate, I thought I was coming out here to put my feet up and now I'm investigating a murder, an attempted murder, and a historic murder."

"Jesus fucking Christ!" Pete replied, "Maybe I should be a naughty boy like you and get kicked out to a nice little quiet village."

Pete and Ken went back a long way, in fact all the way back to their training days. There were not many who knew the real reason for Ken leaving London, but Pete was one.

Ken knew he could trust him.

"So what is it you need to know, old man?"

"It's pretty simple, but strange"

"Okay hit me with it."

"I have a theory. In fact, I have someone working for me who has come up with a theory for my murder and attempted murder. The guy used a crossbow."

"Who did he think he was Robin fucking Hood?" Pete laughed.

"I know right, welcome back to the 1600s," and Ken laughed nervously. "Thing is I have an analyst here and she reckons…"

Pete laughed. "She reckons your cock fits her all right I bet"

Ken laughed nervously again. "We are just good friends."

"Be careful old boy, you will run out of chances."

"I know old man. "Anyway, let me finish the bloody story. She reckons my killer is deaf." There was silence on the phone. "Pete!" Ken snapped. "Don't tell me you've gone deaf too."

"No, old son I haven't gone deaf, maybe got a few goosebumps and I'm a bit chilled but the truth is, there are just rumours. No one's ever seen him, he was never caught, never been anything really. The stories range from he lives in a one room hovel, he lives under a bridge, he lives in the woods, blah blah, you get the picture. A ghost. Anyway, the bottom line is, it was some old guy. Sort of a legend, who at one time did some work in London and either used a knife or a crossbow."

"But how did anyone know he was deaf?"

"I know of three occasions where he was chased and on one occasion cornered. The officer in question did all the usual; Stop, police, bullshit. All he got back was a muffled sound, no words just noises. The guy was completely deaf. As the officer approached him he took out a knife, threw it as accurately as anyone would ever imagine, cut the officer's ear, and it embedded itself in the wall behind. The officer went down, and the guy vanished. Nobody knows who he is, what he is, or where he is."

"Is he still working?"

"Ken this was probably fifteen or even twenty years ago. Nobody has seen or heard anything of him for years. It can't be the same fellow surely. Tell me the M.O."
"Two guys, Range Rover, middle of nowhere. Crossbow bolt to the head for both of them, one dead one barely alive.
"Well if it was him, he is slacking."
"What do you mean?"
"I never knew him to miss, but I'm telling you it was the best part of twenty years ago, it can't be the same guy. He's probably dead by now."
"Thanks Pete."
"Anytime, old man. Next time you're back in the big smoke why don't you drive your tractor around and pop and see us all."
"I might just do that old boy." And he ended the call still no further forward.
He got to the station and made himself another coffee. As he did so his mind flicked across to The Warren. Rabbits live in a warren he said to himself. Warren means underground, he grinned. A building underground. What did the chief super say? 'Dancing girls', there is an underground club somewhere. He smiled to himself "I'm not a fucking detective for nothing."

After three weeks Michelle had had enough. She no longer wanted to go to the hospital. Tommy's condition hadn't changed at all and she was tired of going to the hospital every day. She sent a text to Harvey.
"Can you get all of the boys together, and also all of the bar staff, meet me at the club at midday."

Harvey replied, "No problem."
Michelle had discussed with Valerie that she was now going to take over the club, and at least in the short term run it as best she could with all the help she had. Valerie smiled. "I will just take the profits from the golf club. It ticks along very well by itself, though I have to say I do not trust the new bar manager Rosy one little bit.

Michelle was determined that Tommy was not going to ruin or change her life. She didn't give a fuck about him. After all, whether he was alive, dead or a cabbage, she didn't care, it was now her turn. She arrived at the club dressed immaculately. Knee length skirt, blouse, leather jacket, heels. She unset the alarm and walked in, sitting at the bar, she waited until everybody had arrived.

"I am taking over control of the club," she said boldly. "No, I do not know anything about running a nightclub, yes, I will need all of your help and yes for all those of you that want to carry on there will be a job for you and a pay rise. I'm not interested in drugs, and any of you that are, can leave now. Other than that, this is my place, and I will make it work."

Harvey looked at her. "Are you sure you want to do this Michelle?"

"I *have* to do this Harvey, there's no want about it, I have to do this for me."

"Fair enough." He looked around at the collection of bar staff, backroom staff, and of course his team of bouncers. "So, we are all agreed?"

Everybody nodded.
"Sounds like a great plan!" They all agreed. If nothing else, they all needed jobs. Tommy had always paid well, always looked after them, and even if there had been too much shady business at times, to which most of them had turned a blind eye, they all felt this probably wouldn't be the case anymore.

Valerie decided that if Michelle was going to take control, perhaps she needed to do something about the golf club and that bitch Rosy. She made a call. Rosy answered the phone.
"I am coming in," Valerie said bluntly, "I need to talk to everybody." Just before she hung up the phone she said to Rosy, "My husband confided in you a lot, who do you think killed him?"
Rosy was taken aback. "I have no idea! I think he just caught himself in the wrong place at the wrong time and with the wrong person. Tommy Shelton is a wrong un'."
"I am sure you are right about that," Valerie said sarcastically, "I will see you in an hour."

She swung into the golf club and marched straight to her husband's office. The police had been through everything and could find no trace of anything untoward. Other than the camera, of course, which had led to all of the questioning about Giles and what he may or may not have been up to.
The detective sergeant was getting nowhere. His ghost killer was just that, and it seemed, had completely vanished. Ken decided he wasn't going to look too hard. There were two pieces of shit; one dead, one close to

death, that had got exactly what they deserved. It was a pro hit probably paid for outside of the country and it was too much like hard work to look too hard. He sat at his desk and massively regretted telling Annie. As his thoughts turned to her, she walked through the door. He looked up. "Don't you knock?" He said with a smile.

"I'm sorry, I should have knocked, however, I have just come to tell you that Jack is back in a couple of weeks. I am being transferred to another station. It's a fair few miles from here. And I thought you should know."

Ken's face fell. He looked at her. "I'm going to miss you, we have worked well on this."

"Is that all you're going to miss?"

"No, Annie, I'm going to miss you. A lot."

"You have my phone number, maybe you can take me out for a drink." And she turned on her heel and left.

I know who he is.

    The Signalman didn't care much for anything other than his dog and the boat. The money he had been paid, he decided he would distribute to various charities. Just small donations so as not to alarm anybody. £500 here, £500 there. He already had a box full of money under the floorboards of the boat he certainly didn't need anymore.

    It was a beautiful day and he decided to take the dog and have a walk to the pub up near the lock. He hadn't been there for a week or two wanting to keep quiet and out of the way, but he figured his little furry friend deserved a treat. Nothing would change his life. At nearly 70 he didn't need anything. He didn't give a shit that Tommy was still alive, and he certainly didn't give a shit about the rest of the money. He had done Marco a favour. Marco had been good to him but now they were even.

    Valerie told all the staff including Rosy that the golf club will be up for sale. She had no interest in it, and now with her husband gone she had no interest in sticking around. She marched back to Giles office and looked around at the pictures. Photos of them on cruises and on holidays. She felt the anger building in her. She took off her shoe and smashed each picture very carefully.
Rosy watched from the doorway and didn't quite know what to make of it. Was it the sadness of losing her

husband, or anger at what she had found out. Rosy decided to approach her.

She opened the door. "Are you OK?"

"No, I'm not fucking okay! Everyone thinks he was a fucking angel, but you know as well as I do Giles' liking for young women. For thinking every single person could be bought or paid off."

Rosy smiled. "Yes, I know all of that, I know that he had fucked most of the young girls here, or had his cock sucked at one point or another, and I know that they hoped that they were going to either further their careers, in porn, or at the very least be well rewarded. I know that Giles was a manipulative, clever man and I know that all of it must be hard to take. But, I also know about your lover, and the fact that Giles hated it was so obvious."

"Is that right? And just what the fucking hell else do you know Ms know it all?"

"You and I need to decide what we want to do, and what we want to get out of this." Rosy said abruptly.

"So, before I say anything else. If this goes to the police, I will shoot you myself."

"You wouldn't have the bollocks," Valerie said.

"Don't fucking try me!" Rosy said and walked up to Valerie. "Because believe me, it wouldn't be the first time," she said menacingly.

Valerie stepped back. "Okay, I'm listening."

"Giles has another club. Called 'The Warren'. Part of the reason the young girls were employed here was that I was grooming them for sex. High class hookers. Super exclusive clientele. The coke and everything that was found with Tommy and Giles was meant for the club. It's there, it's all ready to go, it just needs somebody to run it. It can be as straight and legitimate as you want. But once it is open it can't be a secret anymore can it."

"OK. You have my attention, I knew that bastard was up to something, but I didn't know what."

"That's the whole point. Nobody knew. It was a very tight circle, and believe me Giles paid enough money to keep everybody quiet. With no Giles there is no club. If you are selling the golf club that's fine, I don't give a fuck about golf anyway, but I'd like to run the other club. I ran sex clubs in Spain and France. They are very lucrative and with the right management can be very successful. You and I are both strong, determined women. If you want the place to be a classy joint, we can do that. Giles had other plans of dungeons and debauchery, all of that turned him on."

Valerie laughed, "The only thing that fucking turned him on was teenagers."

"They may have turned him on, but he never touched one. There may have been the odd eighteen-year-old barmaid here, but believe me, the one thing Giles never wanted to do was blatantly break the law."

Valerie at least felt relieved if nothing else her opinion of him on that score hadn't changed.

"You best take me to this other club. Let's see what we are dealing with."

The two women left together.

"Gigi, look after the bar," Rosy said as they departed.

As the landlord finished pouring Ken's pint, The Signalman walked in with toffee. Neither of them had a clue who the other was. The landlord looked up, smiled and pointed to one of the pumps, getting a thumbs up from the old man. He walked over to the corner and sat down, patting the chair beside him. The dog jumped up, curled himself around and settled himself down to sleep. Brian took a book out of his pocket. A Stephen Leather novel. He removed the bookmark as the landlord placed the pint in front of him. As he walked back to the bar he passed Ken. Ken looked up.
"What's this, delivery service?" he questioned and laughed.
"No," the landlord said politely, "he's deaf, been coming in here for years, so I always look after him."
Ken's eyes widened "Really?" he said. "What does he do for a living?"
"Oh, he's long since retired. Come to think of it, I don't really know what he does, he always keeps himself to himself. Comes in, has a few pints, reads a book and goes back home with the dog.
"So he's almost invisible, like a ghost."
The landlord laughed, "Well, he's definitely very real, but yes, I suppose if he disappeared tomorrow nobody would know." And he went back to cleaning glasses.
Ken looked at the old man. Occasionally he patted his dog before going back to his novel. Ken's gut instinct was very rarely wrong. Looking at the man in the corner as if butter wouldn't melt in his mouth, a grandad just out for a pint with his dog, what could be more innocent.

Ken smiled to himself. He casually took out his warrant card and showed it to the landlord. Noticing the old man had looked up, he turned around and raised his glass, his warrant card 'accidentally' in his hand. The old man looked back at the detective. Didn't even flinch, raised his glass and carried on reading.
The landlord politely asked, "Is there anything I can help you with officer?"
"I'll just have another one in there."
He left after the second pint. The old man in the corner looked up and nodded. Ken went out to his car. His conscience forced him to sit and wait. It was another hour before the old man and the dog came out of the pub.
Ken decided to follow him. Keeping a good distance. He watched as eventually the old man reached the barge. Just as The Signalman was about to board, he looked around, taking in his surroundings. Ken stepped back.
The Signalman climbed into the boat. Patted Toffee on the head and closed the door.
Ken marched towards the boat. Despite the fact he had a grudging respect, he was still a copper. And he was now one hundred percent certain he had his man.
As he approached, his mobile rang. He looked down. Annie was the name on the screen. Torn between her and his work, he answered the call.
"I need to see you."
"What's wrong?"
"I think I love you," she said, fighting back the tears.
Ken felt shocked; happy, elated, scared. "I will come to you, Give me thirty minutes or so."

"Thanks"

Ken made his way back to the car. The Signalman would wait until tomorrow.

The Signalman smiled at Toffee. He watched intently at the window. Seeing the policeman leave, he signalled to the dog. The copper would be back. It was time for Brian to move on. Not too far, he liked the Tavern. It would be dark in an hour or so. An hour or so was a good enough start. He started the engine, and let the barge chug along the canal at a serene pace.

Ken vowed to return tomorrow. He needed a word with his 'ghost'.

He spent the night with Annie. Talking; crying, shouting, fucking. No, he was not in love with her, but he could be. Yes, he did want to give their relationship a chance. No, there would not be any other women. Yes, he was a bit of a maverick. No, he would never follow the rules. Yes, they did have a chance. Let things run. See what happens. And yes, he did want her.

Bright and early the next morning, the detective came back to the spot where he had been yesterday. He smiled to himself. Looking at the empty space where only a day before the barge had been.

"Goodbye ghost," he said to himself, as he kicked a stone into the canal.

Wind it down.

Six weeks on, there had been very little progress in reality, other than the fact that he knew Charlie Summer had been murdered; he still didn't know where The Warren was. The only man who could really tell him was dead. And it felt like the whole team was flogging a dead horse. He had decided to leave chasing his 'deaf ghost', as Pete had called it. A grudging respect for the old man, despite the fact he was a killer, meant Ken wasn't going to look too hard. He figured The Signalman had probably done his last job, and cleaning up Giles and Tommy really should be commended. He shook his head at the thought. But inside, he knew they had both got what was coming. Still, he was ever optimistic, and ploughed on. He was not expecting the phone call from the chief superintendent.
"Can you come to my office?" was the order. Short, sharp and barked rather aggressively.
Ken made his way to the chief super's office. He knocked on the door and waited.
"Come," was the response.
"Why the fuck does he have to be so antiquated?" The thought again went through Ken's mind.
"Ah, there you are. Take a seat. The divisional chief has been speaking to me. He wants to know what progress we're making."
Ken leaned back in the chair. He had heard this speech one too many times. It came out in different ways but he kind of knew what was coming.

"To be honest Sir, things have gone a little quiet. Also if I'm being perfectly honest with everybody choosing to *keep* quiet, and with the two main people I need to interview, one of them dead, one of them close to death and with no sign of our ghost killer, he smiled to himself, right now I have very little to go on. We are basing our ideas right now on a drug deal that went wrong. Now I can't understand why the drugs were left and not taken, nor can I explain the diamonds, unless of course Tommy Shelton was supposed to be delivering them and never made it. But the truth is we haven't got very far right now. Ironically, the only thing we've managed to prove is that Charlie Summer was murdered and the man who was responsible for that is close to death in hospital."
"I thought that's what you might say Ken. You have accused a very good friend of mine who has sadly passed away of being a paedophile, yet you have no evidence."
"Sir," Ken interrupted.
"Be quiet! You have found images on a laptop of his none of which you can prove are underage girls, is that correct?"
"Yes, Sir."
"You have found out about something called The Warren, but you know nothing about it is that correct?"
"Yes, Sir."
"And you have a ghost killer who may or may not exist."
"Yes, Sir."
"Division has told me to wind down the investigation. We will keep two people on it. But the rest of the team will be wound down and placed on other assignments."

He leaned back in his chair. "And let's be honest Ken, you were brought in to clean up a drug problem. I never knew we had a drug problem, and it turns out that a man I used to play golf with is somehow linked to that drug problem. Ironically, whoever your ghost is with his crossbow has cleared that problem up. Tommy Shelton is definitely a problem but a problem that's close to death. Giles Williams clearly had something in the background, and he is dead, and quite frankly I can't afford the resources on a case that's going nowhere. I'm sure you understand."
Ken stood up abruptly. "I understand alright," and he marched towards the door.
The chief super shouted, "Don't try anything clever. I know all about you and London. You may think you're the best detective in the world, but believe me, whoever is behind this is two steps ahead of you. I appreciate your efforts so far. Now select two of your team and instruct the rest of them to carry on with other duties, the investigation is being wound down."
"Am I at liberty to tell Michelle Shelton and Valerie Williams that?"
"As you wish," the chief superintendent replied, "as you wish."

      Ken left the office seething. These things took time. However, it would seem that time was a commodity Ken didn't have and he couldn't argue against some of the chief superintendent's logic.
The key to most of this was held by Giles Williams, now deceased, and Tommy Shelton, in an induced coma with no prognosis of getting any better. He punched the wall as

he walked down the corridor. As he got back to his office, his phone lit up.

"Do you fancy lunch?"

"Yes I bloody fancy lunch! I fancy you, and I need someone to talk to."

"Shall we say the pub in twenty minutes?"

"Perfect!"

Ken marched out of the station. Entered the pub and ordered a pint of bitter. He needed to gather his thoughts before he spoke to his team. He decided that while he was waiting for Annie, he would make a phone call first to Michelle Shelton.

"Hello DS Nicholson," she said a little sarcastically. "What can I do for you?"

"I will keep it brief. The investigation is being wound down. My chief super does not have the resources to keep chasing after ghosts. Unfortunately, there is little I can do about the Charlie case. We know Tommy was involved, we know probably Tommy killed him or if he didn't, he is certainly responsible for it but without Tommy being around, there isn't much of a case to pursue. As for Giles, my chief super seems to think that we need to let sleeping paedophiles lie. And again, as we have no evidence other than a few images on the laptop, none of which we can prove are underage. He has decided that he is dropping the intensity of the case. I thought you should know."

"I appreciate your call," she ended the call abruptly. Ken made the same call to Valerie Williams and got pretty much the same response.

As he finished the call, Annie walked through the door. He leaped up, his face aglow.

"Thank God I've seen a friendly face! Large sauvignon please and I will have a large rum."

"Sit down Annie. I need to talk to you."

"What's wrong?"

"The chief super is winding down the case. He says that after six weeks and with very little progress he cannot afford the resources. I thought you should know. And there's something else I need you to know. Before you make a complete decision about me."

"Okay," Annie said. Her voice faltering, she was slightly worried.

"I just need you to understand why I ended up here."

Ken proceeded to tell her that he had been working on a heavy case in London. Witness protection, drugs, guns, gangs. He overstepped the mark, and in particular with everything that had been going on recently in terms of the police, he ended up in bed with a victim. "She fully consented, it was not rape. I didn't force her into anything, and she told my superior officers that at the investigation. It's probably the only reason I still have a job. They decided to put me out to grass and I ended up here. I just needed you to know before you make any other decisions about me. I fully understand if it's too much for you to take in."

Annie sunk the other half of her remaining glass of wine. She stood up.

"Thank you for telling me. It may be too much for me to take in." She put her glass on the table and left.

Ken Shrugged his shoulders. "I can't blame you," he said to an empty seat. He finished his rum and made his way back to the station to collect his car.

Michelle was angry. Actually, she was more than angry. She was absolutely seething. She knew Charlie had been killed, and her husband had done it but there was nothing anybody could do. It had been chewing over in her mind. She certainly hadn't paid Tommy a visit for days now. She decided that she probably needed to make an effort. Just to keep up appearances if nothing else. She dressed elegantly and left the house. The drive to the hospital did nothing to calm her. And she didn't really know what she was going to do or say. She parked the car and went inside.
A journey that she had done several times, but this time it felt different. This time she felt angry, stronger, and the truth be told, if she could have turned off all those machines she would have done.

She decided she needed a coffee before she went up to see him. Around fifteen minutes later she decided she had the courage, and made her way to Tommy's room. The police officer on the door acknowledged her. "Good evening, Mrs Shelton," and he nodded towards her. "Good evening," she said politely and made her way inside the room. Tommy's motionless body lay there. She looked at all the machines, the wires, the cables. The anger building and building.
"Why the fuck couldn't you die?!" She said, conscious that the policeman was just outside the door and could be listening at any time. She pulled the chair close to her

husband's body and whispered again, "Why the fuck couldn't you have died?"

She took a deep breath. "Well, the police are winding down their investigation because you, you worthless piece of shit are still lying here and Giles is dead. So they have nobody to talk to. But I am telling you this Tommy Shelton. I know you killed Charlie Summer. I know a copper that has evidence that can prove it. And I am going to make you pay," she spat the words angrily, almost spitting in Tommy's face.

She leaned closer. Just as she was about to speak, Tommy opened his eyes; wide, piercing, and alive with anger.

Michelle reeled back in her chair. Terrified outwardly, she looked at him. His eyes full of hate.

She smiled at him. "You will pay you bastard," she said softly. "You will pay."

This is a work of fiction. Names, characters, business, events and incidents are the products of the author's imagination. Any resemblance to actual persons, living or dead, or actual events is purely coincidental.

I Hope you have enjoyed Bittersweet Revenge enough to want the third book in the series to come to fruition!

Printed in Great Britain
by Amazon